CONFESSIONS

OF A

KAMIKAZE GEISHA

A novel by

M. A. Cooney

THREE HAWKS PRESS

Confessions of a Kamikaze Geisha by Michael A. Cooney

Published by Three Hawks Press
16 Beechwood Lane
Westport, CT 06880

ISBN numbers:
979-8-9864172-0-2 (paperback)
979-8-9864172-1-9 (digital)
979-8-9864172-2-6 (hardcover)

Maps by Mapping Specialists
Cover design and interior design by Rafael Andres

Translator's Introduction

In our rich and varied literature on the Japanese, there are two subjects which have consistently rewarded us with particular insight to these often wondrous and mysterious people. Those two subjects are the geisha and the kamikaze. Independently, each has been explored in detail by a number of our most distinguished scholars. Here for the first time, however, we have been given the opportunity to delve into both simultaneously, and not surprisingly, the results are illuminating in the extreme.

The instrument of our education is the memoir of Funabashi Suzukaze, the so-called "Kamikaze Geisha." During the war, she was renowned as the symbol of Japan's determination to triumph at all costs. By the time of her death in 2006, however, she had largely been forgotten by the general public, and a minor newspaper article here or there was the only notice that was taken. She would have likely remained forgotten had it not been for a serendipitous discovery I made in the fall of 2019 while on a research trip to Kyushu. There one night in a drinking establishment in the small village of Kujirahe, I made the acquaintance of a local fisherman and four or five of his cohorts. Over the course of a few rounds of *sake*, it became known to me that this fisherman, Funabashi Jinbei, was the nephew of a certain woman who had not only been a geisha during the period of the war, but had also been a kamikaze. Towards the end of our convivial evening, Jinbei also mentioned that he was in possession of several notebooks written by his aunt. It seemed she had been living with Jinbei and his wife at the time of her demise.

I must admit that by the following day, under more sober circumstances, I wondered if I hadn't been played for a fool by Mr. Funabashi and his associates, but a quick check on the Internet told me that such a person had in fact existed and that she had indeed originally been from Kyushu. That evening I went back to the same establishment and continued my conversation with Jinbei, explaining to him the potential significance of the notebooks. It took several weeks of further discussions, but eventually Jinbei and his wife did agree to putting them in my care for editing and translation. Several more months of painstaking research verified their authenticity.

There were in total eight notebooks. The writing was in ink on standard manuscript sized paper, and there was virtually no revision, as far as can be told. It is likely, I would conjecture, that she had done earlier drafts and then transferred her final "fair copy" to the notebooks. In my translation I have tried to reproduce as closely as possible not only the content of the original Japanese but the writing style as well. Ms. Funabashi's language reflects her times: the more elaborate tendencies of the pre-war era mixed with the greater liberties of expression that came after the war. Although limited in her formal education, Ms. Funabashi is a fluid and thoughtful writer. It should be noted that the geisha house to which she belonged placed a good deal of emphasis on writing skills, in addition to the traditional skills of entertainment for which such establishments are usually better known. As to why Ms. Funabashi's memoir was never published, we can only speculate. It is certainly possible she simply was not able to get her manuscript accepted for publication when it was completed. It is also possible, of course, that Ms. Funabashi never did attempt to sell the manuscript. Perhaps, in the end, she simply could not bring herself to make public the "confessions" she had privately recorded. We will never know.

In this introduction there is one final issue which I must unfortunately address. It seems there are certain parties in the academic community who claim the notebooks to be forgeries. Has not Winks simply chosen the two most common of Japanese stereotypes and combined them in an effort to line his pockets with cash? Is not Winks the second coming of Edmund Backhouse? These so-called scholars seem to feel it perfectly plausible that the Japanese would fly airplanes into aircraft carriers but somehow not conceivable that they would choose an apprentice geisha as their symbol of national purity. That's absurd, they say. How could that possibly be true?

These accusations do not surprise me. Being a veteran of the academic wars, I am long accustomed to such jealous sniping. I find the association with the British blackguard Backhouse to be particularly galling. His forgery of the diaries of the Chinese court official Jing Shan, written in Beijing in the early 1900's, was extremely amateurish and would have easily been ferreted out as a fake by even the most mildly competent of Chinese specialists— had such specialists existed in England at the time. As for the accusations themselves, my cousin Dr. W.C. Winks, a certified handwriting expert, has perused the notebooks in detail and verified their authenticity beyond any shadow of a doubt, comparing the handwriting therein contained with that of other documents written by Ms. Funabashi (including some in the possession of the U.S. government). W.C. noted in particular the left-to-right slant of the middle stroke of 東 (*higashi,* "east") and other similar "center-pierced" hieroglyphs as being conclusive evidence. There have been requests that other experts be allowed to examine the notebooks, but Jinbei has decided that such handling by other persons of unknown origin would not exhibit the proper respect for the memory of his aunt. I, perhaps not unexpectedly, am in full agreement with his decision.

Japanese words have been Romanized using the simplified Hepburn system (no macrons to indicate long vowels). Following this transcription, pronunciation is straightforward: consonants are pronounced as in English (with *g* always hard), the vowels as in Italian. Thus "geisha" is pronounced *gāy-sha;* "kamikaze" is *ka-mē-ka-zā;* Suzukaze is *su-zu-ka-zā;* and "sake" is *sa-kā.* All Chinese place names and personal names have been Romanized in their modern Pinyin version, the one exception being Chiang Kai-shek (Jiang Jieshi). As for the order of personal names, all have been rendered in accordance with local practice: given name first, surname last for Western names; surname first, given name last for Oriental names.

Maps have been included. Please refer to them as necessary: the narrative will be much more easily followed if the geography is understood.

Although this memoir deals with the period of Japan's Greater East Asia War, it seems relevant parallels might be drawn with wars of other regions and other eras. Indeed, as I labored on this translation over these many months, it struck me more than once that there might be some universal truths found in the story of this humble woman.

T.D. Winks, PhD
Professor of Japanese Studies
Camino Perdido College

July 2022

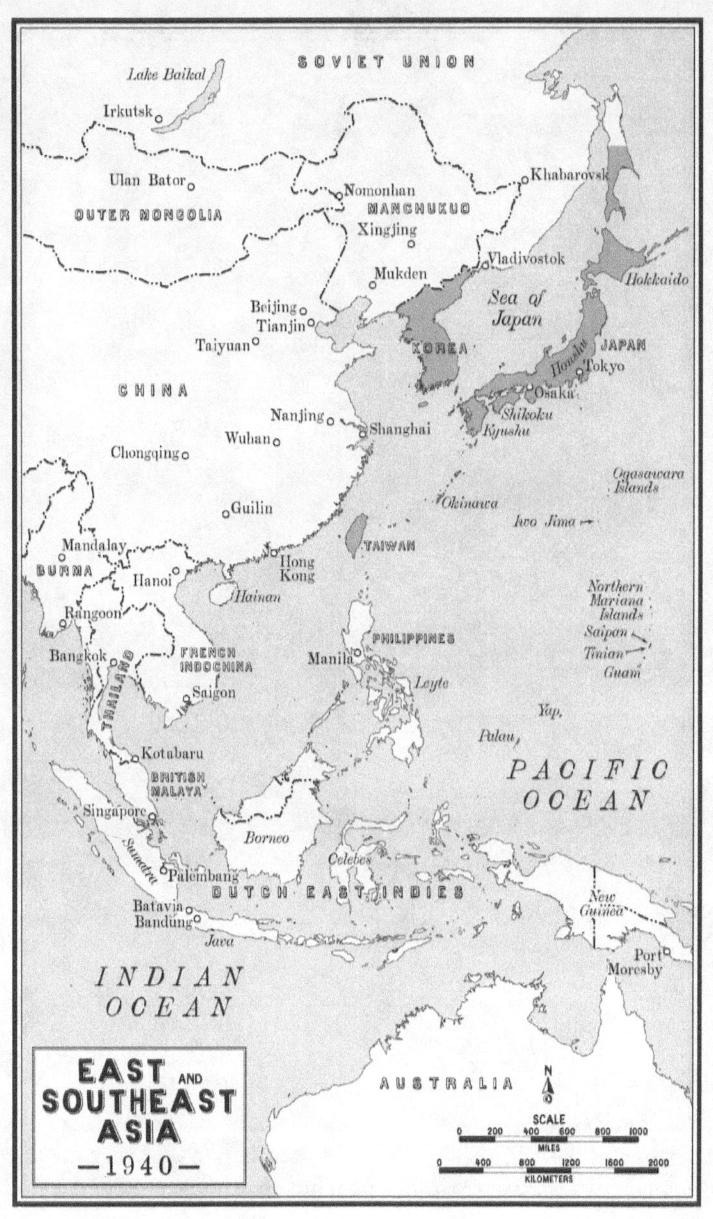

SOVIET UNION
Lake Baikal
Irkutsk
Ulan Bator
OUTER MONGOLIA
Nomonhan
MANCHUKUO
Xingjing
Mukden
Khabarovsk
Vladivostok
Hokkaido
Sea of Japan
Beijing
Tianjin
Taiyuan
KOREA
JAPAN
Honshu
Tokyo
CHINA
Osaka
Nanjing
Wuhan
Shanghai
Shikoku
Kyushu
Chongqing
Guilin
Ogasawara Islands
Okinawa
Iwo Jima →
Mandalay
TAIWAN
BURMA
Hanoi
Hong Kong
Hainan
Northern Mariana Islands
Saipan →
Tinian →
Guam
Rangoon
Bangkok
THAILAND
FRENCH INDOCHINA
Saigon
PHILIPPINES
Manila
Leyte
Yap.
Palau.
Kotabaru
BRITISH MALAYA
PACIFIC OCEAN
Singapore
Sumatra
Borneo
Celebes
Palembang
DUTCH EAST INDIES
New Guinea
Batavia
Bandung
Java
Port Moresby
INDIAN OCEAN
AUSTRALIA
N
EAST AND SOUTHEAST ASIA
—1940—
SCALE
0   200   400   600   800   1000
MILES
0   400   800   1200   1600   2000
KILOMETERS

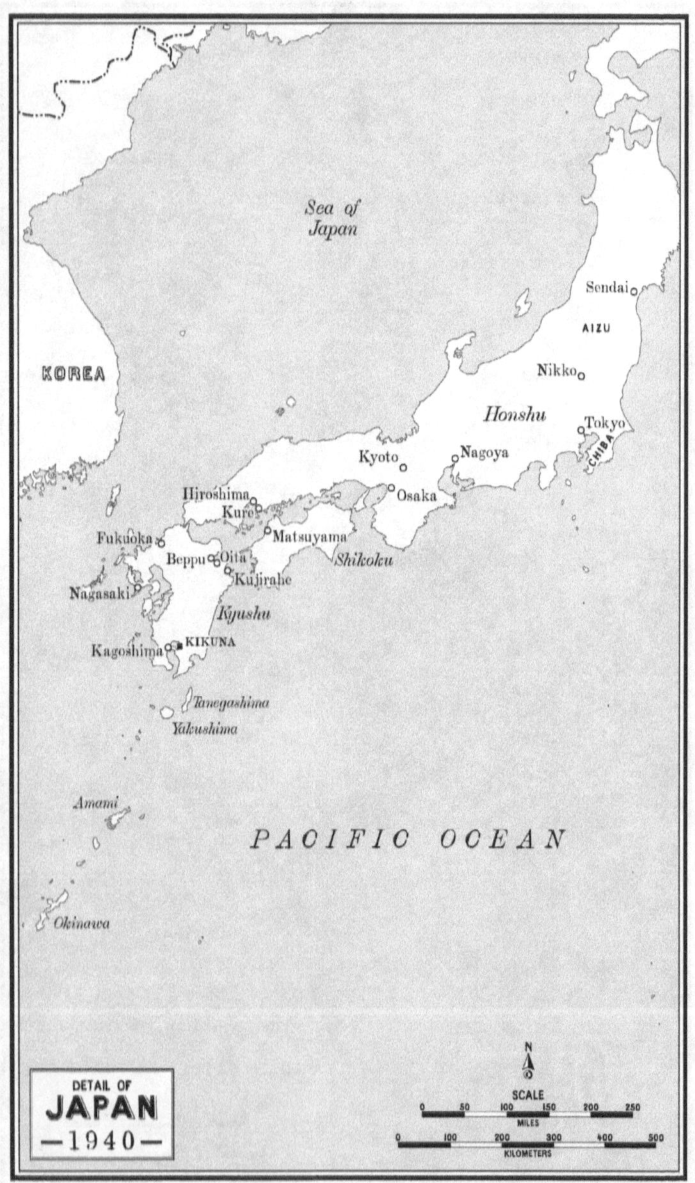

Sea of Japan
KOREA
Sendai
AIZU
Nikko
Honshu
Tokyo
CHIBA
Kyoto
Nagoya
Hiroshima
Kure
Osaka
Fukuoka
Matsuyama
Beppu
Oita
Shikoku
Kujirahe
Nagasaki
Kyushu
Kagoshima
KIKUNA
Tanegashima
Yakushima
Amami
PACIFIC OCEAN
Okinawa
DETAIL OF
JAPAN
—1940—
N
SCALE
0 50 100 150 200 250
MILES
0 100 200 300 400 500
KILOMETERS

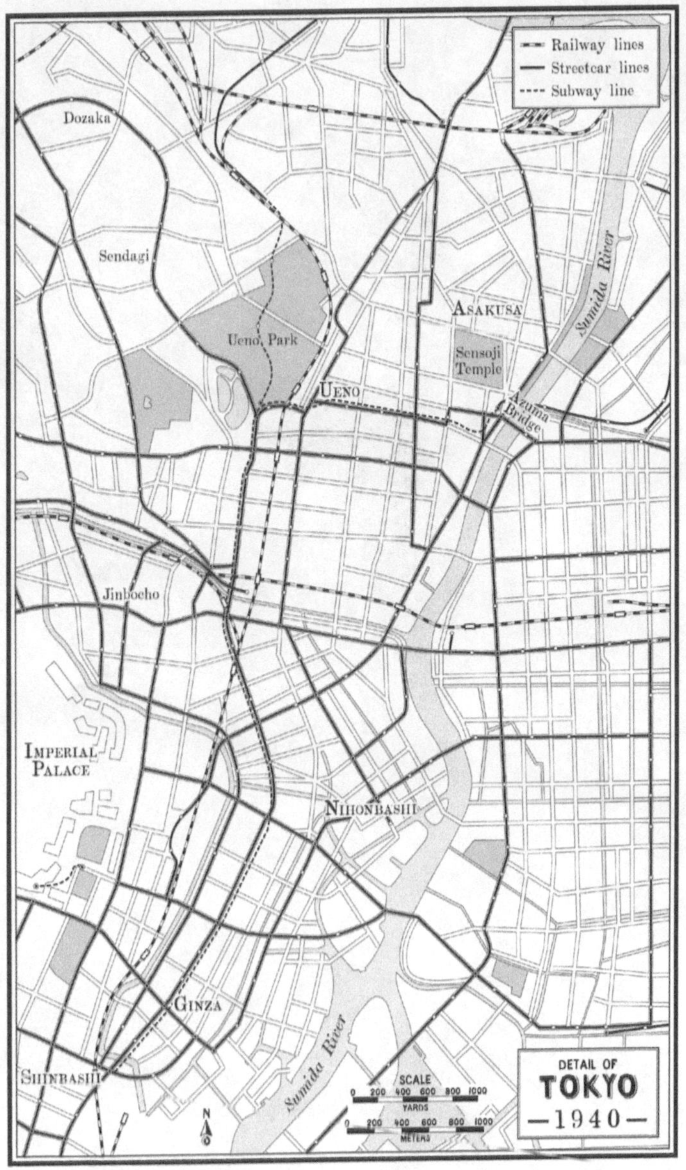

Railway lines
Streetcar lines
Subway line
Dozaka
Sendagi
Ueno Park
Ueno
Asakusa
Sensoji Temple
Azuma Bridge
Sumida River
Jinbocho
Imperial Palace
Nihonbashi
Ginza
Shinbashi
Sumida River
N
SCALE
0 200 400 600 800 1000
YARDS
0 200 400 600 800 1000
METERS
DETAIL OF
TOKYO
—1940—

THE NOTEBOOKS

1

You must remember, my dear Suzu, that all of history is a myth, a fable, simply the telling of a tale, and what is passed down always depends on who is doing the telling.

That's what the Colonel wrote in one of his letters. It was during the war, and he was at the front, in Burma. I didn't give his words much thought at the time. That's just the way the Colonel was. He was a very intelligent man, and he had his own peculiar way of doing and saying things.

As I sit down to write this memoir, however— this history of my life— the Colonel's words have come back to me. Where to start? And how much to tell you, the reader? And how to tell you? And what to say about those whose lives crossed with my own? Will people be upset if I say too much? Or too little? Will they be upset merely by the mention of their name? Will they accuse me of telling the story wrongly? Will they say this or that didn't happen, when I know for a fact that it did? Or will they say I've left out something? That's an especially difficult one. How could I ever hope to include everything? It seems all these questions might have something to do with what the Colonel had to say— although I must admit the connection is not always clear in my mind.

I was born Panko, but have long gone by the name Suzukaze. During the war I was also known as the Maiden Maiko and the Maiden Defender and, finally, the Kamikaze Geisha. People have seen in me what they want to see. Mangetsu was the one who warned me against falling in love with soldiers. If I had followed her advice, much of what follows would not have happened. But how can a girl have any idea of the emotions that will come to rule her heart? How can she control when and with whom she falls in love? She might as well try to control the rising and setting of the sun, or the changing of the seasons. I want to tell you all about those times— about Ummu Sensei, and Taibo, and the trip to China, and the day the war with the Americans started, and the Fuji boys, and that final, climactic assignment with the Commander.

But first I must tell you about the night of my debut, the night I met the Lieutenant and the Minister, for I would not have one day become the Kamikaze Geisha were it not for the events that transpired that evening.

2

Our geisha house was located in the Asakusa district of Tokyo, just north of the Sensoji Temple, not far from the Sumida River. If you've ever been to Tokyo, you've no doubt been to the Sensoji Temple. You would remember the enormous red *torii* gate, with the huge lantern hanging in the middle, and the long arcade of trinket shops leading to the main hall. Asakusa has always been popular with the tourists, even more so in the days before the war. The Sumida was truly the center of the city in those days and Asakusa one of its chief playgrounds, with countless restaurants, bars, movie houses, *rakugo* theaters, and burlesque shows— not to mention the Hanayashiki Amusement Park, right there in the middle of it all. And north of the temple, to its rear, were the *okiya*, the geisha houses.

It was from the front entrance of our house there that I stepped into a rickshaw that fateful summer evening, and set off with Mangetsu.

"Here we go, ladies," our puller said.

And then our vehicle was lifted in the air, and we were off into the Asakusa night, exiting our narrow alley and taking a left and then a right before coming out on to a larger street, and then down the side street that runs parallel to Sensoji's arcade, and then left on to the main road past the enormous gate of the temple, and then on to the Sumida and Azuma Bridge, taking a right before crossing. It was a warm night, and the breeze felt good on my face, and it was exhilarating to be rushing along at such speed, thinking ahead to my debut, only minutes away, and my heart was thumping so hard I thought it might burst.

As we made our turn along the river, I looked over at Mangetsu. Although then still only twenty-two, she had the poise of a veteran geisha and a classically beautiful face that one might find, say, in the long ago paintings of the Heian court. My apprenticeship to her had started two years earlier, and I knew I had been fortunate indeed to have a teacher who had taught me my lessons so well while never being overbearing in any way. Then again, that would not have been fun-loving Mangetsu. It was said the Madame had named her after the full moon that shone the night she first met her, but I'm certain she had also intended some sense of a girl who lived life to its fullest, a girl who drained every last drop of *sake* from every cup offered.

"There will be a very important gentleman there tonight," Mangetsu said softly as we slowed at an intersection.

I nodded gravely, being careful not to make too sudden a movement that might disturb my elegant coiffure. It had taken all day to get me prepared— the costume of a *maiko*, an apprentice, being even more elaborate than that of a full-fledged geisha.

"General Kukihara, Minister of Public Enlightenment."

I nodded again.

"Yes, he's a general and a minister. As I said, a very important man."

Having passed through the intersection, our rickshaw once more began to pick up speed.

"The Madame wants you to spend some time with him," Mangetsu went on after a pause. "It's never too early, I'm sure she's thinking, to cultivate potential patrons."

Mangetsu had mentioned this word "patron" on several other occasions, but neither she nor the Madame nor any of the other girls had ever spoken to me in detail about all that such a relationship might entail. Love, yes. Mangetsu had spoken to me about love. But she had neglected to speak to me about the more intimate physical aspects of such a relationship, and I would remain ignorant of such specifics until, abruptly one day, I received first-hand instruction. There had been some talk among the girls of a patron paying a "significant sum for a first time," but I was still extremely innocent and naive, and all that came to mind was the thought of someone paying money to support my dancing and singing— these, after all, were the skills in which I had been trained. Those of you who hold some of the more common misconceptions about geisha may find this claim difficult to believe, but it is the truth nonetheless. As I look back on it now, I don't think the Madame or Mangetsu were trying to hide anything from me. They might have just assumed that I already knew what would be expected of a young lady entering our profession. Or, they might have felt the timing for such a discussion might be better after I had made my debut. In fact, that's when the conversation with the Madame about these matters did indeed come up.

"What kind of a man is he?" I asked. "This Minister— have you met him?"

"No, no, I haven't," Mangetsu said, looking away.

I shifted forward anxiously in my seat. "What will I talk to him about?"

"You'll be fine," Mangetsu said, patting my knee. "Just remember your coquettish smile."

I lifted my head, recalling the many hours Mangetsu had had me practice this seemingly simple act— seemingly simple except when wearing the heavy cosmetics of a *maiko*. What one has to work with is merely the inference of a smile— an inference ultimately communicated through the shape of one's mouth, but in actuality created through the subtle movement of the fingers, hands, shoulders, eyes— and of course, the heart. While but one of the many skills a *maiko* must master, Mangetsu had taught me it was perhaps the most essential.

"Now let's see that coquettish smile one more time."

And so once more, as I had countless times before, I showed Mangetsu my coquettish smile.

"Yes," she said comfortingly, "that will do. That will be just fine."

I sighed, and the thumping of my heart seemed to quiet a bit.

Mangetsu patted my knee again and smiled slyly. "And there may be one other surprise guest. Who do you think that might be?"

I told her I had no idea.

"The Madame said Grand Champion Taibo may also be there."

I couldn't believe it. All of us girls were huge sumo fans. Taibo himself? He was at the time among the most famous of men in all of Japan, an historic *yokozuna* who had set one record after another.

"Quite a debut for you, Suzu— a minister and a grand champion."

And just about then our rickshaw started to slow down, and I looked up to see there in front of us the most celebrated place of entertainment in all of Asakusa at the time, Nagabashiya.

"Now," Mangetsu said with dramatic emphasis, "we must go on stage."

We came to a halt, and as the front of our vehicle was lowered I grabbed the side-rail to prevent myself from being pitched out on to the street.

"Welcome, welcome," said a fawning little man dressed in a neat blue kimono. Lined up with him at the gate were several serving girls.

"It's the famous Mangetsu," I heard one of them say.

"Yes, and her apprentice," one of the others chimed in.

Having never before attended such an event with Mangetsu, I hadn't realized how well-known she was. And I was her apprentice— once again I felt the magnitude of the moment.

"Right this way," the little man said, and we followed him in through the gate, through a magnificent garden, down a covered passageway, and on into the main building itself. Mangetsu, conscious of my still limited ability to move about in my ornate attire, walked more slowly than I'm certain she usually did, and I was grateful for her thoughtfulness.

Proceeding down several more corridors, we were led into a small room, apparently an antechamber to a larger room, and from there we could hear loud male voices and reciprocal female laughter.

"Are you ready, Miss?" the little man asked.

Mangetsu took a deep breath. "Yes, let's do it."

The little man then got down on his knees, slid open the door, and announced to the assembled guests, "Gentlemen, let me present the magnificent Mangetsu and her apprentice, Suzukaze."

There was applause as Mangetsu entered the tatami-matted room, stopping just inside the doorway to strike a pose and survey the scene. I stood frozen behind her, following my instructions. I was to wait there until she had taken her seat, after which I was to enter and proceed to the opposite end of the room, where the lower ranking guests would be seated. There looked to be about twenty persons present, including two other geisha and one other *maiko*. Most of the men were military officers, but there were also five or six civilians in attendance, including three very large men dressed in kimono— Taibo and two other sumo wrestlers. Taibo had indeed come!

"My, what a collection of men," Mangetsu exclaimed.

The men laughed, and then Mangetsu made her way around the room to a spot next to a middle-aged military man with an odd-looking moustache. Based on the obsequious behavior of those around him, I assumed he must be the Minister. Mangetsu bowed low to him, and then sitting down in formal *seiza* style, put her hands neatly together in front of her, fingers pointed precisely at 45 degrees to each other, and bowed low once more to the entire room, saying, "I am Mangetsu. Your gracious forbearance of my inept entertainments would be eternally appreciated."

There was another round of applause at these words, and then Mangetsu looked at me standing in the doorway and said, "Gentlemen, my apprentice, Suzukaze."

As I heard more applause, this time rippling in my direction, I felt my heart pounding again and I was certain I was about to pass out, but somehow I steadied myself and began my entrance, keeping my eyes all the time on an open seat at the opposite end of the room.

"She's a pretty one," I heard one of the guests say as I passed by him, and the man sitting next to him agreed, "Yes, she certainly is."

I found the open seat and bowed to the gentlemen on either side. "Would this by any chance be my seat?" I asked.

"Yes, I believe it most certainly is," the handsome young army officer to my immediate left was quick to answer.

I extended my hand to balance myself as I went to sit down, and the young officer took my hand and helped me maneuver into position on my cushion.

"Thank you so much," I said, putting the same hand, now disengaged from that of the young officer, over my mouth. "To not even be able to sit down on my own..."

"Not at all," the young officer said.

"Such an embarrassment.."

The young officer nodded and looked deeply into my eyes, and I felt a warm flush come over my entire body, such as I hadn't felt since being alone under a turned-over boat with one of the local boys back in Kujirahe. I turned away, trying to compose myself.

"Well, aren't you a young one," the man to my immediate right said.

I turned a bit more, so that I was now facing the other man. He was much older, bald, his face red, already drunk. "Aren't you going to give me anything to drink?" he asked gruffly.

"Pardon me," I said, bowing deeply, and I picked up the *sake* jar and poured some *sake* for the man. And then I turned back to the young officer and tilted my head slightly and motioned with the *sake* jar, asking him with my eyes if he would like some.

"Ah, thank you," the young officer said, and I felt the warm flush rushing through me once more, reaching even the most extreme of my extremities.

This is what Mangetsu had warned me about. There will be men, she had said, for whom you will feel affection. You must deny those emotions in yourself. You are training to be a geisha, a professional entertainer of men. There will be other wonderful things in your life— fine food and drink, and beautiful clothes, and deeply moving music and dance— but you can not allow yourself the luxury of love. And most especially, you can not allow yourself to fall in love with a soldier. Only tragedy, most assuredly, will come of that. This is what Mangetsu had said to me. And so I turned away again, uncertain of what to do, and I looked quickly about the room— at Mangetsu talking to the grand champion, and one of the other geisha pouring *sake*, and one of the other sumo wrestlers loudly laughing— but this feeling that had grabbed ahold of me was not about to go away so easily. Alas, I realized, before I had even gotten myself properly seated at my very first engagement, I had already fallen in love.

"How about some for yourself?" the young officer asked.

"Pardon?"

"Yourself— how about a little *sake* for yourself?"

I looked down at the *sake* jar in my hand. Lost in my thoughts, I'd forgotten I was even holding it.

"Oh, no... I can't... Here, you please have some more."

I again extended the *sake* jar in the direction of the young officer. He finished what remained in his cup, and then he held out his hand, looking deeply again into my eyes all the while. His head seemed perfectly formed, the hair short but thick with a healthy sheen to it, while the nose was prominent and straight, the lips full, and the eyes soft and inviting. As he reached across, his broad chest pushed against the confines of his uniform, and I could sense the strength of his shoulders and arms and wrists— and even his long, elegant fingers— in his grasp of the cup. I noticed my hand was shaking as I poured from the *sake* jar.

The young officer smiled. "Now tell me again— what's your name?"

"Suzukaze."

"How do you write it?"

"With the characters for chimes and wind."

"Chimes in the wind. It's a pretty name."

I gave him a coquettish smile, just as I had earlier practiced with Mangetsu, and then I bowed in appreciation of the compliment.

"Will you be performing tonight... singing or dancing?"

"Oh, no... I'm afraid I'm still... in training."

"I see..."

"Yes, tonight is actually... my first time..."

"Your first time to attend such an event as this?"

"Yes..."

"A night to remember, then."

"Yes..."

I smiled again, and the young officer smiled back at me, and then he turned on his cushion to look at the front of the room, and as he did so his leg lightly brushed mine, and I shifted my weight ever so slightly so that my leg would stay pressed against his.

"How about a dance?" I now heard the Minister call out from the other end of the room. "With the famous Mangetsu here, we must have a dance. How about 'Love Suicide at Shinbashi?'"

Mangetsu slowly stood up. "Would you mind accompanying me?" she asked the two other geisha.

The other geisha nodded their assent, and then one of them picked up her samisen and began to tune it. The song the Minister had requested was very popular at the time. The story was about a young couple, an army officer and a bar girl from the Shinbashi section of Tokyo who fall madly in love but can not marry because of their difference in social class. Unable to bear their situation any longer, they commit suicide by jumping in front of a streetcar. The lyrics of the song are as follows:

Is not our existence
but a drop of dew upon the iris blade,
a fragile blossom on the cherry tree?
Oh, this sorrowful life:
why must I love you so?
Hold me tightly now
as the clanging bells draw near,
our transport to the other world,
our vehicle to eternal bliss.

"I apologize for what I am certain will be a most inadequate performance," Mangetsu said, and then she nodded to the other geisha, and the one started to play her samisen and the other to sing.

Mangetsu struck a pose, and then she began her dance, subtly reenacting the story— the meeting of the young couple, their intense love for each other, their tragic end. Mangetsu's interpretation had a mesmerizing effect on those present— absolute silence, catatonic expressions, and a final bubbling up of tears into the eyes of all. I found myself becoming the bar girl, feeling a passion so fierce that nothing else mattered, contemplating a death that would make my lover mine forever. And then I turned my head and stole a quick look at the young officer, and I was certain the story was my own.

The silence continued for quite some time, and then wiping away a tear, the Minister said, "Here, here, magnificent!" and there were several other cries of "magnificent!" and then a round of applause. After the war, the Americans would often ask me about the popularity of "feudalistic" songs such as this. It seems they never could understand how it is that love and death placed so near one another is what most powerfully moves the heart.

"Enough of sad stories," Taibo now said, standing up to reveal his full height and girth, which were both considerable. "Time for some games."

"And what game would you like to play?" Mangetsu asked.

"How about a drinking game?" the grand champion replied, extending his enormous hand out in front of him in a sweeping motion. "We'll go around the room, with the young ladies asking questions of the men. If the man answers the question wrong, he must drink three cups of *sake*. If he answers it correctly, the young lady must drink one cup."

"And we can ask any question we like?" Mangetsu asked.

"Yes, any question you like."

"Very well, let's begin then."

Mangetsu started and she put her first question to Taibo. It had to do with *The Tale of Genji.* To be specific, she asked him how many lovers Genji had had over the course of the story. The Yokozuna allowed as how it was unlikely that an effeminate royal prince would have more lovers than a grand champion sumo wrestler, and since his count now stood at

162, he figured Genji might have had half of that number, or 81. In response to this answer, Mangetsu laughed lightly and told the grand champion that he had greatly underestimated the prowess of royal princes, or at least this particular royal prince. The correct answer was 344. Taibo burst out laughing and declared that couldn't be the correct answer, but he was a good sport and quickly downed his three cups of *sake*.

In this way, the game proceeded around the room, with Mangetsu asking a few questions and then the other two geisha and then the other *maiko*, and then finally my turn came to ask a question. I'm afraid I proved to be a miserable failure at this game. Whereas the other girls had all asked difficult questions that had virtually no chance of a correct answer, I was able to think of only simple questions. It so happened that my first question went to the Minister. That was just the way in which the order came around. I was in an absolute panic— what was an appropriate question to put to a minister? The only thing that came to mind was: when do the cherry blossoms bloom? This was a very silly question, of course, one easily answered by anyone. There was a loud roar of laughter from the crowd. The Minister gave the correct answer, April, and then he motioned for me to drink my penalty. I felt myself shaking as I picked up my *sake* cup, and then someone pointed out that it was empty, and there was another roar of laughter, and then the young officer gently touched my hand and came to my rescue, picking up the *sake* jar and pouring some *sake* into my cup. I had never had a drop of alcohol before in my life. I found the taste bitter, and soon felt light-headed and hot.

"And your next question?" one of the other sumo wrestlers shouted out at me.

"Yes, your next question," the thin, balding man to my other side insisted.

I can't remember now what my next question was. Something also silly and easily answerable. I was forced to drink one more cup of *sake*, and then there was one more question and one more cup of *sake*. I think that was it, three cups of *sake*, although there might have been a fourth. I can't be certain. What I do know is I felt even more light-headed and hot, and then I seemed to reach some sort of a high plateau and simply felt good, or as I would later come to understand, intoxicated.

"I haven't met such a charming young lady in ages," the Minister declared. "Come down here and talk to me."

Complying with the Minister's command, I wobbled to my feet— with the generous assistance once more of the young officer— and made my way slowly to the other side of the room. Looking at Mangetsu, I could see she was rightly worried about my condition. I sat down next to the Minister, giving him my best coquettish smile.

"Yes, very charming," he said again.

He had a distinctly round face dominated by the odd-looking moustache, which ended abruptly on both sides of his nose without extending properly across his full lip. Although he was then sitting, he would later stand and I would see that he was of average height with a solidly built upper body on surprisingly spindly legs.

"Don't you think so, Mushitani?"

Mushitani was evidently the gentleman sitting to the other side of me.

"Yes, sir, absolutely charming."

"A fine example of what is best in the young ladies of our nation."

"Yes, sir, my thoughts exactly."

The Minister then pointed at the *sake* jar in front of me. "Let's have some more of that *sake*," he said. "I think it will taste especially good coming from your hands."

I picked up the jar and poured some *sake* for the Minister, and he drank it, and then taking the jar from me, he insisted I have some. I hesitated to pick up my cup, but he insisted again, and I put out my cup and he filled it and I drank it.

"Where are you from, girl?"

I tried to speak, but no words would come out.

"Kyushu," Mangetsu intervened helpfully, "she's from Kyushu."

"Ah, Kyushu," the Minister said enthusiastically, "perfect! And how appropriate— I'm also from Kyushu."

"Is that so, sir?" Mangetsu said with exaggerated interest.

"Yes, Kagoshima."

Mangetsu leaned forward deferentially. "Some of our nation's finest leaders are from Kagoshima."

The Minister laughed. "It depends on one's definition of 'finest,' I suppose," he said. But now is not the time for politics."

"No, of course not," Mangetsu agreed apologetically.

"And how long have you been in Tokyo?" the Minister asked, turning to me again.

"Since the age of nine," I managed to say softly.

"You've grown used to the big city then?"

I paused for a moment before saying, "I'm afraid I'm still just a small-town girl at heart, sir."

The Minister roared with laughter. Now that I think back on it, it was a rather clever thing to say. I don't know where the words came from. They just seemed to pop into my head.

"There's something special about you," the Minister then said, taking one of my hands in his. "Yes, something special..."

"Isn't it just that she's young?" Mangetsu interjected playfully.

"No," the Minister said, "something more than that. I

can't quite put my finger on it..."

I stayed perhaps fifteen or twenty minutes by the Minister's side. As Mangetsu had assured me, there was no need to say much. I poured more *sake* and produced more winning smiles, while Mangetsu and the Minister did the talking. Then at an appropriate point in the conversation, Mangetsu tilted her head towards the other end of the room, and I knew it was time to go back to my own seat.

"Please excuse me," I said, standing up.

"Yes, something special," the Minister mused to himself one last time.

I walked back to my place, and the young officer gave me his hand and again helped me to sit down. Once more I felt the warm flush rushing through me from head to toe. I didn't quite know what to do. It was by no means pleasant duty, but I found myself talking at length with the thin, bald man on my other side so as to not say something horribly stupid to the young officer and leave a bad impression. But I couldn't help myself either from turning around from time to time to look at him. I would pretend that one of the other men had caught my attention, or that I was checking to see if the Minister was calling me again. Then Mangetsu motioned for me to change seats.

"Leaving so soon, Chimes in the Wind?" the young officer asked.

I bowed low, smiled awkwardly, and then walked away, truly at a loss for words. My next assignment was between Taibo's two compatriots, the two other sumo wrestlers. In like fashion to the grand champion, the two men were gigantic, and I felt very much like a sapling between two fully grown cedars. I'm afraid I wasn't very good company, my mind occupied as it still was with thoughts of the young officer. I tried not to look in his direction, but couldn't help myself, and soon I saw that one of the other geisha had taken my place. She was older, perhaps the same age as Mangetsu, stunningly beautiful and evidently quite charming, as the young officer appeared totally infatuated with her. Oh, I was such a fool! To fall in love on my very first night of entertainment— and with a soldier!

Abruptly later in the evening the Minister stood and declared he was leaving. Everyone else staggered to their feet and followed him out of the room, down the several corridors, and out into the garden. I scurried behind with Mangetsu and the other geisha, trying to keep up as best I could. I had a very difficult time getting my *pokkuri* footwear on at the doorway, almost falling over, and by the time I got to the garden everyone else was already out on the street. I was in an absolute panic, as to not give our guests a proper farewell would be a serious failure of service on my part. When I finally did get to the street, the Minister was just getting into the backseat of his chauffeur-driven car. He turned to say one last word to the others in his party, and as he did so he spotted me.

"Young Suzukaze, come over here," he said, beckoning with his hand. "Aren't you going to see me off?"

I walked to his car as quickly as I could, feeling quite humiliated, but the Minister had no intention of scolding me. "Work hard," he said with a smile. "I'm certain you'll make a fine geisha one day."

I bowed low, greatly relieved.

Then turning to Mangetsu, he said, "Mushitani will be in touch with the Madame. Please pass on my regards."

"Most certainly, sir," Mangetsu replied with a flourish.

"Yes, something special," the Minister murmured one final time.

And then the chauffeur began to close the door, and I

bowed low again, very low indeed. The year was 1939. I was fifteen years old, and I had just made a strong impression on one of our nation's most esteemed leaders. I could have had no idea then how this would come to affect my entire life.

"Make sure," Mangetsu said, whispering in my ear, "to see off your other guests as well."

"Yes, of course," I said earnestly.

Where was the young officer? I looked about, but he was nowhere to be seen. Then farther down the street I saw a lone figure striding purposefully towards the next intersection. I took a few steps in the same direction and stopped, and then just as he came to the corner, the young officer turned and looked back. I bowed low and the young officer waved.

"Suzu..."

I turned back towards Mangetsu.

"You must..."

I nodded, and then turned back once more in the other direction, but he was already gone around the corner.

3

The morning after my debut I wasn't feeling at all well. I knew I had drunk too much *sake*, but I hadn't slept much either. I'd been awake all night thinking of the young officer. It was truly extraordinary, this feeling that had taken ahold of me.

"Did you meet any interesting men?"

That was the first thing Hoshi asked me. Oh, I so wanted to talk to her about the young officer, but I knew I couldn't. I talked to Hoshi about everything, but this was simply one thing I couldn't talk to her about.

"Yokozuna Taibo was there," I said instead.

"Really, the grand champion himself?"

"Yes, the grand champion himself."

Hoshi was my very best friend among the eight girls of the house, the same age as I was and, if possible, even more naive and gullible. The two of us shared a room. While I was from Kyushu, down south, Hoshi was from Yamagata, up north. When we had first met it was all we could do to make ourselves understood to each other, our accents being so different. But what we had shared was the challenge of adjusting to a new and demanding situation, and it wasn't long at all before we became quite close. While perhaps not among the first rank of beauties in our house, Hoshi was still very attractive, with a sparkling and slightly zany personality that would later prove to always make her a success with the men. The Madame had very much known what she was doing when she named her Hoshi, "star."

"What did you think of him?" she asked.

"He was a lot of fun. Huge… and a lot of fun."

"Did you talk to him?"

"No, there was a minister I was assigned to," I said, exaggerating my role somewhat.

"A minister?"

"Yes, the Minister of Public Enlightenment— General Kukihara. He's an army officer and a minister."

"Is that so?" Hoshi said, rolling up her futon. "He sounds very important."

"Yes, very important."

"But what does he do?"

"Do?"

"Yes, what does the Minister of Public Enlightenment do?"

I must admit that until this point I had given this

question no thought. What indeed did the Minister of Public Enlightenment do? I ventured, after a long pause, to say I really had no idea, but whatever it was he did it must be a good thing, as the public clearly needed enlightening. Hoshi agreed— it must be a good thing— and we left it at that.

"Will you see him again?" Hoshi asked.

I said I thought it was a possibility, but of course another meeting with the Minister was the farthest thing from my mind at that moment. It's horrible, this thing called love. All that day I had no energy to do even the simplest of tasks. I couldn't stop thinking of the young officer, and yet I knew nothing about him— where he was from, or where he was based, or even his name. I wasn't able to get anything more than soup down at breakfast, and when I washed my face I saw I was very pale, perhaps even vaguely green. How long would this affliction last? Would it be two or three days? A week? A month? A year? Mangetsu of course had said nothing about this, having warned me against falling in love in the first place. I wondered if Hoshi and the other girls in the house could tell that I had been stricken, as for example one could readily identify a person with a fever. I knew the only cure was to see him, but I also realized this was impossible. I couldn't very well ask Mangetsu to help me contact him. She'd immediately know I was in love with him. And then again, who was to say he was even interested in me? He had, after all, appeared completely captivated by that geisha who'd sat next to him after I'd moved. No, I told myself, there was nothing to do but endure this yearning until it finally went away, however long that might take.

Late that afternoon I was called in to see the Madame. Mangetsu was with her, and it seemed she had already given a report on the proceedings of the previous evening.

"You've done well, Suzu," the Madame said. "It's no

easy feat, charming the likes of the Minister of Public Enlightenment."

Although then in her mid-forties, the Madame could have easily passed for ten years younger— the smooth, firm skin, the abundant hair pulled up on top of her head in the style common to her generation, the taller than average figure that was always carried with such graceful poise.

"I tried to follow Mangetsu's instructions as best I could," I said humbly.

"But one never knows how these things... will develop," the Madame continued. "Once the alcohol has worn off... men can be quite fickle. Isn't that so, Mangetsu?"

"Yes, most assuredly," Mangetsu quickly agreed.

The Madame went on to say I would have a busy entertainment schedule over the next several months. A wide net must be cast, and out of that process she was confident a number of "qualified candidates" to be my "patron" would emerge. The key was to not appear too eager, she emphasized. Again, there was no explanation of what exactly my duties and responsibilities to my "patron" might be, and I didn't ask for a clarification. The Madame had always treated me well, and I just assumed whatever she had in mind would be in the best interests of me and our house. In closing, the Madame reminded me again that it was only because of my position as a member of her house that I would have access to such influential and well-off men.

"And tomorrow night we'll see Colonel Yamanaka, right?"

The Madame nodded affirmatively to Mangetsu's question. "Yes, Colonel Yamanaka. Just a small gathering... You seem to be one of his favorites, Mangetsu."

Mangetsu smiled mischievously. "He likes to drink and he likes to talk, and so, yes, we get along well."

The Madame put a finger to the side of her face in a

reflective pose. "He's always been a bit of an odd bird... We go back quite a ways together and... I don't know that he should have ever been in the army... A strange choice for him... More of a scholar, a thinker... His father was an army man— I think that's what it was."

"You just never know, do you?"

"No, you don't... And now look at him— a colonel in charge of all those troops!"

Mangetsu leaned forward. "Do you think he'll be interested in Suzu?"

The Madame paused. "He might be... I don't know what his current situation is— if you know what I mean."

Mangetsu nodded in understanding. As for myself, as I say, I truly at this point was still in the dark as to what any of this really meant.

The following evening Mangetsu and I once more set off in a rickshaw, this time for our assignment with the Colonel. As the Madame had indicated, it was a much smaller gathering, just the Colonel and four other men. It seemed they all had been in the same graduating class at the Army Academy. I quickly found the Madame and Mangetsu's description of the Colonel to be accurate. He indeed liked to drink and talk. And he also liked to sing.

"Let's play some music," he bellowed not long after we arrived.

This being a smaller and less formal group, Mangetsu had informed me beforehand that it would be a perfect opportunity to make my performing debut. I would play the samisen while she sang. But the Colonel threw off our plans by insisting he would sing instead of Mangetsu. She could dance, he said. This left us trying to find a song in my limited repertoire that the Colonel would know. Fortunately, after an exchange of three or four titles that were not a match, we did find one— "Spring Snow in Aizu." Or, I should say more precisely, we found one the Colonel claimed to know. I must give the Colonel high marks for his enthusiasm, but his phrasing and cadence were completely off, and his mastery of the lyrics spotty. I did my best to complement the Colonel's idiosyncrasies but, alas, not very successfully, I'm afraid. Thankfully, no one seemed to care. Least of all the Colonel. They were all too drunk.

"Splendid!" the Colonel declared when we were done.

And then he had me sit down next to him and pour him more *sake*. Similar to the Minister, he wanted to know where I was from originally, and when I told him Kyushu he was also quite intrigued. I expected he might then tell me that he, too, was from Kyushu, but it turned out he was in fact from Aizu. That's why he had chosen the song he had. Avoiding false flattery about any other aspect of his rendition, I told him honestly how clearly evident his passion was for his home region.

"Passion!" he roared, the creases around his eyes crinkling up in a warm and agreeable way. "Passion— a word with such deep meaning coming from such a young lass!"

I bowed my head, mortified. I of course should never have taken such license in speaking to someone of the Colonel's standing. Mangetsu stepped in to apologize. But again similar to the Minister, the Colonel saw my gaucherie as merely "charming." And then he asked if I'd ever been to Aizu, and I said I hadn't, and he went on to tell me how beautiful it was, with its stunning mountains and swiftly running rivers.

"Yamanaka, you boast too much about Aizu," one of the other officers yelled out.

"You're just jealous, Tanaka" the Colonel yelled back. "And with good reason— how could Chiba ever compare with

Aizu?"

"You may have your mountains," the other officer retorted, "but we have our seashores."

The Colonel laughed, shaking his head. "Fair enough, I suppose, fair enough..." And all the others laughed as well.

"When are you headed back to China?" another of the officers asked the Colonel.

"It looks like early next month," the Colonel replied.

There then ensued a general discussion about our nation's liberation of China. It was all going well, from what I could tell, but there seemed to be a consensus that some nasty character by the name of Chiang Kai-shek was standing in the way of a final resolution.

"If only he had the interests of his own people in mind," one of the officers summed up.

That evening Mangetsu and I played several more songs— without further interference from the Colonel, I must add. Each piece was seemingly well received, although I must stress the inebriated state of our audience likely accounted for a less than stringent standard of judgment. As the gathering was wrapping up, the Colonel insisted on sharing one last cup of *sake* with me. Mindful of my earlier bad experience with alcohol, I had skillfully avoided more than a cup or two until that point, but the Colonel was determined I share this one last drink with him, and I did.

"I'm wondering," the Colonel then said, leaning forward, peering closely into my eyes, "if you wouldn't mind exchanging letters with me from time to time."

I was stunned. Why would a man of his stature wish to send me letters?

"I'm going back to China," he went on, "and I want to write to you."

I looked over at Mangetsu. What in the world was I

supposed to say? "But I'm only an ignorant girl," I finally blurted out.

"No, no," the Colonel said, putting his hand softly to my face, "you are much more than that... There is something special about you, something special..."

There was that word again— "special." The Minister had used it, and now the Colonel. I was completely baffled. What was it that they could possibly see in me?

Apparently taking the Colonel's request as a joke, Mangetsu then playfully referenced *Genji*, saying, "Of course our young Murasaki would be happy to exchange letters with you."

But the Colonel didn't smile. "It's very important," he said, his gaze not wavering. "And you'll write me back?"

Again, I didn't know what to say. I bowed low, and he seemed to take this as my consent to his proposition, saying happily, "Very well, very well."

In the rickshaw on the way home Mangetsu spoke about how the Colonel was indeed a likeable "odd bird" and how it was his wont to play practical jokes like this. I shouldn't give his strange request a second thought, she said. But the following week the Colonel apparently spoke directly to the Madame, making it crystal clear his request was not in jest. The Madame had been hoping for a proposition of a different sort, she later told me, but it was always possible this was a first step in that desired direction, and she had agreed to the exchange of letters. Thus began my curious correspondence with a man who was destined to become one of our nation's most acclaimed military heroes, for you see this Colonel Yamanaka was the one and same Colonel Yamanaka who only three years later became known as the "Viper of Burma" for his valiant actions in the defeat of the British forces in that Southeast Asian colony.

4

Where to start? And how much to tell you, the reader? What to include and what to leave out? These are the questions I posed at the start of my tale. I must go on to relate what happened with the Lieutenant and the Minister and the Colonel, but I'm afraid it won't all make sense unless I first go back and explain how it was that I came to be at our geisha house in Asakusa. Unless I do that, there may be those, too, who will accuse me of trying to hide something— especially if they were to discover through their own investigations that my family history was not at all in line with what was publicized at the time. And so let me briefly tell you about that earlier period of my life.

I was born in the small fishing village of Kujirahe on the island of Kyushu in 1924. It seems my mother was quite fertile and my father more than sufficiently virile, as five children were produced in five years. Then two years later I came along, and after me there were no more. By the time I was born, the family was in increasingly desperate straits. It is said my father took one look at me and declared I would be called "Panko," or "Breadcrumbs," for that's all they would be able to afford to feed me. You might think I am pulling your leg, but if you check my birth record you will see that Panko is indeed my official and proper name.

Although we were poor, my parents always found a way to make ends meet, and we were in general a very happy family. My father was a carpenter— a short, round man with whiskers that ran down both sides of his face but didn't cover his chin. He would often put me on his lap and rock me back and forth, holding me tightly up to his face and tickling me with the whiskers. It was my father who instilled in me my life-long love of stories. He was always telling one story or another, invariably beginning with "long, long ago," even if telling a story about something that had happened the week before. My mother was relatively tall for a woman of her generation, actually a bit taller than my father, and thin, with oddly beautiful features. She was mostly a quiet person who would listen patiently as my father told his stories, smiling knowingly and nodding, and in her little voice telling my father that he had just told the same story a few days before when, in fact, he had.

I was close with all of my brothers and sisters, but especially so with Tomo, who was also the closest to me in age. We were always together, the two youngest. This was true when we were very small, but it was also the case as we got older. Even after we started going to school, we were always together. Tomo's friends were the only friends I had. There were three or four boys, and we had great fun together doing the things that boys do. I must confess I was particularly fond of one of the boys. His name was Sumio. He was tall and thin, and actually quite awkward, but he was always very kind to me, and for some reason I liked him in a special way. He was the boy I mentioned earlier in my narrative, the boy I was with underneath the turned-over boat on the beach. You might say, I suppose, that he was my first love. We were only seven or eight, and nothing happened of course, but I do clearly remember the sensation of that warm flush spreading over me.

Then when I was nine, our mother died, and our world was turned upside down. It was a fever, a sudden and severe fever, and she was dead within a week. Even today, I have no idea what the cause was. Day after day we could see her slipping away right before our very eyes, but there was nothing we could do. Our mother's death was very hard on all of us, but particularly so on our father. He grew quiet and depressed and quickly lost weight, so that where he had once been round and lively, he was now gaunt and listless. He no longer tickled us with his whiskers or told us any of his stories, and he started to do strange things he had never done before— talking to himself, and sitting half-naked in the middle of the street, and howling at the moon. My brothers and sisters and I didn't know what to do. We tried talking to him, and making him special meals, and massaging his legs and back, but there was no improvement in his condition. We weren't the only ones who could see he was in a severe decline. Out of concern, neighbors and friends made visits to our house with increasing frequency.

Finally, five months after our mother died, a delegation of family members showed up. Tomo and I were told we would be taken back to Tokyo to live with these people. As for our two older brothers, they would be sent to work on a fishing boat in a neighboring village, while our two older sisters would be sent away to work at an inn. And our father, our poor father, my eldest brother told me, was being sent to a special house for crazy people. I didn't really know then what "crazy" meant. My brother told me it meant Father was sick in the head because our mother had died, and there was a special place where they took care of people like that. But it wouldn't be for long, he said. Father would soon get better, and then we would all be together again in Kujirahe.

The next morning, before we left for Tokyo, we met with our father one last time. He looked so old and beaten, and when he saw us tears started to stream down his cheeks. And then for one brief moment, he seemed to regain his senses and become his old self— like the old man in one of his stories who becomes a young man again in the presence of his princess. I was overcome by tears then too, and even today, if I let my mind drift, I can feel the coarseness of his beard on my soft skin and the mixing of his tears with mine. I felt sure we would be together once more soon, just as my eldest brother had said, but neither Tomo nor I ever saw our father again. It seems he died sometime in the next year or so, although we didn't find that out until many years later.

Our relatives lived in the Sendagi section of Tokyo, in those days a newer and well-off area of the city, up and away from Asakusa and the older downtown part of the city by the rivers. These people were quite rich, with a large house and many servants, and you would have thought we would have had a good life there. But this was not the case, as Tomo and I were not allowed to go to school, instead being forced to work in the house all day. I thought it strange that we could be treated so poorly by our relatives— in fact, no different than any of the servants— but Tomo told me it was not unusual for relatives to treat each other badly. Unfortunately, he said, it was human nature.

Then one April day, shortly after I turned twelve, the mother of the family sat me down and said she had "something important to talk to me about." We would be seeing a woman in Asakusa who was in the entertainment business, she said, and if everything went well I would be going to live with her. The following week we made our visit. I evidently created a proper impression, as I was told a mere three days later to gather my meager belongings and ready myself to move to Asakusa. It was difficult leaving Tomo, but we would still be only a few kilometers apart, and there was certainly no sorrow in parting from my relatives.

As you have no doubt surmised, this new home of mine

was in fact the Madame's geisha house. It was only some months later that I learned the true circumstances behind my move. It was then the Madame told me about the debt I now owed the house. It seemed there had been an exchange of money— that I had in effect been sold for a goodly sum by my kind relatives— and that the money paid by the house had now become my personal debt. The Madame tried to put a positive slant on her explanation, saying it was better not to think of this as an obligation hanging over my head but rather as an investment in myself. In the years to come I would repay the house through my earnings as a geisha, and once the money had been fully repaid, I would be free to leave and lead my own life.

Despite the Madame's gentle approach, the news that I had been sold still came as quite a shock. Then, and many times in the years since, I have wondered what my life would have been like if my mother hadn't died. Perhaps I would have never left Kujirahe. Perhaps I would have married Sumio, and had children with him, and spent my entire life in that small fishing village. Who can say? But each of us has his or her own fate, and mine was not to stay in Kujirahe. No, for better or worse, mine was to go to Tokyo, and become a *maiko*, and apprentice myself to Mangetsu, and meet the Lieutenant and the Minister and the Colonel.

And one day become the Kamikaze Geisha.

5

In the days following my debut, my obsession with the young officer never abated. I honestly began to think death might be preferable to the pain of this longing. Hoshi took notice of the change in my eating and sleeping patterns, but attributed the cause of my malaise to the stress of my new schedule. I don't think she at all suspected I might be in love. I don't think, at that time, she had yet experienced love and having had no such experience, she was not able to recognize the symptoms.

And then one day the gods intervened.

My brother Tomo, who by then was also living in Asakusa, was the medium of their communication. Tomo was, in fact, working at one of the vaudeville theaters. He had joined the troupe there about a year after I had joined our geisha house, and he was actually training as an apprentice to the great "Enoken," Enomoto Ken'ichi, then the most popular comedian in all of Japan— although Furukawa Roppa certainly had his fans. It was difficult for me to believe my own brother was training to be a comedian under such a well-known star, but this was indeed the truth. He told me he had started as a ticket taker and general jack-of-all-trades, but had then one day been "discovered" by Enoken. Discovering new performers was one of Enoken's many talents, Tomo said.

On the day in question, Hoshi and I went to a matinee performance at Tomo's theatre. Enoken sang and danced and performed several skits. Tomo was in one of the skits, a longer piece set in the Tokyo of a hundred years earlier, about a country bumpkin merchant coming up to the big city. Enoken played the part of the merchant, while Tomo played his servant. It truly was an amusing skit, with the merchant putting on airs and acting as though he knew everything there was to know about the city, when in fact he knew nothing. Tomo's role was not large, consisting mostly of trailing after his master, carrying his belongings and doing considerable bowing. But he did have one line he repeated a number of times, always getting a laugh: "Yes, sire, it is exactly as you say."

After the performance, Hoshi left. She had an engagement she had to prepare for. I waited for Tomo as he swept up the theater, and when he was done we went to a coffee shop for a snack. Our route took us down the Nakamise arcade until we came to the grand Kaminari Gate, and then we crossed the avenue and went down one alley and then another until we came to our destination, the "Tour Eiffel." Whenever we got together, we usually went there. There were various photos of Paris on the walls, and the menu was in French. The waiters even wore French-style berets.

After we'd ordered our café au lait and cake, Tomo told me he had some news to pass on to me. He said it with a very serious face, and I was certain he must have word of some tragic happening, perhaps the death of one of our long-separated siblings. But what he had to say was in fact something very different.

"It seems you have a secret admirer."

At these words from Tomo, my emotions were all aflutter. I immediately thought of the young officer, of course, but it was too much to hope he actually held feelings similar to my own or that, if he did, he would have expressed them to anyone.

"One of my friends in the troupe came to me the other day," Tomo went on, "and said there was someone out front who wanted to talk to me. I went out to the lobby of the theater and there was an army officer. I presume you know who I'm talking about."

So it was indeed the officer. My heart soared.

"He asked if I was the brother of the *maiko* Suzukaze."

It didn't seem real. I'd been pining away for him, but had resigned myself to never seeing him again, and now for him to try and get in touch with me...

"He said his name was Lieutenant Nogi."

"Lieutenant Nogi?"

"Yes, Lieutenant Nogi."

I had a name for him now. It was a nice name, Nogi. I wondered what his bottom name might be.

"What else did he say?"

One of the waiters wearing a beret came over at this point with our café au lait and cake. He was very precise about how he put the coffee out on the table, and then the cake.

"He said he'd like to see you," Tomo said, picking up his spoon and stirring his coffee.

I tried to appear as nonchalant as possible, as though the request from this lieutenant meant nothing.

"He said he's leaving for China next week, going back to the front."

"Really..."

"Yes, back to the front in China somewhere. I don't remember the name of the place."

So, he was home on leave. How long had he been in China, and how long had he been home? And how long would he be back in China once he left again?

"Where did you meet this lieutenant anyway?"

"At Nagabashiya, the night of my debut."

"He was a customer?"

"Yes…"

Tomo took a sip of his coffee, and then he sat forward in his seat. "Why didn't he just contact you directly himself?"

I looked down, hesitating. "I suppose," I said after a moment, "he didn't want to make it a matter of business."

Tomo took a moment of his own to process this. "Somehow he found out I was your brother."

"It appears so, doesn't it?"

"Is this something you're allowed to do?"

"Meet with a customer on my own, you mean?"

"Yes…"

It was forbidden I fall in love, and yet I had, and now my love had sought me out and if I did see him, nothing good would come of it. I knew this, but there was nothing to be done about it. I couldn't help myself. I had to see him.

"He's going back to China, back to the war," I said, looking down again. "I'll see him just one time. It's the least I can do for one of our men in uniform."

I didn't know if Tomo could tell I was in love with him— I didn't know how experienced my older brother might be in such matters— but he in any event chose to say nothing directly to dissuade me. He instead asked when would be a convenient time for me to meet. I thought about it a moment, and said the day after the next. I was not entertaining that evening, and I could tell the Madame I was going to see a *rakugo* performance with my brother. I knew Hoshi had a planned engagement, so there would be no curiosity as to why I didn't invite her along.

"You're sure you want to do this?" Tomo asked as we were leaving the coffee shop.

"Yes," I said, "I'm sure. After all, *isn't our existence but a drop of dew upon the iris blade?*"

But I'm afraid the poetic reference was lost on Tomo.

6

Over the next two days I gave considerable thought to what I would wear when I met the Lieutenant. He had only seen me in my elaborate *maiko* costume, and I was very much afraid he would be disappointed when he saw me in civilian attire. Since the Madame knew I was going to the theater, there would be no questions asked about making myself reasonably presentable. Still, I had to be careful not to overdo it and create suspicion. I had two informal summer kimono, one with a pattern of blue waves on a white background and the other with a pattern of green bamboo shoots on a pastel blue. I went back and forth between the wave pattern and the bamboo shoot pattern, thinking first one and then the other would make me appear older, or more sophisticated, or more casual in a fashionably *iki* sort of way. In the end I decided to wear the somewhat more understated wave pattern and give it an accent with my choice of *obi*, the decorative sash I would wear across my midsection.

As I stood in front of the mirror putting up my hair on the appointed day, I did in fact begin to have second thoughts about going. If anyone were to see us together, I was certain there would be severe consequences. For one thing, the Madame would immediately know I had lied to her. And if I would go so far as to risk lying, it had to mean there was something of significance going on between Tomo and the Lieutenant. In other words, we had not just happened to meet on the street by chance. Was it really worth it? He would be going back to China in a few days. I might never see him again. He might be killed. I didn't even really know him. But then again, what were the chances of anyone seeing us in Jinbocho? That's where we would be meeting. I was certain the Lieutenant had chosen to meet there precisely because it was very unlikely anyone from our house would be anywhere near there. And what could come of meeting him this one time? We would have a cup of coffee somewhere and chat, and then part. But at least I would have seen him again. And in the end I knew I had no choice but to go— I was in love, after all.

"Who will be performing?" the Madame asked as I was on my way out.

"Harudanji," I said, perhaps too quickly. Tomo had made certain to tell me who would be performing.

"Your brother will be sure to pick up something from him."

"Yes, that's what he said."

Harudanji was at the time a well-known practitioner of the traditional art of *rakugo* story telling. The Madame was right— Tomo would have had much to learn from him, if we had in fact been going to the *rakugo* theater.

"Getting something to eat afterwards?"

"Yes, we thought we might get some dinner."

The Madame nodded, and I slid open the door and bowed, and then I slid the door back shut and started off down the street. Exiting our narrow alley, I made my way out to the main avenue, Asakusa Dori, and there I caught the streetcar for Asakusabashi. It was early evening, just about 4:30, and the streetcar was packed with students and housewives and men of every description. A young mother was standing next to me, one child strapped to her back while she gently but persistently scolded her other child, who was clinging to her skirt. Across the car a man was speaking excitedly to his younger colleague about a business meeting they had evidently just come from. In the back, one young soldier was telling a story to his buddy, who was laughing and making comments in turn. Other people read the evening newspaper or simply stood or sat with nondescript expressions on their faces. None of them knew I was going to see my Lieutenant.

At Asakusabashi I transferred to another streetcar, this one less full, and I was able to get a seat for the ride over to Jinbocho. I got off a stop early and walked up the street past the bookshops that stood there one after another. The farther I walked, the harder my heart pounded and the drier my mouth became. I wondered again if I should really go through with it. I could still turn back. All I had to do was turn around and walk back in the other direction. But I kept moving forward, putting one foot in front of the other, inevitably coming closer to our arranged meeting place. I looked up at a clock across the street and saw I was still ten minutes early, and then I stopped in front of one of the bookshops and picked up a book from an outside rack and flipped through it.

"Looking for anything in particular?" a clerk asked, coming outside.

"No, not really," I said, quickly putting the book back.

"Feel free to look around."

I thanked the clerk, and then I walked on toward the next intersection, toward the Iwanami bookshop, where we were to meet, and as I got closer I could see the Lieutenant was already there waiting, standing tall in his uniform, his cap at a jaunty angle, a cigarette in his hand. He hadn't seen me yet, and one last time I almost turned back, but then he spotted me and raised his hand and started walking toward me.

"It was good of you to come," he said, smiling and looking

me over from head to toe. "You really are beautiful."

I could feel my face turning red as I bowed in greeting.

"Have any trouble finding the place?"

"No, I've been here before with my brother."

He nodded and told me he knew the area well. It seemed he had been a student at Nihon University, and had lived in a boarding house nearby. He tossed his cigarette on the sidewalk and stubbed it out, and then we started walking back in the direction from which I had just come. I was in a daze— it seemed unreal that he was actually there, walking by my side.

"I just wanted to pick up a book of poems," he said. "You mind?"

"No, of course not."

We walked past the bookshop at which I had just briefly stopped and went into the shop right after it. The Lieutenant seemed to know specifically what he was looking for, heading directly for a particular section and browsing through the books there. The shop was very small, with books piled everywhere, and I stood in a corner at the front, trying to stay out of the way of the other customers while I waited for the Lieutenant.

"Are you hungry?" he asked as we left.

"A little," I lied, really having no appetite at all.

He said there was a good *yakitori* spot he knew nearby, and he suggested we go there. Walking back to the main intersection, we crossed and started up the hill until we came to a small alley, and at the end of the alley was the *yakitori* shop. It was a large shop as such shops go, crowded and smoky. We sat at a small table in the back, and the Lieutenant ordered a few different types of skewered chicken and a bottle of beer with two glasses.

"Oh, I can't drink," I said.

"Just a little," he insisted, "nothing more than you had the other night."

"But I had too much the other night."

He told me not to worry, that I would be fine, and then the skewered chicken came out with the beer and the two glasses, and the Lieutenant poured some beer for me and I took a sip, and same as the night of my debut I felt light-headed and hot, and I could feel my face turning red again. He wanted to know everything about me— where I'd been born, and how many brothers and sisters I had, and how I'd come to Tokyo, and how I'd come to be at our geisha house. I tried to answer his questions as honestly as I could, but I didn't want him to think my origins too extremely humble, and so I told him I was from the city of Oita, not the fishing village of Kujirahe, and I told him my father was a merchant, not a carpenter, and I told him I had been discovered by the Madame during one of her recruiting trips around the country. It was not just any girl, after all, who could become a geisha in Asakusa.

"No, indeed not," he agreed.

"And how about you?" I asked. "Where are you from?"

He said he was from right there in Tokyo, from Kameido, just the other side of the Sumida River, not far from Asakusa. In fact, he said his parents' home was very near Kameido Tenjin, the well-known shrine. But he didn't want to talk about himself too much, and he turned the conversation back to me again, asking me about the training I was doing in song and dance. I told him I was a poor dancer, and he laughed, and then I told him I was somewhat better at singing and playing the samisen, and he seemed pleased to hear that.

"You're a romantic," he said.

"Why do you say that?"

"All musicians are romantics. You're a romantic."

The Lieutenant was drinking at a much faster pace than I was, and later, in addition to the beer, he had *sake*, and his face also began to turn red. He loosened his collar, and I could see a scar starting at the front of the base of his neck reaching down toward his chest, and I thought it likely he had gotten the scar while he was away at the war. I said my brother had told me he'd been in China, and I asked him where in China, and he said he'd been in the center of the country, in Wuhan. I didn't recognize the name at first, but then I remembered there had been a large battle there the year before, a big victory for our brave troops.

"I'm sorry," he said. "I shouldn't have asked you to come."

"No," I blurted out, "I was so happy to hear from you."

There were four students at a nearby table, and they started to sing, a patriotic song popular at the time.

"One of them must have been called up," the Lieutenant said, glancing in their direction.

He apologized again for asking me to come, but said he hadn't had a choice, that he had had to see me. I probably wouldn't understand— he didn't expect me to— but once a man had seen what he had seen, there was something sacred about love. There was a need to fight death with love, to find the perfect girl, the perfect love. The moment he had seen me, he had known I was that girl, and he had known too, right at that moment, that I felt the same deep emotions for him. As the words kept coming from his lips, I started feeling light-headed, and then he leaned across the table and took hold of my hand and looked deeply into my eyes, and I thought I might swoon right then and there.

"I know you've got to get back," he said.

"Yes," I managed to say, "I can't be too late."

He said he had a friend who lived nearby, and he asked if I wouldn't mind going by there on the way back to the streetcar stop. It would only be a few minutes out of the way. He wouldn't have asked, but it might be the last chance he would have to see this friend— at least in this world.

How could I refuse? He paid the bill, and we left the *yakitori* shop and continued down the alley, and then we took a right and headed up another alley, and there was a small boarding house there, and the Lieutenant walked in ahead of me and got a key out of the mailbox and led the way up the stairs to the second floor. At the end of the hall he slid open the door of the room there, and we went in. It was a small room, six mats. No one was there. I didn't ask why. Then the Lieutenant grabbed me in his arms, and I buried my head in his chest. What happened after that is a blur in my memory. There seems to have been some awkward fumbling about— even perhaps some partial exposure of my modestly accented bosom— before I found myself on my backside with the Lieutenant on top of me. I remember, with sudden insight, realizing how the mechanics work between a man and a woman and, for a very brief moment, wondering whether it wouldn't be better to stop, but then I recalled that refrain again— *but a drop of dew upon the iris blade*— and I gave myself to him in complete and sincere surrender.

He would leave for the front in three more days, he said. His new posting was to Taiyuan, in the province of Shanxi. I made certain to memorize the name of the city. He promised to write. That wouldn't be a problem, I told him— we'd pretend he was a cousin. Walking back down the hill to the main avenue, we said our farewells and then I boarded a streetcar and stretched out the window and waved to him as he gradually receded in the distance, his figure finally disappearing as we turned a corner. Oh, my true love! My feelings were all in a jumble. I was certain I had just experienced a depth of emotion never before experienced by any other girl in the entire history of the human race. And yet, with a chilling clarity, putting two and two together, I then also suddenly realized I might have given away for nothing that which was to have gone to a so-called "patron" for a significant sum. Most certainly, without any shadow of a doubt, my career as a geisha was now over before it had even begun.

7

Over the next several days I gave considerable thought to going in to see the Madame and confessing all that had happened. I was positive that in the end, in one way or another, the whole story would in any case be revealed. Better to be forthcoming about it than found out like a common criminal. It wasn't, after all, as though I had murdered someone. It was simply a matter of true love. But human nature being what it is, I put off my confession day after day, coming up with one excuse after another.

Finally my hesitations were, as it was, overcome by events. The development of which I speak occurred ten days after my tryst with the Lieutenant. I was called in to see the Madame, and I was certain then that I had been found out. Our conversation took place in the Western-style parlor. You might think it odd for there to be a Western-style parlor in such a traditional establishment as ours, but evidently the Madame had decided it appropriate to add such a room a few years earlier. Even the Emperor, after all, had taken to wearing Western-style uniforms.

"I have something of great importance to talk to you

about," she began.

I immediately hung my head, prepared for the worst, but I should have known the Madame would have spoken to me in the more formal setting of one of the Japanese-style rooms if she had intended to conduct an inquisition.

"We have had a request from Minister Kukihara," she went on.

"The Minister?"

"Yes, the Minister."

I thought back to my debut, recalling all that had happened that nerve-wracking evening. The Madame paused, and I could see she was searching for words.

"I assume you know," she finally continued, "what goes on between a man and a woman... when they sleep together..."

As I have previously mentioned, I had not had the foggiest until a few days earlier, but of course I could not say that to the Madame.

"I'm sorry," I said, "but I'm afraid..."

The Madame looked surprised that I could be so innocent, and then proceeded to give me a brief explanation.

"Really?" I said when she had finished. "It doesn't seem that..."

"Yes, I know," the Madame said with a sigh, "but that's what's done. It's not as bad as it sounds. Most women get used to it. I dare say some even grow to enjoy it after a while."

I shook my head. "I can't imagine..."

"But in your case..."

The Madame's voice trailed off, and I could see she was again searching for words. In my case? What was so different about my case?

"But we'll talk about that in a moment. I'm getting ahead of myself."

The Madame went on to tell me that a girl's first

experience was a very significant event in her life, and that participating as the male partner was highly valued by certain men. In the world of the geisha, this first experience was called the *mizuage,* or "raising from the water," so described because, just as a merchant would "raise his goods from the water"— unload his goods from a boat and put them out for sale— so would this girl now be ready for presentation. The word would be put out to worthy potential patrons that the *maiko* in question was available and allow these men an opportunity to make a financial proposition. Yes, as I had feared, I had given away for nothing that which was to have gone to the highest bidder for a significant sum.

"But in your case," the Madame said, using those words again, "we've had a preemptive offer from the Minister."

Now I was done for. A preemptive offer? A preemptive offer to buy something that had already been given away? I was just about to confess, but then the Madame continued, not allowing me to get a word in.

"And he's attached a very peculiar condition."

"A peculiar condition?"

"Yes... as part of the arrangement, we must agree to maintain your maidenhood."

This was very peculiar indeed. To maintain that which had already been lost? I was just again about to confess, but once more the Madame started talking before I could say anything.

"I don't know how you feel about all this."

How was I supposed to feel? She had no notion... "I just don't understand," I said. "Why would he pay for something he's not going to..."

"You see," the Madame said, choosing her words carefully, "the Minister seems to think that you are... blessed in a special way."

Blessed? The Lieutenant had used the word "sacred." Now the Minister was using the word "blessed." The Lieutenant had found it necessary to consecrate our love in a physical union. Now the Minister wished to sanctify yet another love in a platonic relationship. It was all too much to make sense of. My head was spinning.

"He said you should be 'preserved for the good of the nation.'"

Preserved for the good of the nation? What on earth...

"Suzu..."

"Yes..."

"You see, they feel that in this holy mission upon which our nation is now embarked, we must use all of our resources, and in the words of the Minister, 'What is more pure and powerful than the preserved maidenhood of a young woman?'"

"Really..."

I took a couple of deep breaths, trying to digest all of what the Madame had said. And then it suddenly struck me— if the Minister would not be sampling the goods, he would have no idea if they were damaged or not. The "peculiar condition" which he had attached just might be my saving grace.

"Suzu..."

The Madame was once more trying to regain my attention.

"Yes..."

"You understand what I am saying?"

I looked at the Madame, and then I looked down at the floor and slowly thought everything through one more time.

"Suzu..."

"Yes," I said, looking up, "I don't know... I'm not sure... The Minister of Public Enlightenment... I mean... am I really worthy of this?"

"In this life," the Madame said, taking my hand in hers, "one's destination is often not clear. Nonetheless, one must set off on the journey."

I nodded, and then unexpectedly, my eyes filled with tears.

"There, there, now," the Madame said, stroking my hand. "I know it's a lot to take in all at one time." And then turning towards the small altar that stood in the alcove behind her, she said, "Let's pray to the gods."

And the Madame and I bowed our heads and put our hands together and silently prayed, my prayers perhaps being expressed more fervently, I supposed, than those of the Madame.

8

Later that same day, the Madame took Mangetsu aside and talked to her about the decision that had been made concerning my status.

"It must be the first case ever in the long history of our nation," Mangetsu said, when told the news, "of a maiden still being a maiden after undergoing a *mizuage*."

"Yes, I think that is quite likely," the Madame agreed.

Mangetsu asked rather pointedly if I would still be her apprentice, and the Madame said that would still be the case, and Mangetsu then asked it there would be a need to modify my training at all, and the Madame said she didn't know. Captain Mushitani, Minister Kukihara's chief aide, would be coming by the following day to outline the specifics of my new role.

The Captain did indeed come the next afternoon, arriving at precisely 3:00, the appointed hour. The Madame and I were waiting for him in the Western-style parlor. Takako, our chief housekeeper, showed him in, and I immediately recognized him from the night of my debut. He was the officer who had been sitting next to the Minister. He was a short, thin man with a bald head and what appeared to be a poor imitation of his superior officer's facial hair— a scraggly stubble that, similar to the Minister's moustache, ended abruptly on both sides of his nose without extending properly across his full lip. He was perspiring profusely.

"Would you like a cold drink?" the Madame offered solicitously after the standard greetings had been exchanged.

"Yes, yes, thank you," the Captain answered.

The Madame, no doubt worried about the aftereffects of the bodily fluids that would be seeping into her sofa, cringed as the Captain sat down. Takako left to fetch the cold drinks.

"This is indeed a tremendous opportunity to serve our nation," the Captain exclaimed, placing his cap and his briefcase carefully on the seat next to him.

"We are most grateful," the Madame replied, bowing low, "that our humble house might be able make even this small contribution."

I bowed low as well, my hands shaking, fearful of what was to come.

"You do understand the magnitude of your new position?" the Captain asked, turning his attention to me.

I bowed low once more, uncertain what to say.

"You mentioned something over the phone about an explanation of the duties," the Madame interceded.

"Yes, yes, the duties," the Captain said with a gleam in his eyes. "The duties..." He then proceeded to open his briefcase and take out some papers. He put his glasses on and studied the papers for a moment, and then he began to read out loud:

Article One: The maiko Funabashi Suzukaze shall henceforth be known as the Maiden Maiko.

Article Two: The Maiden Maiko shall be pure and perfect, and her maidenhood preserved for the good of the nation.

Article Three: The Maiden Maiko's house shall henceforth be known as the House of Sugutatsu. The House shall be commended throughout the land for its role in the upbringing of the Maiden Maiko, and the illustrious history of the House shall be taught to all school children within the confines of our great empire.

Neither the Madame nor I knew how to respond to this declaration from the Captain. Finally, the Madame managed to say, "The illustrious history of the House?"

Just at that moment Takako came in with glasses of cold wheat tea and put them out on the table.

"Yes," the Captain said, picking up his drink, "I expected you might have some questions about that."

He then went on to explain that, given the prominent role the Maiden Maiko would be playing in the affairs of the nation, it would be necessary for her House to have an appropriate origin story. He himself, he said with pride of ownership, had created one— in consultation with the Minister, of course. It went something like this: The then current master, Sugutatsu Ikuzo, was the twelfth in a direct line of descendants from the founder of the house, Sugutatsu Sugeimon, a well-known tea master and political figure of the eighteenth century. Sugeimon had been appointed to his position as master of the house by the eighth Tokugawa shogun, Yoshimune himself, the only case of a geisha house master ever being so appointed. Yoshimune, feeling the entertainers of the time lacked integrity and a deeper sense of meaning in their lives— that they needed more of a Zen-like discipline, a balance of the chrysanthemum with the sword— had decided to found a geisha house that would promote the principles of bushido, the "way of the warrior," in addition to the traditional skills of singing and dancing. With this in mind, he had ordered Sugeimon to set up an *okiya* in Asakusa, and placing an emphasis on the moral rectitude he felt should be central to the new house, he had ordained that the name of the new establishment would be Sugutatsu, "quick to stand up" or "upright." It was this extraordinary relationship with the very upper echelons of the ruling class that accounted for the distinctive status of Sugutatsu. It was also why Sugutatsu was presently the only *okiya* in the nation with a master as well as a madame.

The Madame was clearly flabbergasted. "But we don't have a master," she protested.

The Captain smiled blithely. "No, I wouldn't think you would. But that won't present a problem. I'm certain we can find the right man for the job."

I could see the panic on the Madame's face. The right man for the job? Was the Captain proposing to install an unknown man in her house in a position of authority? Who would this man be and what degree of control would he have over her affairs? The Madame's recovery was swift and impressive.

"No, we don't currently have a master," she said slowly, "but we might indeed have an appropriate candidate for the position."

The Captain leaned forward.

"He is in fact a baron," the Madame continued, "a man of superior character and vision."

"A baron," the Captain said loudly, clearly impressed by the title.

"Yes," the Madame repeated, "a man of superior character and vision."

"Might I ask his name?" the Captain inquired.

The Madame paused for a moment before saying in a hushed tone, "I think it best that I first consult with the gentleman. As I'm certain you can appreciate, sir, discretion is paramount in such matters."

As I listened to the Madame speak with such conviction, I wondered whom she might have in mind. She did indeed have a wide circle of clients and acquaintances, and it was more than possible she would have known a gentleman of high station fit for the role. You can only imagine my surprise then when I later learned the person to whom she was referring was Mr. Takeda Ryunosuke. Mr. Takeda was in fact a baron, but it would have been problematic, I dare say, to find anyone who would have agreed he was a "man of superior character and vision." Mangetsu said he had been one of the Madame's patrons when she was young. He had evidently been quite handsome and witty then, as well as being a man of title and means, but over the years he had made some poor investments and indulged in drink, and by this time he had become a pathetic figure of derision among all the girls of the house. The Madame, however, still apparently had a soft spot for him, even allowing him to stay some nights at the house, however drunk and reduced in circumstances he might have been. Despite his deficiencies, it seems the Madame had calculated she could manage him, and that made him a preferable choice to anyone the Captain might have sought to force on her. Over the next week or so she was somehow able to convince the Captain and his superiors at the Ministry that Mr. Takeda was "the right man for the job." I think they must have been quite blinded by the title of "baron"— as well as the Madame's outstanding abilities of persuasion. And thus it was that Mr. Takeda Ryunosuke became the Master of the House of Sugutatsu.

The day of his visit the Captain did also, as the Madame had expected, speak in some detail about the plans for the education of the Maiden Maiko. Apparently the Ministry had arranged for Unmu Sensei, a Grand Master of All Things Japanese, to be my personal tutor. The Sensei was not only a Shinto and Zen priest, the Captain explained, but also a 10th dan in kendo, judo, and aikido as well as a highly respected scholar of Japanese history and culture.

"You do understand the magnitude of your new position?" the Captain asked again when his explanation was complete.

I thought my head was going to explode. What in the world had I gotten myself into?

"Suzu...," the Madame prompted.

"Yes, sir," I said, my voice quavering, "I understand."

"Very well," the Captain nodded, a sense of satisfaction in his tone. "Your training will begin next week."

"Yes, sir," I responded, bowing as low as I possibly could.

9

Mangetsu had clearly been miffed that she had not been consulted before my appointment as the Maiden Maiko. This annoyance was not to last long, however— that was not Mangetsu's character. By the next day she had accepted my new role, and in fact was expressing pride that it was her apprentice who had been selected for this significant duty.

"It's all due to your thoughtful instruction," I would say without fail in response.

All the other girls of the house were also excited about my selection. Although, not surprisingly, they were also puzzled by the arrangement that had been made with the Minister. Why would he pay for something of which he had no intention of availing himself? This, of course, was the same question I had asked the Madame. Koyo, to whom Hoshi was apprenticed, said there was something similar in the Christian religion— the mother of their god was a maiden. A number of the girls doubted this assertion. Certainly this would be an impossibility. But Koyo maintained that this was indeed what the Christians believed and I, for one, felt she was most likely right, as Koyo was very well read and almost always right in such matters.

"Strange what some people will believe as part of their religion," Hoshi said.

"Strange indeed," all the other girls agreed.

I recalled again how the Lieutenant had said our love was "sacred," while the Minister had maintained I was "blessed." Now I was being compared to the mother of a god? Was there no end to the holy designations people wished to attach to me?

That following Monday, as the Captain had indicated, my training with Unmu Sensei began. Takako showed him into the room where the Madame and I were waiting, and without saying a word or acknowledging our presence, he sat down in a rigid posture on his knees on the tatami-matted floor and closed his eyes. He was a small, ancient man dressed in the simple white robe of an ascetic. Five minutes passed, then ten, as he remained silent and motionless. The Madame tilted her head toward me in puzzlement a few times, finally instructing me in a whisper to take up the same rigid posture as the Sensei and close my eyes. As I moved to take my position, the Madame quietly left the room. I sat there for what seemed an eternity, keeping my eyes shut, trying to stay as motionless as possible, and then suddenly, extremely close to the vicinity of my right ear, there came the sound of an explosive "Hah!"

I collapsed in shock on my side and, opening my eyes, looked up to see the Sensei standing over me. "Even in winter, water runs only downhill," he shouted, and then he walked to the other side of the room and sat down in a relaxed posture. Attempting to regain my composure, I sat up, smoothing my kimono and straightening my hair. As the Sensei stared deeply into my eyes, I was certain he could see I was not worthy of this position I had been given— that I was in love and not ready to attain a higher consciousness, that I was in fact not even a maiden. But he said nothing about these fears of mine. Instead, he launched directly into an account of the founding of our great nation.

Thus spake Ummu:

"In ancient times there existed only the gods, and the gods existed only in the sky, and to the land below, there being no land but only sea, the gods did not descend. Until one day a male god and a female god became desirous of eloping, and there being no such place to which to elope, they decided they would create such a place and with the objective of creating this place they attempted to mate, but not being experienced in such matters the first attempt was a failure, and the land to which they wished to elope was not created. Yet being of stout heart and mind, the male god and the female god attempted to mate once more, and this time they were successful and the issue of their coupling was a small island to which they proceeded to descend.

"There being no plants or animals on the island or fish in the sea, the male god and the female god created such as were necessary through further conjugal efforts— having become quite practiced now in such methods— and their island flourished and multiplied with life, sentient and non-sentient alike, and their island having thus become confining to the spirit, the male god and the female god became desirous of new lands and such were created in the same method as heretofore described.

"And these lands they so created they named Yamato, and of the beings created some were human, and these human beings became known as the people of Yamato."

With these words, Ummu concluded his chronicle. So that was how the people of Japan were created, I said to myself, as direct descendants of the gods. It was only many years later, after the war, when the Americans came to Japan, that I learned that they were also specially created by the gods, albeit their own gods of course, and that being specially created by the gods might not count for as much as I had once thought. At the time, however, this was a significant discovery for me, one which would come to greatly influence my life over the next several years.

At the beginning of my third week of training with Unmu Sensei, the new Master of the House of Sugutatsu— the aforementioned Mr. Takeda Ryunosuke— also began to attend my sessions. He had taken up residence in Sugutatsu by then, and the Madame explained to me that she had told the Ministry that the Master had insisted on attending. This was in fact not true, but she felt the Ministry would feel less inclined to question the fitness of the Master for his new role if he were attending my training sessions.

That first day the Sensei— whose name of Unmu was written with the characters for "clouds" and "fog"— took no notice of the Master, who lay hungover in a corner of the room the entire two-hour session. As the week progressed, the Sensei remained oblivious to the Master's presence, but I did notice a slow improvement in the condition of the Master himself. Day by day he was less hungover, and by the end of that first week he was even sitting up in the meditative posture taken by the Sensei— not for long periods, I must add, nor in a pose in any way approaching what might be acceptable, but at least he was sitting up. Thereafter, the further transformation of the Master was dramatically fast, as he gave up drink completely and submitted himself to the most rigorous of physical and spiritual training. Such were the powers of the Sensei. All of us at Sugutatsu were stunned, most especially so the Madame.

"It's a miracle sent from the gods," she said.

As those early days of training passed, I had hopes that I might be able to sometimes engage in informal conversation with the Sensei— some casual comments about the weather, for instance, or an exchange about my plans for the coming evening— but it seems the Sensei had reached such a high level of enlightenment that he was able to communicate only in aphorisms and "lecture speak." Rare indeed are such individuals, and I knew I must feel privileged to be his pupil.

10

On almost a daily basis over those first few weeks I again considered confessing. The whole thing was overwhelming. Who was I but little Panko from Kujirahe? And yet now I was promised to the Minister of Public Enlightenment and was being trained to be the Maiden Maiko by Unmu Sensei, a Grand Master of All Things Japanese. And I wasn't even a maiden! How long could I keep up this ruse? Surely I would be found out. Wasn't it better to just confess and get it over with? I came to think there might even be a chance the Madame would be understanding. After all, she had been a girl herself once, and perhaps she had experienced similar emotions of love for a young man, perhaps even for the Master. She might, in fact, still even be in love with him— despite the rules of the house. How else to account for the kind attitude she had maintained toward him even after he had sunken to the depths of dissipation? But in the end, I could not confess. I realized matters had gone too far by then. Such a confession would now be a humiliation not only for myself but for our house as well. The Madame's reputation and business would be ruined. My sisters at Sugutatsu would all be out of work. And what, in any event, were the true chances of being found out? Much less than my fears had led me to believe, I concluded, after calmer consideration of the situation. No, I had no choice but to grit my teeth and make my best efforts to become the embodiment of the Minister's vision for me.

By this time more than a month had elapsed since the Lieutenant had left for China. Day after day I waited for the mail to arrive, yearning desperately for a letter from my true love. But day after day no such letter arrived. I speculated as to why. There were numerous possibilities. Perhaps he had written, but the letter had been delayed. Perhaps he had written, but the letter had been sent to the wrong address. Perhaps he had written, but the letter had been lost. Perhaps he was in combat, and in no position to write. Perhaps, the gods forbid, he had been wounded. Perhaps, the gods forbid, he was dead. Perhaps, the gods forbid, he had never had any intention of writing and had already forgotten me. But it had only been a little more than a month, I told myself over and over, and I focused on the more positive possibilities, shutting out the negative. He was in a war zone, after all, and it couldn't be easy to get mail in and out. He was alive and well. I was certain of it— the gods would see to it. And he was still very much in love with me. I knew that too. That night he had been so passionate and his declarations of love so sincere. A girl knows these things in her heart. Still, it was hard, very hard, not to hear from him.

And then, about this same time, I received my first letter from the Colonel. It was special delivery. The Madame handed the letter over to me herself, saying she had not opened it. It was a private matter, she said, between me and the Colonel, and she would always respect that privacy. I was to find the Colonel liked to write long, descriptive letters. Over the next several years he would write me often, recording his views about everything under the sun— from military operations to politics, to the local climate and plants and animals, to his feelings for me. I fear it may be a breach of confidence to reveal the contents of these letters now, but he is dead and many years have passed and I feel my own story would be incomplete if I were not to do so, and so I will quote a passage here, and more in the pages to come. This is how the first letter began:

August 6, 1939

My dear Suzukaze,

I am writing to you from Taiyuan in Shanxi Province.

Please look at a map and see where this is. First find Beijing and then take your finger and move southwest until you come to the city of Shijiazhuang, and then from there go west until you come to Taiyuan. I want you to know where I am. That is important to me.

You may still think it odd that a man of my age and position would choose to write letters to a young lady of your age and position, but I wish to tell you again that it is very necessary for me. To put it bluntly, I have no one else in whom I can confide. I want you to take that in the right way. I don't mean that I have chosen you because there was no one else; rather, I have chosen you because you are special. I told you that the night of our first meeting, and I will say it again here. You must believe me when I say you are the very core and essence of our nation, our very heartbeat. You must believe that.

This war will not end anytime soon. There were many victories in the early days, with our forces driving south from Beijing and west from Shanghai, climaxing in the grand battle of Wuhan. We had more than 300,000 men on the ground there, and it is said the Chinese forces numbered more than a million. I don't know if the people back home realize the scale of this war. But that was the last great victory, in the fall of last year. The Chinese withdrew then into the hinterlands, taking their capital with them. After we took Nanjing, they moved the capital to Wuhan, and when we took Wuhan they moved it once more, this time to Chongqing, in the mountains, ever further down the Yangze River. It's a very large country, China. Now we control the big cities, the ports, and the railways, but there's still much we don't control. The Communists hide in the mountains near here and ambush our troops and attack the railroads. They and other guerrilla forces like them will not easily disappear. As I say, this war will not end anytime soon.

I don't know how long I'll be in Taiyuan. Essentially I have been banished here because of my past loyalties within our army. Unfortunately, the army is like any other organization— jealousies and rivalries drive everything. While other officers are winning glory on battlefields far to the south, I have been relegated to garrison duty here. It is the same with the other officers in my faction. They have also all been banished to marginal theaters or given assignments where failure is assured. I must not think too deeply about these things, but rather accept them as part of the reality of my present life. If I am fortunate, more opportunities will arise in the future for me to serve our nation in a meaningful way.

The Colonel went on to write about several other things. But what caught my attention of course was the mention of Taiyuan. That was the same city where the Lieutenant was based. I'd memorized the name that night, the night we'd been together, and later I'd found it on a map. It was located right where the Colonel said it was, southwest by west of Beijing. So the two of them, the Lieutenant and the Colonel, were in the same city. I immediately wondered if they were in the same unit. Was the Colonel perhaps even the Lieutenant's commanding officer? Did they know each other? No, no, that would all be too much of a coincidence.

Not at all likely, I told myself. But why was there no letter from the Lieutenant when the Colonel's had come through posthaste? All the same questions once more assailed me. Had his letter been delivered to the wrong address or simply lost? The Colonel's had arrived special delivery, but maybe the Lieutenant's mail was not afforded such special care. And again, the other negative possibilities crept into my mind—had he been wounded or killed, did he no longer care for me?

11

Through the hot and humid month of August so my days passed, training in the morning with the Sensei and entertaining in the evening, while constantly brooding about the Lieutenant. Then near the end of the month I was told by the Madame that the entire house would be going to Nikko for four days. Apparently Unmu Sensei had scheduled his summer retreat in the mountains for that time, and the Ministry thought it would be a very good idea for me to accompany him. They also felt, the Madame said, that it would be a perfect opportunity for the rest of the girls to get some basic training. The other girls would never be expected to follow the stringent regimen of the Maiden Maiko, she emphasized, but there was an "illustrious history" that now existed for the House of Sugutatsu, and it would be necessary to "keep up appearances" to some degree.

The day of our departure I was up early after another restless night. For me, the trip to Nikko would be a welcome break.

"How long is the train ride?" Hoshi asked as we picked

up our travel bags and headed downstairs.

"About three hours," I said.

"At least it will be cooler there."

"Yes, cooler."

We joined the others congregating in the foyer. All the eight girls of the house would be going on the trip, in addition to the Madame and the Master. Takako was directing traffic, getting bags stacked up in a corner and ushering girls out on to the street. She must have then been in her late forties, although I thought of her already as an old woman. She was round and not very tall, and had a mothering way about her that sometimes irritated the girls, but we knew at heart she was a good person. Outside it was a bright, sunny day, and Hoshi and I quickly put up our parasols to protect ourselves. A few minutes later the Madame and the Master came down and joined us outside.

"Take good care of the house while we're gone," the Madame said to Takako.

"Don't worry about a thing," Takako replied, bowing low.

And then we were off, the Madame leading our procession followed by the girls of the house, with the Master trailing after. We all wore nice kimono— nothing of the finer sort the Madame, for example, would wear when meeting someone for business purposes, and certainly far removed from the elaborate attire we would wear when entertaining, but still kimono made with superior craftsmanship using first-rate material. It would do no good to look shabby in public, even when on an excursion such as this. As for the Master, he was also wearing a kimono. He had always worn Western clothing, but within the last week or so he had taken to wearing kimono. It was part of his transformation.

It was only about a six or seven minute walk to the train station. From there the express departed directly for Nikko.

As was true everywhere one went at the time, there was a distinctly patriotic air about the station. Our rising sun flag was much in evidence, as were posters praising our fighting men while exhorting those of us not in the military to pitch in and do our share to support them. Here and there milling about were also groups of young men in uniform, some in the army, some in the navy. The men in their uniforms only served to intensify my thoughts of the Lieutenant.

"It's track number four," the Madame said once we were inside.

Hoshi wanted to buy a luncheon box for herself, so we quickly went to the kiosk at the head of the platform before boarding.

"Aren't you getting anything?" she asked.

"No, nothing," I said.

"You're sure?"

"Yes, very sure…"

On the train we sat with Mangetsu and Koyo. As I mentioned earlier, Hoshi was apprenticed to Koyo, who was two years older than Mangetsu and had come to Sugutatsu before her, but they were both from Toyama, across the mountains from Tokyo, on the side that faces Korea, and perhaps because of that they seemed to have much in common and were quite close. Not that their personalities were similar. No, they were actually quite different, Mangetsu being more outgoing, while Koyo had a quiet sophistication about her that was unmatched by any other girl in the house. She was also beautiful in a different way, taller and thinner, her legs shapely and her face— in line with her name of "red leaf"— pretty in a stunningly modern way.

"Did you see Mr. Fukunaga last night?" Mangetsu asked Koyo not long after we departed the station.

"No, the night before. Last night I was entertaining some

customers in the Ginza."

"And how is he?"

"Oh, he was in high spirits. Business is good, evidently."

Mr. Fukunaga was Koyo's "patron."

"Are you still going with him to the seaside next month?"

"Yes, to his place in Kamakura."

Mangetsu had told me that Mr. Fukunaga was chairman of a munitions company. They made bombs and bullets and guns and things of that nature and sold them to the army. It was a good business to be in, Mangetsu said, especially since the start of the liberation of China two years before.

"And what about your Mr. Mizuno?" Koyo asked Mangetsu. "How's he doing?"

"Oh, him?" Mangetsu said with a playful wave of her hand. "He's fine, I suppose…"

Mr. Mizuno was Mangetsu's current patron and president of a textile company. It seems he had large contracts to sell uniforms to both the army and navy.

"How about the two of you? Will you be going somewhere?"

"Now why would I want to do that?" Mangetsu said with a laugh. "Spend a week at the beach with the same man? It might be fine for you, but it's not for me…"

Koyo laughed in turn. "No, it wouldn't be, would it?"

It had only been about three months since Mr. Mizuno had become Mangetsu's patron. Before that there had been a Mr. Kodama, and before that a Mr. Ito, and before that a Mr. Hirayama. Mangetsu was very popular with all the men, it seemed. I'd rather liked Mr. Kodama. I'd had to deliver small things to him a few times for Mangetsu, and he'd taken the time to talk to me, and on one occasion he'd even given me a small gift, a box of sweets. But then one day Mangetsu had told me she was no longer seeing him. That was also when she had warned me against falling in love.

"Suzu," Koyo said, handing me her thermos, "why don't you pour everyone some tea."

I reached down and took some porcelain teacups out of my bag, and as I did so Koyo asked the Madame and the Master if they would also like some. The two of them were sitting across from us, on the other side of the aisle.

"Yes," the Madame said, "that would be good. Let's have some tea."

But the Master said nothing, simply shaking his head while continuing to look out the window, seemingly deep in thought. As the sun struck his face I noted again how thick his hair was— long and streaked with grey, combed straight back— and how prominent his nose, large and curving down at its end like the beak of a hawk, his thin face making the nose that much more prominent. I could see how he might have been considered handsome when he was younger.

"How about a tangerine?" Mangetsu asked the Madame.

"Yes, now that would be nice, too, wouldn't it?"

I poured out tea for everyone and passed out the cups, and then Mangetsu gave me a tangerine for the Madame and I handed it over to her.

"Aren't you going to have one yourself?" she asked.

"Thank you," I replied, "maybe I will."

I took a tangerine out of Mangetsu's bag and peeled off the outer cover, and then I broke off a piece and peeled back the inner skin and sucked out the fruit. It tasted surprisingly good, I must say.

"Some more tea?" I asked the Madame, motioning with the thermos.

"No, I'm fine, thank you," she said with a polite smile.

After we'd had our tea and tangerine, it got quiet, with some of the girls nodding off and taking naps. I looked out the window, watching as the city gradually disappeared and the farmland of the countryside began. The rice fields were green and full of water, stretching on kilometer after kilometer as we made our way north, broken up here and there by farmhouses and small stands of trees and the occasional village. Later the train started climbing as we moved into the foothills of the mountains, and we ran along a river, and in and out of several tunnels, and we climbed higher, and finally just short of three hours after we had left Asakusa, we arrived in Nikko.

"You can already feel how much cooler the air is," Hoshi said, as we pulled into the station.

"Yes, yes, you can," I agreed.

Outside a fleet of rickshaws was waiting for us. The Madame instructed us to split up two girls to a vehicle, and Hoshi and I chose a rickshaw near the end of the procession.

"Up from Tokyo?" our puller asked.

"Yes," Hoshi answered.

"First time to Nikko?"

He was by no means a young man, his skin tanned dark, deeply grooved wrinkles on both sides of his face, his hair heavily sprinkled with grey. Already so many of the younger men were gone to the war.

"Yes, yes, it is."

The man rubbed the back of his head. "I've never seen so many pretty girls at one time. Are you all from the same school or something?"

"Something like that," Hoshi said, tilting her head and smiling.

"It's kind of a nice thing," the man said, rubbing the back of his head once more, "to see so many pretty girls."

Then he turned around and reached down and picked up the two shafts of the rickshaw, and lifting us in the air, we were off down the road, quickly leaving the town and heading out into the countryside. The muffled spinning of the wheels and the soft footfalls of the puller were the only sounds to be heard as we passed between open fields and bamboo groves, and I found myself very much looking forward to our time away from the hubbub of the big city.

12

After about twenty minutes we came to the entrance of a small trail and our puller let us off, and from there we hiked up a steep slope some forty minutes until we came to the rustic temple where we would be staying. Unmu Sensei, wearing only a small loincloth wrapped about his thin frame, welcomed us at the gate.

"When one has climbed a mountain," he declared, "one can see farther."

Surprisingly, at this point it was the Master, not the Madame, who stepped forward to represent us, getting down on his knees and bowing low, saying, "We offer our humble gratitude for the gracious spirit that would allow such worthless beings as ourselves to set foot on these sacred grounds."

"There, there," the Sensei responded, "rise up now and enter, for the worthless shall be worthy, and the worthy shall be worthless, and twixt the two no difference shall be made."

As I indicated earlier, the Master's progress in such a short period of time had truly been extraordinary, and by this point I think the Madame was already quite happy to step back and let the Master take the lead in matters concerning the Sensei. Although always very respectful of Unmu, I don't think she ever saw him in quite the same light as many others.

Following this exchange between the two gentlemen, we all walked on into the temple grounds and across to the entranceway of the temple itself. There we removed our footwear and washed our feet before stepping up inside. The Sensei then led us down a corridor to a large room with a well-polished wooden floor, and sitting down in formal style, he motioned for us to do the same, and we followed his example, positioning ourselves directly across from him in two neat lines of five each. Fifteen minutes of silence ensued, not a word spoken, as the Sensei looked at each of us, now for a few seconds, then for a minute or more, and then back again, moving his gaze from person to person. It seemed his eyes rested on me more than on any of the others, despite my several weeks of training with him, and I wondered, I must confess, if he was trying to remember who I was. Certainly this might be a case of overthinking on my part, certainly it is more than likely that he did remember who I was, but again, given the level of enlightenment he had reached, it was a possibility that could not be ruled out. And once more I noted with humility how privileged I was to to be his pupil.

At the end of the fifteen minutes, the Sensei stood slowly and walked out of the room, and the Madame told us to get ourselves changed. I looked about and found the Master had already disappeared, presumably to another room to also change. Thin white robes were gotten out of the closet, and we took off our kimono and put on the robes. The Madame then informed us of the rules that would be in place during our stay at the temple— no talking or eating from sunrise until we took our bath at the end of the day before dinner. Ummu Sensei would give us instruction during the day. A small breakfast would be taken before sunrise, and in the evening we would have another modest meal, followed by a lecture.

As soon as we had all changed, the Sensei reappeared and motioned for us to follow him, which we did, marching back down the corridor and on to the temple grounds once more, all of us without our footwear. The Master had rejoined us by this point, dressed in his own white robe. The Sensei then led us through a series of exercises, raising his hands above his head and to the side and down to his toes and back again. When he was done leading the calisthenics, Ummu lay down on his back and stared upward.

"Remember," he declared, "it is not necessary for any man to hold up the sky."

The Sensei then jumped to his feet and started off at a trot out of the grounds of the temple and up the trail, taking all of us girls with him farther up the mountain. The Madame and the Master stayed behind. It was a struggle for us to keep up, and the Sensei soon slowed down and started walking, going up the mountain and across the mountain and down the mountain and then back across again. We'd been gone more than three hours when we finally arrived back at the temple. It was a difficult hike, and there was definitely some grumbling in the ranks, but it was a muted grumbling and none of it was directed at me. The other girls knew I had not sought out the position of Maiden Maiko— it was the Minister who had come looking for me. And besides, there was now the prestige and attendant benefits that came with the new designation our *okiya* had been given as the House of Sugutatsu. All of the girls were quite well aware of this.

After our hike, we finished up our training for the day with a light introductory session to judo, and then before dinner we bathed in a nearby stream. Proper modesty was maintained by having the Master and the Sensei bathe downstream while the women bathed upstream in a small pool behind some conveniently placed boulders. It was a hot day, even at that altitude in the mountains, and the water was cool and refreshing. I looked about, watching the girls getting in and out of the water, sunning themselves on the rocks. Each was attractive in her own way. Mangetsu was standing nearby, her body half submerged, a small cloth towel held modestly in front, and I was reminded again of the fullness of her figure— her bosom and derrière both being well endowed— and I couldn't help but think that the Madame may have also had this "fullness" in mind when she had named her. Koyo sat on an adjacent ledge, her beautiful long legs dangling in the water, the two of them talking.

"Oh, this feels so good," Hoshi said, swimming over to my side.

She then ducked under the water, swam several strokes, and burst on to the surface again. I laughed at Hoshi's playfulness, and then I got out of the water and sat on a nearby rock by myself, looking around again and imagining what the other girls saw when they looked at me. Although then only fifteen, I had already essentially attained the proportions of my adult self. I think it's safe to say that while the other girls would not have thought of me as a classic beauty in the way of Mangetsu or a modern beauty in the manner of Koyo, they would have still judged me to be quite attractive. In the years to come I would be told on more than one occasion that my large round eyes, well-shaped nose, slightly prominent cheek bones, modestly accented bosom and derrière, and shapely legs— each contributing in its own way— accounted for my "distinctive good looks." I don't mean to be boastful, but in a record such as this I feel it is best to not be falsely modest, seeing that one's looks could significantly affect the twists and turns of the tale.

Dinner that evening was simple— roots and twigs and the leaves of various plants mixed with the spleen and liver of a wild boar that Ummu had ensnared and slaughtered the day before. "The lives of all sentient beings are sacred," Ummu declared, as he chewed vigorously on the remains of the boar.

After dinner the Master was sitting by himself in a corner of the courtyard of the temple. I thought of approaching him, but couldn't bring myself to do it. Although we had been in training together for several weeks, we rarely spoke to each other. Our sessions with the Sensei were always very full and intense, and when they were finished, the Master would quickly retreat to his room. When I saw him about the house on other occasions, we would exchange polite greetings but never more than that. I wished I knew more about him. I wondered if he had ever been married. Was he maybe even married now but no longer living with his wife? And I wondered if he had any children, and if he did, how many and where they were living. And I wondered what had happened to make him so fond of drink. Had it just been a matter of losing his fortune? Or had there been other factors? And more than anything, I wondered about the relationship between him and the Madame. For the most part they were not together. I didn't see them take meals together, or sit together in the evening, or take walks together. As I say, the Master would do his training in the morning with the Sensei and me, and then most of the rest of the day he would stay alone in his study. Occasionally he would go out for walks by himself. It was whispered by some of the girls that they had seen him sometimes slip into the Madame's bedroom at night, but I didn't know if this was true— I didn't know if rumors were being circulated just for rumor's sake. Mangetsu had said they'd been lovers when they were younger, and we knew the Madame had sometimes allowed the Master to stay overnight in the days when he'd been down on his luck and always drunk. But what about now? What about now that they were living in the same house and the Master was no longer a derelict but rather the Master of the House of Sugutatsu? How did they see each other now in the sober light of day many years after they had first been intimate with each other?

I had no answer to these questions.

13

That evening there was a lecture from Unmu Sensei. All of us were already sitting in formal posture on the tatami-matted floor when the Sensei entered. As was his usual practice, he made no acknowledgement of our presence, instead proceeding directly to the front of the room where a water-ink painting of a waterfall hung on the wall. It was difficult to be certain, but he appeared to be counting the drops of water splashing up from the rocks on which the water was falling. He then paused for a moment, seeming to do some calculations, and then he nodded and turned to us and sat down and began to speak as only he could speak.

Thus spake Unmu:

"In ancient times there existed only the gods, and the gods existed only in the sky, and to the land below, there being no land but only sea, the gods did not descend. Until one day one male god and one female god..."

It was the lecture on the founding of Japan. By now each and every one of these words was familiar to me, as he had started each of my training sessions at Sugutatsu with this same lecture. As I well knew by then, the Sensei was a proponent of a national school of thought that promoted "the uniquely native aspects of Japanese culture." Many of his lectures harkened back to the earliest days of the nation, before even the introduction of things Chinese. It was such a pure and beautiful time. And now these moving lessons were to be shared with my sisters. I felt a sense of contentment at this thought.

During the rest of our time in Nikko we continued a similar pattern of training each day— up before dawn, a physical workout of some sort, a meditative session, another physical workout, another meditative session, a cold bath, our evening meal, and then Ummu's lecture. At least once a day we would also practice calligraphy and composition. Throughout my time at Sugutatsu, not just during this trip to Nikko, there was a great deal of emphasis placed on writing skills, particularly on the writing of poetry. In my early days my abilities were quite limited, as I had only finished the fourth grade in Kujirahe and had had no further formal schooling since coming to Tokyo. I seemed, however, to have an innate knack for putting pen or brush to paper, and over the course of my first few years at Sugutatsu I made rapid progress. It is this basic training in the art of writing that has allowed me to tackle this memoir. As to how skilled a level I have ultimately been able to attain, I will let you be the judge.

In addition to our mountain hikes, the other physical workouts in which we engaged consisted of judo and kendo. Upon our return to Sugutatsu all of the girls would continue to train in these two disciplines. As the Madame had said, the other girls would not be expected to train in the same manner as the Maiden Maiko, but now as members of the "esteemed" House of Sugutatsu it was incumbent on all of us to obtain at least a certain degree of competency in a martial art. It is interesting to note that, over time, most of the girls came to feel this additional training actually helped them with their dance routines. Although in my own case, I must admit dance continued to be the weakest of my skills, despite my own continued considerable progress in not only judo and kendo but aikido as well. Everyone has a weakness, I suppose, something at which they will never excel no matter how much they practice. Mine— as you may remember I had admitted to the Lieutenant— was dance. On the other hand, when it came to the samisen, I was an above-average performer. I think even Koyo, who was quite good, would have recognized me as the superior player. If one is lucky, the gods give back in one talent what they've taken away in another. As the Madame had known even before I myself did, I had an ear for music. It was with this in mind that she had given me the name Suzukaze, or "chimes in the wind," saying, "you will be joyous and musical and give much solace to those around you." My entire life I have tried to live up to the spirit of those words.

The lectures for the rest of the week continued our education in the history of Japan. The final night covered the coming of the Americans up until the present time.

Thus spake Ummu:

"And so it was that ships one day appeared off our coast, bereft of sail but sailing nonetheless, their locomotion propelled by mysterious smoke-emitting machines. And these ships made their way close upon Edo, and on that city they trained their guns and threatened our great nation save we open our ports and agree to trade with them. And having no choice in the matter, our nation then lacking in these so-called 'black ships' and the related science, we opened our ports and agreed to trade with these people, who called themselves Americans.

"And these Americans, being of clever disposition, devised a treaty whereby they exchanged two of our coins for one of theirs, and allowed such that there was no duty on their goods imported into our nation, and allowed that no man of their nation should be tried in our courts, even should that man murder a man of our nation or rape one of our women. And this we called the unequal treaty. And upon the signing of this treaty, there appeared ships from all the nations of Europe— from England and France and Russia and Germany and other nations too numerous to enumerate— demanding that they be given the same rights as those accorded the Americans. And this, too, we agreed to because we had no choice. And having been so laid upon by these so-called Western nations, though some be to our east and some be to our west, we determined that we would contest these nations in all aspects of social intercourse— be it martial or economic or scientific— and having thus so determined, we engaged foreign experts in all fields to come to our nation and from these experts we derived expertise, and upon so mastering this expertise we added to it so as to be more expert than the experts, and thus enable ourselves to beat the Westerners at their own game, as it were. And having so made preparations, we surveyed our surroundings and found that the Western nations had divided the world among themselves, with one nation taking India and another Indochina and another the grand southern archipelago of the Pacific and another Hawaii and so on, with China being divvied up among all of the Western nations, seeing that she had one-quarter of the world's population and many riches and was worthy of such special attention.

"And having thus surveyed our surroundings, we determined to wage war against China, so that we might liberate her from the Western nations and pass on our expertise and so return her to her past glories. And having so determined, we waged war against China and the results of the war were favorable towards our nation, and having been so favored, we came into possession of Korea and Taiwan and the Liaodong Peninsula, having thus gained territories where we might begin the education and uplifting of our Asian brothers. But the Russians were not pleased with this turn of events and conspired with the French and Germans to have us return Liaodong to the Chinese, whereupon the Russians took it for their own, and so it was that we harbored a bitterness in our hearts against the Russians and ten years later waged war on the Russians and took back Liaodong, and so wrought our rightful revenge.

"And the Russians, being not a clever people, then forced their ways on the Manchurians in the same manner, compelling our nation to intervene once more and take the Manchurians under our wing, providing aid and comfort to them in the formation of their new nation, Manchukuo. And so it is that we come to today, where many of the people of Asia still lie under the yoke of Western oppression, waiting for our great nation to take up the sacred mission of their liberation. And in this task we shall prevail, for it is only we who possess the spirit of Yamato."

So that was the horrible position in which our nation now found itself. I could only imagine all the millions of people in China, and the millions in India— and the millions in all the other countries whose names I did not even yet know— suffering under the tyranny of the Westerners, and it was almost more than I could bear. And as I looked about at the other girls, I could see that they had been similarly moved, all of them almost in tears. At least our men were now in China setting out on this sacred mission to liberate

Asia from these devious Westerners.

The following morning we arose early for our departure to Tokyo. On the train on the way back I gave much thought again to what the Sensei had said about the Westerners. It all seemed so distant and overwhelming, and the more I thought about it, the more my head hurt. How could our little nation take on so much? Yes, we were the people of Yamato, but how could we face down all of those barbaric Westerners by ourselves? Still, there had to be a way. Ummu wouldn't have said all those things unless there was a way. Certainly our leaders and all of the handsome young men in their uniforms would take care of everything. Certainly they would. That's what I told myself.

What I didn't know— what I couldn't know then— was the role I myself would come to play in this momentous undertaking.

14

The ceremony for my *mizuage* was held on September 28th of that year, 1939. It was the first full moon after the autumn equinox. In choosing the date for such a significant event, Unmu Sensei had declared, it was necessary to pay heed to the movement of both the sun and the moon. It was a sunny, brisk day. I remember that clearly. I woke up early that morning and threw open the shutters and the windows, and let the fresh air pour into the room Hoshi and I shared.

"Well, the big day is finally here," Hoshi said, poking her head out from her covers, "if you can call it a big day— since nothing is going to happen."

"Well, that's not exactly right," I said defensively. "There is going to be a ceremony."

"Yes, you've got all the celebrities coming and you're going to have a ceremony... and then nothing's going to happen."

"What can I say? At least you've got your own *mizuage* sorted out now too."

"Yes, at last..."

Hoshi had had a more difficult time finding a patron than I had. Of course in my own case I hadn't even really had to try to promote interest among potential candidates, as Hoshi had pointed out to me on numerous occasions. You've got that "preemptive offer" from the Minister, she would say teasingly, and then she would repeat what everyone else had said, about it being so strange that a man would pay such a large amount of money to do nothing. She said she'd talked to Koyo about it a number of times, and Koyo had said it was a symptom of the times we lived in— everyone was just a little bit crazy. As for Hoshi herself, she had initially had only two proposals, one from a Dr. Kusano and the other from a General Okada. She had not been at all pleased, as it looked as though her choice would be between a sleazy doctor and a geriatric general, but then Yokozuna Taibo had stepped into the ring, so to speak. At first Hoshi had also been reluctant to accept the grand champion's proposal— the thought of attending to such a substantial man must have indeed been daunting— but after spending further time with the Yokozuna and coming to appreciate even more his humor and his gentler side, Hoshi had acquiesced. As both the Madame and Koyo vigorously pointed out, he was an historic grand champion after all, and it would be quite an honor for Hoshi to have such a man be the one to take her maidenhood. Hoshi's *mizuage* would be held in December, on the fourteenth, the 236th anniversary of the deaths of the 47 *ronin*.

"So tell me again who's coming today," Hoshi said, getting up.

I went through the list with her once more— the Minister of Public Enlightenment, and Ummu Sensei, and Captain Mushitani, and some journalists.

"And, as you know," I added, "Yokozuna Taibo will also be there."

"Yes, so I understand," Hoshi said, smiling.

The Madame had made certain to explain to me the role of each of the gentlemen attending. The Minister would of course be there as my "patron," my partner in the non-union we were consecrating, but he would also be there to give the ceremony the official sanction of the government. The Sensei would be there to perform the religious rites, and the Captain would be there to direct the journalists in recording everything for posterity. As for Taibo, the Minister had thought his presence would give added weight, so to speak, to the ceremony, since he was not only a well-known national figure but a representative of the highest values of the Shinto religion. There would also now be the additional connection to the House of Sugutatsu, with the Yokozuna becoming Hoshi's patron.

That afternoon Ummu Sensei was the first of the celebrities to arrive. He came a little bit after lunch, showing up at the front gate dressed in the attire of a pilgrim— a straw conical hat, a white robe, white leggings, straw sandals, and a wooden staff. The Master went running out to the gate to greet him, while the Madame and I waited in the foyer.

"Sensei," the Master said, bowing low, "on this special day you honor our humble abode with your presence."

Looking up at the sky, Unmu stroked his face and then

walked past the Master directly into the foyer, declaring, "In the autumn, the leaves fall."

Soon after the Sensei's arrival, he and I began our preparatory meditation together, just the two of us for more than three hours. I wore my white supplicant robe, while he stripped down to his loincloth. There was no instruction, no riddles, no shouting of incantations to the gods— just the two of us sitting in silence in formal style, our legs folded underneath us on the hard wooden floor. I tried hard to empty my mind, to enter a state of nothingness, of *mu*, but I'm afraid thoughts kept entering my head from the left and the right like a revolving door at a busy department store. Up until this point I had fantasized that my life would not change much from what it had been— despite the obvious expectations of the Minister— but now as I sat there with the Sensei for this extended period of time, it was no longer possible to escape the reality of what I faced. Highly respected gentlemen such as those attending this ceremony would not be spending their precious time on something of this nature unless they did indeed have significant plans for me. What those plans might be, I had no idea, and that unknown was quite a frightening thing. In ancient times, Koyo had said to me, maidens in many areas of the world had often been sacrificed to appease the gods. At least we lived in the modern era, she'd added soothingly. Little did I know then how ironic these words would later sound to me.

At the end of our time together, Ummu stood up slowly and put his hand on the top of my head and said, "Go forth my child with the blessings of the gods, for the path which you have chosen will not be easy."

When the Sensei was gone, Takako came rushing to my side with two other servants of the house. I could barely stand up on my own.

"Oh, poor girl," Takako said, "and now we must get you ready for the ceremony itself."

The two other women got under one arm each and helped to take me to the bathhouse. There they undressed me and got me into the bath, and when I was done with my bath, they wrapped me in a towel and laid me out on a table and massaged my legs until eventually I could feel the blood flowing again.

"That's better now, isn't it?" Takako said, motioning for the women to stand me up.

We went upstairs after that, and first the women helped me to dry and arrange my hair, and then they helped me to apply my white makeup— to my face and the front and back of my neck— and then on my own I applied my liner, to my eyebrows and the corners of my eyes, and lastly I applied my lipstick, a very bright red lipstick that was a favorite of all the girls.

"Just perfect," Takako said when I was done.

Then Takako directed the other women to prepare my undergarments, and the women got the undergarments out and dressed me in them, two layers of white followed by one of red, and then Takako asked the women to take the kimono that had been selected for this special day off its rack. It was a white kimono made of the highest grade silk, with long sweeping sleeves and a distinctive pattern of autumnal foliage, and the women put it on me, adjusting it to my frame the way a kimono must always be adjusted, with some padding added here and there, and sashes used to pull up and down and back and forth as necessary. When the kimono was fitted as snuggly as possible, the *obi* was added— a large and quite ornate sash that ran from near the top of my back down to the back of my knee, in the style common to all *maiko*. And then finally, to top it all off, two exquisite *kanzashi*, decorative hairpins, were placed in my hair, one to the left side and the other to the right.

"Oh, you look so beautiful," Takako said, standing back and clapping her hands in satisfaction when the last *kanzashi* had been placed.

"Yes, indeed," the two other women exclaimed, "so beautiful!"

I stood in front of the full-length mirror and took a look myself, and had to agree the picture I presented would likely charm even the most demanding of men. The Minister would be pleased.

Shortly after I was ready, the Madame came up to say Captain Mushitani had arrived with the journalists. The Madame and the Master and I would meet with them in the Western-style parlor.

"Perfect!" the Captain exclaimed when he saw me.

I hadn't seen him since the day he had first come to Sugutatsu to explain the duties of the "Maiden Maiko," as he had informed me I would thenceforth be known. I had forgotten how small he was and, to put it bluntly, unattractive. Even though the weather had cooled by then, he was still perspiring heavily.

"These gentlemen will be interviewing you," the Captain said, sitting down in the exact same spot he had on his earlier visit. The Madame once more cringed, knowing full well Takako would not be happy about having to sanitize the sofa again.

The three gentlemen— Messrs. Wada, Tada, and Yada— were from three of the leading news organizations in the land. They had "their fingers on the pulse of the nation," the Captain said. They began by asking some questions about my background, about my family and where I'd been born, and when I had answered these questions they proceeded to put several others to me, mostly having to do with my "personal preference and habits," as they put it. To tell the truth, the Captain had prepared me for the interview ahead of time, using the Master to convey the answers he wished me to give. Following this script, I told the journalists I had been born in Kagoshima, not Kujirahe, and that I was from a samurai family, not the daughter of a carpenter. I even casually mentioned I was a distant relative of the great samurai leader Saigo Takamori. When I'd first been told I should answer in this way, I'd questioned the Master, asking him why it was necessary. He'd told me the Captain had explained to him that sometimes such "small adjustments" were called for "in pursuit of the greater truth." In this case we were trying to "create patriotic sentiment" in support of the "sacred mission of the nation." If such "adjustments" were necessary in order to produce this result, wasn't this the right thing to do? It was difficult to argue with such logic. And then I'd thought back to the "small adjustments" I had made in my own telling of my life history to the Lieutenant, and his contention made even more sense to me.

At the end of the interview, the pressmen asked some questions about the war in China. They wanted, for example, to know if I supported our troops' efforts there. I told them, of course, that I most certainly did, and they seemed to be particularly pleased with that answer.

"She is wise beyond her years," the Captain said, smiling broadly, and the three gentlemen nodded enthusiastically in agreement.

"As only to be expected of the Maiden Maiko," Mr. Wada exclaimed.

After the interview session was finished, we all proceeded to the large Japanese-style room where the ceremony was to be held. Yokozuna Taibo arrived soon thereafter. His enormous frame filled the entire doorway as he entered, and he looked even larger once he had taken his place next to the tiny Captain. Then the rest of the household, including Takako and the other servants, came down to join us. I noticed Taibo make a point of spotting Hoshi and giving her a friendly nod. In his own way, I knew he was in love with her.

And then General Kukihara, the Minister of Public Enlightenment himself, arrived. As with the Captain, I had not seen the Minister for some time— in his case, since the night of my debut. Again I took note of his solidly built upper body on top of the surprisingly spindly legs. The spindly legs looked even spindlier in the light of day, and he looked older than I had remembered.

"Maiden Maiko," he said with a touch of drama, "it is so good to see you again."

I bowed humbly, saying nothing.

"And you must be the Master of the esteemed House of Sugutatsu," the Minister said, turning to the Master.

"It is indeed an honor," the Master replied, "for your excellency to visit our humble abode on such an auspicious day."

The Minister looked at the Madame and winked, saying under his breath, "An excellent choice— a baron, nonetheless."

The Madame bowed low, saying nothing.

"Isn't she perfect!" the Minister then proclaimed, extending an arm in my direction.

"Exactly the word I used," the Captain quickly agreed in his toadying way.

It was utterly embarrassing to be praised in this fashion in front of my sisters, all of whom were well aware of my numerous imperfections. I had no idea what to do or say.

"Your sacrifice for the nation," the Minister went on, "is

indeed a magnificent gesture."

I truly did not understand what he meant. I didn't understand what any of them meant— their desire to "preserve me for the good of the nation." Why did they wish to "preserve me" and why was it "for the good of the nation?" All I knew at that moment was that their commitment to their ideals— whatever those might be— was saving me from having my affair with the Lieutenant found out. And that single fact was enough for me to do anything. Or as it is perhaps better put in this case, nothing.

"Mushitani, the scroll!"

"Yes, sir!"

The Captain handed the Minister a scroll, and the Minister unscrolled the scroll and began to read:

> *In recognition of your unsullied state*
> *and your spiritual contributions*
> *to the sacred efforts of our nation*
> *to liberate the peoples of Asia, and by so*
> *doing, bring peace and stability to the world,*
> *you are hereby honored as the Maiden Maiko.*

> *General Kukihara Yujiro*
> *Minister of Public Enlightenment*
> *September 28, 1939*

When the presentation was done, the Captain brought the journalists forward to take photos. They asked me to pose now one way and then another before having me stand together first with the Minister for several more shots, and then with both the Minister and the Master at the same time.

After all the photos were taken, at long last Ummu Sensei made his entrance. He was wearing the same pilgrim's attire he had worn when he had arrived earlier in the day, but he soon removed his conical straw hat and then his robe and then his leggings, so that once more he stood before us in only his loincloth. Then he went over to where Taibo was standing and squatted down in front of him and made as though he were going to charge at him, as one would at the start of a sumo bout. The Yokozuna momentarily flinched, and then he smiled.

"When insane men charge, even grand champions flinch," Ummu declared.

Then the Sensei lay down in front of us, perfectly still, and went to sleep. After a few moments, out of the corner of my eye, I could see the Minister make an inquiring face to the Captain, and the Captain in turn indicate he had no clue as to what Ummu was up to. When five minutes had passed, the Sensei then suddenly jumped to his feet and motioned for me and the Minister to come forward. Then taking some bamboo rushes in his hands, he gently beat both of us about the shoulders and after that, picking up a small bowl, he sprinkled water on our feet and our heads.

"For the sake of this non-union" Ummu then intoned, "go forth and do nothing, for in nothing, the purity of the nation shall be preserved."

With that, the Minister and I exchanged cups of *sake* and the ceremony was complete.

"A celebratory dinner will now be served," the Madame said, and all of us followed her out of the room and down the corridor to another room, where the reception, if you will, was to be held.

"Ah, what a wonderful occasion," the Minister exclaimed, as he took his seat. "The prime minister will be pleased when I make my report."

"Yes, sir, he no doubt will be," the Captain agreed enthusiastically.

"Bring in the food and drink," the Madame ordered, and Takako in turn instructed the serving girls to begin their serving.

The Minister and I were placed at the head of the room, as would be done for a newly married couple. To the other side of the Minister sat the Madame, while to my other side sat the Master, the two of them positioned as though the were the *nakodo*, the "go-betweens." Mangetsu was designated to take care of the Captain, while Hoshi was of course paired up with Taibo. Koyo would take the lead in entertaining Messrs. Wada, Tada, and Yada, with assistance from the other girls.

Not long after the banquet had begun, the Minister was clearly already starting to feel the effects of the alcohol.

"So many possibilities," he said, holding out his *sake* cup to the Madame. "So much to be done."

"We feel most inadequate," the Madame humbly replied.

"Places to go, people to see," the Minister went on.

"We will do our best to fulfill your expectations," the Master said, reaching across to refill the Minister's cup yet again.

The Minister in turn tried to fill the Master's cup, but the Master had his cup turned over, and the Madame explained that the Master had totally given up alcohol in his pursuit of a higher level of understanding of the teachings of Unmu Sensei.

"Most admirable," the Minister said, seemingly not completely convinced that a man need go quite that far in the pursuit of anything. Then turning to me, he asked, "How would you like to go to China?"

I lowered my head shyly, not certain how to respond.

"China?" the Madame said.

"Yes, China— a little tour to raise the morale of our troops." The Minister sat back then and smiled. "Nothing's settled yet, but just think of the possibilities... all that we can do with our little Maiden Maiko."

China? They were going to send me to China?

"It would be an honor, sir," the Master said.

"Yes, an honor," the Madame dutifully concurred.

China? They were going to send me to China? And then it suddenly occurred to me that a trip to China might mean a reunion with the Lieutenant. Maybe we would be sent to Taiyuan. Maybe I would see the Lieutenant. Maybe the gods would intervene again. If I was being sent to China, surely they would. My spirits were lifted all at once.

As the evening progressed, a good deal more alcohol was consumed and the mood of the party became very jovial and relaxed. Koyo and the other girls made origami animals in various lewd positions for the journalists, while Mangetsu and the Captain exchanged chopstick tricks, and Taibo and Hoshi made lovey-dovey in their own little world.

"Ah, a night to remember," the Minister said, taking hold of my hand.

And then at the end of the evening, as the guests were getting ready to leave, Mangetsu stood and said, "We've prepared a special performance for our younger sister's special day."

I was truly moved, and again embarrassed, that my older sisters would go to such trouble for me— truly moved. Koyo then played the samisen and sang while Mangetsu and Hoshi danced. The words went like this:

> *To give not*
> *that which was to be given.*
> *To take not*
> *that which was to be taken.*
> *Oh, such trial,*
> *such hardship*

> *as the nightingale sings*
> *o'er the banks of the Sumida*
> *and the sound of your footfall fades.*
> *And now, is it not but*
> *the sun also rising?*

The others departed then, and I was taken by the Madame and Takako to a specially prepared room, and there my elaborate costume was removed and replaced with a simple white yukata. Two futon had already been laid out, one on each side of the room.

"Usually I would give some final words of encouragement," the Madame said, "but that will not be necessary in this case."

I was then left alone for several minutes before the Minister came in, dressed in his own simple white yukata. I stood modestly, my head bowed, and the Minister came to my side and put his hands on my shoulders and breathed his liquored breath into my ears, first one and then the other, and for a moment I thought that perhaps all this talk of preserving my purity had been so much nonsense generated simply for my gullible consumption. But then the Minister backed away and gestured for me to lie down in my futon and he went to his own and lay down, and we were as two very separate beings, apart and alone. I still had my doubts at that point about what might occur over the course of a very long night, especially given the inebriated state of the Minister, but these doubts soon dissipated, as who to my wondering eyes should appear but Ummu Sensei. I had no idea whether the Madame had sent him in order to ensure the Minister upheld his own conditions for the *mizuage*, or whether he had wandered in on his own, but the results were the same, as the Sensei lay down in the middle of the room, right between the Minister and me, and it was very clear that as long as he was there, nothing untoward would happen.

"Sweet dreams," Ummu said, and then soon he was asleep.

It was indeed a seemingly endless night, as both gentlemen snored loudly, not always simultaneously but constantly, with one starting up as soon as the other stopped. As the hours passed, my thoughts turned to the Lieutenant and I recalled our short time together— and imagined the time yet to come. Oh, my love, you needn't worry. I am preserving myself, yes— not for our nation, but for you, and when you return united we shall be. I thought of our future life together and laid it all out in my head— a quiet place in the countryside, six little children running about, the Lieutenant managing a workforce of ten to twelve men on our estate. It took me all night to sketch in the details, and when I was done it was a very clear picture indeed— one that I was certain would one day come to fruition. Yes, I had no doubts about that then, no doubts at all.

15

Five days later, ten copies each of three different magazines were special delivered to our house. My photo was on the cover of all of the magazines and inside each was an article on the *mizuage* ceremony accompanied by numerous additional photos, some of the ceremony itself and some of the banquet that followed, including some of the special performance my sisters had prepared for me. The headline for all of the articles was the same:

Maiden Maiko Preserves Self for Good of Nation

I raced through the pieces, anxious to see what the respected journalists had written about me. The article by Mr. Yada, similar to the ones written by Messrs. Wada and Tada, started in this fashion:

"To give not is to give all." Such are the words of Ummu Sensei, esteemed monk of the Kosenji Temple in Nikko— words which could be used to describe the patriotic actions taken this week by a young apprentice geisha in Asakusa. The young lady in question is Miss Suzukaze of the House of Sugutatsu and the actions— in point of fact, the non-actions— taken by her set an example which we would all be good to follow.

The column went on to set out the historical connection between the House of Sugutatsu and the shogunal court— including the fact that the current master, Baron Sugutatsu Ikuzo, was the twelfth in a direct line of descendants from the founder of the house, Sugutatsu Sugeimon, a well-known tea master and political figure who had been appointed to his position by the eighth Tokugawa shogun, Yoshimune, the only case of a geisha house master ever being so appointed. The given narrative was just as the Captain had outlined to us when he had said the House of Sugutatsu would now need an "origin story." The piece also gave an account in some detail of my *mizuage*— including the preparatory meditative session with Ummu, the presentation of the scroll by the Minister, the religious ceremony itself, and the reception that followed. As for the Maiden Maiko, I was described as the "daughter of a samurai family from the city of Kagoshima, a true representative of all that is finest in the women of Satsuma."

Hoshi was reading over my shoulder. "You're not from Kagoshima," she said.

"I know..."

"And what's this about being the daughter of a samurai family?"

"Yes, yes, I know..."

I had to explain that the Ministry— through the Captain and the Master— had told me how in certain cases "small adjustments" had to be made "in pursuit of the greater truth."

"And what's the 'greater truth' in this case?" Hoshi asked.

I told her it was the "creation of patriotic sentiment," and she asked what was meant by that, and I said I wasn't exactly sure, but whatever it was, it was "for the good of the nation."

Hoshi thought about this for a moment, and then said, "So they said it was all right to lie if it was for the good of the nation."

Now she was twisting my words. I had to tell her emphatically that that was not what they had said. They had said it was all right to "make small adjustments," not that it was all right to lie. There was a world of difference. Hoshi looked like she wanted to argue the point further, but then thought better of it, and simply nodded. I was only relaying what the Ministry— through the Captain and the Master— had told me, after all, and it didn't seem a good idea to question the words of the Ministry.

"There's more," she said, and we both went back to reading the article.

Down below there was a section on my "personal preferences." It said my favorite food was mountain vegetables, which I had "grown to love while in training at Ummu Sensei's temple," and that my favorite song was our noble nation's anthem. It also said I didn't go to movies, especially Western movies, as they might "weaken my spiritual core." As for my "personal habits," it said I rose at four o'clock each morning and did "an hour of meditation, followed by another hour of martial arts training." The column finished with a flourish, praising me again for "giving not" and my "support of the troops."

"Looks like there's a lot of 'adjustments' in there," Hoshi said with a straight face when we were done reading.

"Yes, quite a few," I had to agree.

I must say I was somewhat disappointed that Mr. Yada had not used more of the actual phrases I had spoken, but in reading the piece closely I could see how the adjustments that had been made were not all that large. I certainly wouldn't have said mountain vegetables were my favorite food, but then again I didn't dislike them; and while I wouldn't have listed our national anthem as my absolute favorite tune, I did certainly appreciate its emotional appeal; and while I didn't rise at four to do my meditation and martial arts training, I did do both slightly later in the morning; and while I did go to the movies once in a while— and in fact had somewhat of a weakness for Robert Taylor and Clark Gable, if I must be excruciatingly honest— I did not go all that often, and I hadn't seen a Western movie for at least a month at the time of the interview.

"Well, looks like you're famous now," Hoshi said.

"It'll be just these three articles," I demurred. "You wait and see."

But as I had feared, all of the esteemed gentlemen did indeed have plans for me, and these first articles were followed by requests from numerous other publications. The impact on my entertaining schedule was immediate. Night after night I was called out to various locations all about the city— not just Asakusa, but the Ginza and Shinbashi and Akasaka as well, and even a few times to locations near Jinbocho— the site, as you will recall, of my assignation with the Lieutenant. On these visits near Jinbocho I was always fearful that someone would remember seeing me with the

Lieutenant, but then I would remind myself that in my *maiko* disguise there was little chance of that.

I was invariably accompanied by Mangetsu, of course, and sometimes by Koyo and Hoshi or some of the other girls of the house. You might think there would have been some jealousy on the part of my sisters, but there was in fact very little. This was not the "Sugutatsu Way," where there was always a true esprit de corps, each of us pulling for the other. It must also be said that everyone shared in my popularity, bookings going up for all the other girls as well, and this meant increased financial gain for all of us— a fact that certainly would have taken the edge off whatever jealousy might have existed.

"The next time around, I'm not giving up my maidenhood so easily," Mangetsu joked late one night after we'd returned home from an evening of entertaining.

"That goes for me too," Koyo chimed in.

We were sitting in the Western-style parlor, the three of us and Hoshi. As usual, Mangetsu had drunk a bit more than she should have and was in very good spirits. She'd opened another bottle of *sake*, a particularly high-grade product from Niigata that she'd received from one of her customers that evening, and she was sharing it with the rest of us. I don't wish to leave the impression that this is something we did every night, but once in a while, as the mood struck, Mangetsu would gather us around for an extra cup or two after we got home.

"Yes, a distinctly unusual situation," Mangetsu said, pouring for Koyo.

"Yes," Koyo agreed, "most unusual…"

"Never in the long history of our nation…"

"Undoubtedly a first…"

"A most remarkable man— to pay so much to do nothing."

"Yes, remarkable…"

"You just never know with men…"

"I thought I'd seen everything, but…"

"I suppose he's just that kind of a man…"

"That kind of a man?" I asked.

"Someday you'll know what I mean…," Mangetsu replied, pouring more *sake* for both herself and Koyo.

Koyo laughed. "It is going to be a while, isn't it?"

Mangetsu smiled. "Yes, I'm afraid her experiences will be limited for now."

"In the meantime," Koyo said slyly, "we'll have to teach her about the different kinds of men."

"Yes, I suppose so… About the funny men, and the smart men."

"And the vain men, and the undependable men."

"And the boring men."

"And the men you can't wait to see."

"And the men you never want to see again."

Mangetsu and Koyo broke out in laughter, and Hoshi and I, not feeling by any means knowledgeable enough to share in the humor, nonetheless joined in.

"But the one lesson about men I've already taught her," Mangetsu said, turning mock serious, "is that you can't fall in love. No, you can't fall in love. Isn't that right, Suzu?"

I blushed and nodded. "Yes, my older sister has taught me this lesson well."

Hoshi leaned forward and picked up the *sake* jar and poured for Mangetsu. "But," she asked, raising her voice, "what about the other way around?"

"The other way around?"

"Yes, is it permitted to make your patron love you?"

There was a momentary silence.

"Of course," Koyo replied sharply. "Have you learned

nothing of what I've taught you? It is not only permitted, it is required. We are geisha, after all."

Hoshi hung her head, and Mangetsu started to laugh. "Oh, you little fool. Here, have some more *sake*. Our older sister didn't mean anything by it."

Mangetsu often called Hoshi "little fool" in an affectionate way. She poured her more *sake*, and Hoshi looked up and smiled, and then all four of us laughed together.

"And now it's Hoshi's turn," Koyo said.

"Yes," Mangetsu added, "and with the grand champion as the patron, I doubt we will have another case of a maiden *mizuage*."

"No, most definitely not."

Not long after, our two older sisters said good night and went upstairs, and as Hoshi and I picked up the cups and dishes and took them into the kitchen, I thought back over this discussion we had had about love. Had neither Mangetsu nor Koyo truly never fallen in love? It didn't seem possible. It had happened to me so quickly, my very first night of entertainment. What about all the men they had met over the years? How could it be that they had not fallen in love with any of them? Was I the peculiar one? Was I the rare exception? Was there something wrong with me? I didn't think so. What about all those patrons Mangetsu had had? What about Mr. Mizuno, and Mr. Kodama, and Mr. Ito, and Mr. Hirayama? And I was sure there had been other men before those gentlemen, before I'd come to Sugutatsu. What about all of them? How could it be that she hadn't fallen in love with any of them, while I had fallen so instantaneously for the Lieutenant? Perhaps my love for the Lieutenant was one kind of love, and the affection Mangetsu had for her patrons was another. She might say she wasn't in love, that she was only acting, putting on a performance worthy of a skilled geisha, but was that really the case? Even if her love for a man lasted only a short time, wasn't it still love? Wasn't it just as true a love as my love for the Lieutenant— a love I was certain would last forever. With Koyo, too, I was sure she had to have known love, although not in the same way as Mangetsu. There were fewer patrons. She was more particular about her men. That's what Hoshi had said, and I knew she was right. Hoshi entertained with her more. She knew her better. I must admit I didn't know about Koyo's current patron, about Mr. Fukunaga, about whether she was in love with him. She'd come back from her week at his seaside place in Kamakura, and it's true that I could observe no clear difference in her appearance or behavior— no extra color in the cheeks or added inclination to chat about her time at her lover's secret hideaway. That may have just been Koyo— she always did tend to keep things to herself— but then again, perhaps she simply wasn't in love with him. I'd heard from Hoshi though that Koyo had most definitely been in love with an earlier patron, a Mr. Kawano, the president of a smaller company, a handsome and kind man whose company had evidently gone bankrupt. He had then no longer been able to afford Koyo and their relationship had ended and, Hoshi said, she had heard from *maiko* in other houses that Koyo had been completely heartbroken. The incident had apparently occurred several years before. I could understand why Mangetsu had warned me against falling in love. In our profession it was no doubt a risky proposition. But as I had also learned, how can a girl have any idea of the emotions that might come to rule her heart? How can she control when and with whom she falls in love? She might as well try to control the rising and setting of the sun.

Or the changing of the seasons.

16

Over the next several weeks I was in limbo. There continued to be no letters from the Lieutenant, and there was also no further word from the Minister or the Captain about a trip to China. My emotions were all over the place. I just couldn't stop thinking about why there were no letters. Day after day I reminded myself of the unreliability of the mail, about a letter possibly being lost or going to a wrong address. But I must also admit that, as time passed, I more frequently questioned the Lieutenant's commitment to me. Were my feelings for him stronger than his feelings for me? Could I trust all those sweet words he had thrown my way? When a man had seen what he had seen... a need to fight death with love, to find the perfect girl, the perfect love. Had he found another perfect girl in China? And I thought, too, he must have by then seen the articles about the Maiden Maiko. He was the one person who knew with absolute certainty I was not a maiden. And yet here I was being celebrated throughout the nation for my purity and my resolution "to give not" in support of our troops. I'd had no chance to explain to him. Would he think I'd been brazen enough to volunteer? Would he think I was a complete fraud, a girl of no principles? How could he love such a girl? But then again and again I would force away these thoughts, toss them out of my mind. He had said he loved me, and he had expressed it in the most passionate way possible. There was really no reason to doubt him. I was being irrational, hysterical. I was ashamed of myself. If only he could have been nearer. Why this distance? Why this secrecy? Why? Why? Why?

As I say, my emotions were all over the place. It was a difficult time.

All this while, I did ironically continue to receive letters from the Colonel. There was some vague consolation in this, knowing he was writing from the same city where the Lieutenant was. When the Colonel wrote about the weather, I imagined it was the same weather the Lieutenant was experiencing. When the Colonel wrote about enemy movements in the area, I imagined they were the same enemy movements the Lieutenant was taking note of. When the Colonel wrote about a local restaurant he had visited, I imagined it was the same restaurant the Lieutenant might have visited. But of course these were not the Lieutenant's words I was reading. They were the Colonel's.

As I had promised, I did write letters back to the Colonel, but they were never long and I'm afraid what I did write must have appeared very childish. I just didn't know what to write. Needless to say, there was actually quite a bit going on in my life at the time— my designation as the Maiden Maiko, my training with Unmu Sensei, our trip to Nikko, the ceremony for my *mizuage*— but I didn't feel I could open up to the Colonel about any of this. With such an eminent gentleman, I wanted to be careful not to overstep my bounds. I did write about our trip to Nikko, but I was careful to not disclose any details that would reveal the purpose of the trip.

It goes without saying then that the Colonel was totally taken aback when he learned of my designation as the Maiden Maiko. This is what he wrote:

"...You can only imagine my utter shock when I received my copy of Weekly World yesterday and found

your photo on the cover. I was surprised, but somehow it was not surprising. As I said the night we met, there is something special about you, and evidently I am not the only one who has sensed this..."

The Colonel went on to congratulate me and write about other matters, but at the end of his letter he came back to my appointment as the Maiden Maiko, writing this:

"...and so I urge you to be cautious. You are still very young and have much to learn about the darker side of human nature. Always be courteous, always be kind, but also know that you cannot always be trusting. Unfortunately, when people ask you to do things, you must always question their motives. I am sorry to burden you with the cynicism of an older man, but in the position in which you have now been put, it is best you be aware of these realities."

At the time these words meant little to me. As the years passed, however, I often came to recall them and reflect on their meaning. The Colonel had had a good sense of the perils that lay ahead for me.

Then at last, in the second week of December, we had a visit from Captain Mushitani informing us that we would indeed be going to China. The trip was set for the beginning of April, and I would be accompanied by the Madame, Mangetsu, Koyo, and Hoshi. I was thrilled, of course, that the Madame and my sisters would be coming with me to lend support. But the other pressing matter on my mind, I need not tell you, was the itinerary. Where in China would we be going? I put the question to the Captain and waited on tenterhooks for his reply. We would first sail to Tianjin, he said, and then go on to Beijing, and then south to Wuhan, and then east to Shanghai, and then from there sail home. My spirits were dashed. There had been no mention of Taiyuan. But then the Captain retraced the route in his head and said he had forgotten one place— Taiyuan. It had been added at the last minute by the Minister himself. He didn't know why it had been added, but... But of course I knew why. The gods had told him to add it! I was ecstatic. The gods had arranged for me to go to Taiyuan, and if they were sending me there, they would no doubt also arrange for me to see the Lieutenant! My mind quickly raced ahead. I would be surrounded by the Madame and my sisters and the Colonel and many other military types, I was sure. How would I be able to get away? I didn't know. I had no idea. But surely the gods would arrange for that as well. Surely they wouldn't be so cruel as to put us that near each other and then not allow us to meet. Tears came to my eyes despite myself.

"It is indeed moving," the Captain said, "to see your devotion to our cause."

I'm afraid I didn't listen too closely to the rest of what he had to say— something about entertaining the very men who were risking their lives for our nation, and the need for Ummu Sensei to accompany us to provide spiritual support. The only thing that mattered was seeing my true love again.

Hoshi and Mangetsu and Koyo were also very excited about going to China— not for the same reasons I had, of course, but in the way most young women could be expected to be excited by the prospect of travel abroad. They all wanted to know what the weather would be like, as that would affect what we would be able to wear. The weather up north might still be rather cold at the beginning of April, the Madame said, especially at night, but we should expect the weather in Wuhan and Shanghai to be spring-like, perhaps even quite warm on certain days. Our conclusion was we would be able to wear the same kimono we would wear in Tokyo in the spring, but we would take extra undergarments to stay warm as necessary. Koyo proposed we study Chinese, and the Madame agreed it was a good idea. The Chinese were our fellow Asian brothers and sisters, after all, and it was only right that we learn some of their language— even if only some basic phrases. The Madame hired a tutor, a Chinese woman originally from Beijing, and two times a week Mandarin lessons were added to our schedule.

As it so happened, my brother Tomo had just come back from his own trip to China. He had been there entertaining the troops with Enoken. I wanted to tell him about my plans and get his impressions of the country, and so we arranged to meet at our usual coffee shop, the "Tour Eiffel." All he wanted to talk about was the girls. It seemed he had met quite a few while traveling as part of the entourage of his well-known mentor.

"Are the Chinese girls prettier?" I asked.

"It depends on the girl," he replied diplomatically.

I outlined our itinerary, and then I just couldn't help myself— I told him I thought the Lieutenant he had arranged for me to meet just might be based in Taiyuan, one of the stops on our trip. Tomo's face grew cloudy when he heard this.

"Nothing went on between the two of you that night, right?" he asked in a loud whisper.

I gasped. "Of course not. What kind of a girl do you think I am?"

Tomo sat back in his seat. "Sorry, it was just the look on your face..."

"The look on my face?"

"You just seemed kind of... excited..."

I exhaled loudly and put on my best expression of

exasperation. "I simply thought it was an extraordinary coincidence, that's all."

"I see... You're not going to see him then?"

"Of course not. I don't even know him... And who are you anyway— the Secret Police?"

Tomo laughed. "I should know better than to get my younger sister riled up."

I would have to be more careful, I told myself. Even with my own brother, I would have to be more careful. Oh, I so wish I could have told him the truth, but of course I couldn't. And I wondered again if Tomo himself had ever truly been in love.

17

It was just about this same time, too, that Hoshi's *mizuage* was held. As I mentioned earlier, I do remember the exact date, December 14th, as it was the 236th anniversary of the deaths of the 47 *ronin*. Taibo evidently was the one who suggested the date, wishing to honor the patriots of an earlier age. As those of you familiar with the story will recall— and who is not familiar with this story— the 47 samurai in question became *ronin*, masterless samurai, after the suicide of their lord, a suicide imposed by the shogunal court following an incident with a spiteful court official. In order to exhibit their extreme loyalty, the 47 *ronin* followed their lord into death, taking their own lives after justifiably assassinating the offending functionary. For the House of Sugutatsu, this story now had a special resonance, given our bushido ideals, but Hoshi told me the Madame had actually been opposed to the date, feeling that a date with a more romantic association would be more appropriate. Ultimately, however, she was in no position to overrule the Yokozuna and the Ministry, who were delighted with the choice.

I must confess of my own jealousy when I saw Hoshi's hair done up in the *fukumage* style the day after her *mizuage*— the readily recognizable sign of a girl who had now become a woman. Even though I had also made my own passage through this critical gate, I was not allowed to tell anyone and in the eyes of all remained a juvenile.

"So...," I said to Hoshi the next morning.

"So what?" Hoshi replied coyly.

"So how was it?"

"Wouldn't you like to know?"

Oh, such frustration. I felt like blurting out my secret right then and there. How could her 200 kilo sumo wrestler ever compare to my Lieutenant?

"Let's just say we successfully exchanged more than clever puns," Hoshi said after a further pause.

And I had to agree it was probably best to leave it at that.

The end of the year is always a very busy time for geisha, and that year was no different than any other, with all of us entertaining daily right up until the 30th. The 31st was a day of rest, and then late that evening we had dinner for all the members of the household. This was always a quiet dinner at which we would be urged by the Madame to reflect on the past year, and after the dinner— after the large bell of Sensoji had struck midnight— the entire household would make the short walk over to the temple, and there we would welcome in the new year, saying our prayers and making our resolutions. But that year, the year we rung in 1940, we didn't go to Sensoji after dinner. We instead went quietly to bed shortly after midnight, and the next morning all of us got up early and went to Yasukuni. We were to accompany Minister Kukihara on his official visit to our national shrine.

"The gods will be very pleased," the Minister said, "that the Maiden Maiko has come to pay homage at Yasukuni, where so many of our fallen heroes lie."

The weight of the Minister's expectations fell heavily on my slender shoulders. Up until this point there had been press interviews and instances of special recognition during evenings of entertainment, but nothing this religious in nature in such a formal setting. I felt most inadequate, as I am certain you can imagine. As we approached the main hall of the shrine, the Minister at the head of our procession, there were a number of photographers lined up on either side. While all the other girls were dressed up colorfully, I stood apart in my more understated kimono, white with splashes of a camellia pattern, and it was clear the photographers were focusing most of their attention on me. When I reached the offering box, I tossed in my coins and put my hands together in prayer, overwhelmed by thoughts of all the soldiers and sailors who had given their lives in the service of the Emperor and would now rest here for eternity. Later, near the end of the war, I would be with many other young men whose souls were also fated to find their way to Yasukuni.

"You performed your duties well," the Minister said approvingly as we walked out through the *torii* gate and exited the shrine.

I nodded modestly, acknowledging the Minister's words, but it was difficult to ignore the feelings that stirred inside me of unworthiness and guilt. Who was I— a carpenter's daughter from a backward fishing village, neither pure nor perfect— who was I to be standing in front of the gods praying for the souls of our martyrs? These disquieting feelings would stay with me throughout my time as the

Maiden Maiko and later as the Kamikaze Geisha, but were perhaps felt most acutely on these occasions when I visited Yasukuni or other sacred places of worship. I must confess, however, that I did also allow myself to wonder if perhaps the gods were in some way understanding of my circumstances. I was only in this position, after all, because of a true and sincere love. Wasn't it proof of the gods' understanding that they were arranging for me to see the Lieutenant again? But of course one can never know with certainty the true intent of the gods. Right up until my final mission with the Commander, I would never know.

After the New Year we kept up our usual schedule of entertaining and training, and before we knew it, it was time to leave for China. The Master would not be going with us. It had been the Ministry's decision. For national security reasons, the Captain said, the Master and the Madame of the House of Sugutatsu could not both be gone overseas at the same time. The Madame would need to directly supervise the Maiden Maiko during this trip, and therefore it would have to be the Master who stayed home. The Master didn't come right out and say anything, but we all knew he was disappointed. This would be an important mission for the nation, with the critical participation of both the Sensei and the Maiden Maiko, and as the Master of the House of Sugutatsu it would have been his great honor and privilege to travel with the troupe. Instead, he would be home by himself.

And I felt that had to be of some concern to the Madame.

18

On April 6, 1940 we boarded our ship in Yokohama. We would sail to Tianjin, and then from there travel by train to Beijing. I had made sure to study our route beforehand: down through the Inland Sea past Osaka and Kobe and Hiroshima and then around the end of Honshu, almost touching my native Kyushu as we passed through the Straits of Shimonoseki, and then from there across the Yellow Sea and up the west coast of Korea and on to Bohai Bay, and finally Tianjin.

"Aren't you the lucky girl," Mangetsu said to Hoshi as we waved from the railing of the ship to well-wishers on the dock.

"It's not every girl," Koyo sniffed, "who can bring her patron along."

"No, it's not, is it?" Mangetsu said, continuing with her teasing.

Much to Hoshi's delight, we had found out shortly before our departure that Yokozuna Taibo would accompany us on the tour. The military authorities had evidently felt that as a popular grand champion his presence would also help to raise the spirits of our men at the front.

"Where's the Sensei?"

As the ship's crew made final preparations to disengage the gangway, the Madame was frantically scanning the crowd. Ummu had decided to get to the port on his own, leaving early that morning in order to say prayers at Kanda Myojin Shrine.

"There, there he is," Hoshi cried out.

And indeed there he was, approaching at a hurried pace along the dock, his wooden staff held high in one hand, his straw conical hat in the other. Reaching the ship, he sprinted up the gangway, nodded slightly to the sailor standing at the top and then, spotting the Madame, walked in her direction.

"When ships depart," Ummu declared, "even monks must be on time."

None of us girls had ever been at sea before, and we very much enjoyed being on the ship, exploring the nooks and crannies of the vessel and sitting outside on the deck when the weather permitted. On our last day things were less pleasant, however, as we ran into a violent storm and everyone got sick, even Taibo and the Sensei. All of us found our own little spot with our own little bucket and retched uncontrollably for several hours until the storm passed. I was surprised to see the Yokozuna and the Sensei standing not far away just as sick, if not more so, than any of us. I suppose I thought the Yokozuna's strength and the Sensei's spirit would spare them the suffering the rest of us were subjected to, but such was not the case. It seems the sea is a great leveler of men.

As we left the open ocean and made our way up the river to Tianjin itself, I was surprised to see that the city looked much more like Europe than China. A businessman standing next to me explained that Tianjin was a so-called "treaty port," a city that had been chosen as a trading center for the Western nations. Each country had its own section of the city.

"There's the old Belgian and Russian concessions," he said, gesturing to the right side of the river, "and there's the old German concession," he said, pointing to the left side.

And as we went a little bit farther up the river he pointed out the British and French sections on the left side, and then finally the Italian section on the right side and the Japanese on the left. I must say I did feel some sense of pride, seeing our own designated area right there with all of the European powers.

We were met at the dock in Tianjin by several members of the press. They all wanted photos and comments from Taibo of course, but the requests to me were just as numerous.

"Maiden Maiko, how was your voyage?" one of the pressmen yelled out.

I was embarrassed to be singled out in this fashion with both of my older sisters standing right there by my side, but there was nothing to be done about it.

"Answer the question," Mangetsu said.

"Go ahead," Koyo added.

"Quite pleasant," I replied. "I particularly enjoyed our passage through the Inland Sea."

"Are you still determined to preserve yourself for the good of the nation?" another asked.

"Yes, of course," I said.

"What are your expectations for this trip?" yet another queried.

"Simply to support our troops."

"She's a natural," one of the reporters said to the Madame as our impromptu gathering was breaking up.

"She's got all the boys eating out of her hand," another added.

"Is that so?" the Madame said, skepticism in her voice.

I knew she didn't want my fame to go to my head. But she needn't have worried. All the bother about me meant nothing. Nothing at all. In my heart, I was still just a carpenter's daughter from Kujirahe, little Panko, and that's who I would always be.

We only stayed in Tianjin one night. Our hotel was in the

Japanese section of the city, and that afternoon Hoshi and I took a walk. We might have been in Tokyo or Yokohama, what with all the Japanese street signs and Japanese shops and Japanese people— not just sailors and soldiers, but businessmen and housewives and even children. We decided to go into one of the shops. A clerk, a serious looking man in his twenties, came out to take care of us. He asked if we had just come from Japan and we said that we had, and then we asked him how long he had been in Tianjin and he said he'd been there five years. We bought a few postcards, and then as we were leaving the shop the clerk recognized me and asked if he could take a photo with me, and I said that would be fine, and he went and got his camera and asked Hoshi to take a shot. He thanked me as we left, saying he would "treasure the photo forever." It was startling indeed to see that my fame had even spread to the continent.

We went on to the French section, with its main street named "Rue de France," and we found a coffee shop there called the "Tour Eiffel," and I wondered if there was a Tour Eiffel coffee shop in every city in the world. Beyond the coffee shop there was a large fence with what looked like a military base behind it, and out front at the gate there were two French guards. I must say I was confused. Ummu Sensei had said our men were in China to throw out the Westerners, but the Westerners were still here— at least in Tianjin. It was all a bit more complicated than I could take in at the time. What I understood later was that the war with the Westerners themselves did not start until the following year, after Pearl Harbor.

The Madame had given us strict orders not to enter the British section, and so when we came to the end of the French section we turned around. It seems there had been some sort of incident between the Japanese and the British in Tianjin the summer before, and the Madame thought it might still be dangerous for us to be there. We caught the streetcar on the way back, recrossing the French section and then the Japanese section until we came to the end of the line and the border with the Chinese section of the city. We didn't go any farther, choosing instead to stand at the wall and look over into the Chinese section. My first impression of this "real China" was that it was very foreign. I don't know why, but I suppose I was expecting something more familiar. After all, we are the same Asian race as the Chinese and it is said much of our culture originated in China. The fact that everyone looked like us and we could read most of the Chinese characters we saw on billboards and storefronts made it all that much more disorienting. It was as though I had woken up at home in Japan one day and found that everyone else was wearing different clothes and eating different food and speaking a different language. Hoshi was disappointed she couldn't understand a word, despite our three months of language lessons.

The next morning we were taken by car to the train station, which was in the Chinese section of the city. The streets were narrow, crowded with rickshaws and street vendors and donkey carts. Our driver kept honking his horn, trying to move the competing vehicles out of our way. Once or twice we almost hit people.

"This is really quite frightening," Koyo shouted over the din.

"Just close your eyes," Mangetsu yelled.

"They're already closed!" Koyo shouted back.

We arrived at the station, and a second car with Taibo, Ummu, and the Madame pulled up behind us. A few moments later a third car arrived with our handlers, Mr. Wakinuma and Mr. Ma. Mr. Wakinuma was a specialist in public relations, while Mr. Ma was our interpreter.

"What a lucky man I am," Mr. Wakinuma had said when he met us for the first time. "It's not every day a man gets to accompany a group of beautiful geisha on a tour of China."

He was a dandy, dressed up in a double-breasted suit and spats, his hat at an arrogant angle, two gold rings on his right hand. He had a lecherous mustache to go with his get-up, and I had disliked him immediately.

"This whole thing about you being a maiden," he'd said, "that's just a publicity stunt, isn't it? You're not really a maiden, are you?"

Mr. Ma, on the other hand, was a lovely man. He spoke very good Japanese, and was very polite. He said he had graduated from a university in Tokyo, from Keio. Later in our trip, due to circumstances beyond our control, he and I were to get to know each other far better than either one of us had intended.

The landscape from Tianjin to Beijing was very flat. That was the strongest impression I had as we chugged along on our steam train, the morning sun filtering through the patchy ground fog. Farmers were out plowing their fields, and on the road that ran parallel to the train tracks there seemed to be more donkey carts than cars. We four girls were sitting together in one seat facing each other, while the Madame and Taibo and Mr. Wakinuma sat together in another. Ummu Sensei and Mr. Ma were together in a third seat, just the two of them, with the Sensei sitting by the window gazing out.

You might be asking yourself why Taibo and Hoshi didn't sit together, but the matter of their liaison was confidential— as well it should be, Hoshi being the professional that she was— and so the two of them would never appear in public as a couple per se, even though it was common knowledge among those in the know that they were a couple. Sometimes during the course of our journey I would look over at Hoshi's bed in the middle of the night and see that she was not there. There was never any doubt as to where she had gone, but we never talked about it, not even once. I was not so fortunate to have my own Lieutenant by my side, but I was not jealous of Hoshi. She had her sumo wrestler, and I was happy for her.

After about two hours we could see the walls of Beijing rising in the distance, standing alone on the great plain.

"Ah," Mr. Wakinuma said, turning around in his seat to face us, "Kublai Khan's capital— the ancient city of intrigue."

"Are we going to be able to do any shopping?" Mangetsu asked. She was our most serious shopper.

"Of course," Mr. Wakinuma said, "I know some very good spots."

"But first," the Madame said, also turning around, "we must ready ourselves to perform with the Beijing Opera. And ready we must be. We will be representing our nation, and our performances must be perfect."

"Yes, indeed," Koyo agreed vigorously, "perfect!"

19

In Beijing we stayed at the Beijing Hotel, right off of Tiananmen Square. As soon as we were settled in our room, I asked Hoshi if she wanted to go for a walk and she said she did and we went out of the hotel and down the avenue to the square. To our right was the grand gate itself, Tiananmen, the "Gate of Heavenly Peace"— the entrance to the imperial palace, the so-called "Forbidden City"— and to our left the square stretched several hundred meters in a long rectangle.

At the other end we could see another gate, which we were later told was the Gate of China.

"Is that where the emperor lives?" Hoshi asked, pointing towards the Tiananmen Gate.

"Not any more," I said authoritatively.

"How can you be so sure?"

"Mr. Ma told me."

"Oh, he did, did he?"

"Yes, he did."

It was true. I'd spent some time with Mr. Ma at the hotel in Tianjin and he'd told me a few things about the recent history of China.

"The emperor was thrown out in 1912," I continued, "and a republic was formed then."

"No wonder the country's in chaos. How can you have order without an emperor?"

"I know," I was quick to agree, "no emperor, no order."

Hoshi started walking towards the Tiananmen Gate, and I followed her.

"So anyone can go in now?" she asked.

"Yes, that's what Mr. Ma told me."

Hoshi looked up at the top of the gate, her mouth open. "To think the emperor himself used to live here, and now we can just walk in."

"Yes, amazing, isn't it?"

The first of our performances with the Beijing Opera was a week later. There were to be five in total, all held at a large theatre not far from our hotel. We spent the week in intense practice, working on our own routines while also coordinating the show with the troupe from the Beijing Opera. The leader of the Beijing troupe was a Mr. Liu. He was a tall, thin man with a long, intense face— although he could be quite charming when he smiled.

I must say that after the first day of joint practice, our little band was in shock. Frankly, we were overwhelmed by the intensity and brilliance of the Beijing troupe. We had never seen anything like it before in our lives. The costumes and masks were very colorful— somewhat like our *kabuki*— but it was their shrill music and gymnastics that truly left us gasping for air. By comparison, our routines seemed too subtle, perhaps even in danger of being perceived as dull.

As it turned out, however, we needn't have been so concerned, as our performance on opening night was well received. Mr. Wakinuma acted as the master of ceremonies, with Mr. Ma providing the translation. Most of the audience was composed of Japanese troops, but there were also a significant number of Chinese in attendance. As Mr. Wakinuma said in his introduction, this was a night, after all, to celebrate "the friendship between the peoples of our two great nations."

The Chinese troupe first performed scenes from two of their most famous operas, *Farewell my Concubine* and *When Dragons Die.* During rehearsals Mr. Liu had explained the basic storyline of both operas to us. In *Farewell my Concubine,* the King of Chu is surrounded by the armies of the King of Han. Seeing that the end is near, the king calls for his favorite concubine, Consort Yu. Yu begs to die alongside her master, but the king strongly refuses her request. Later, while he is preoccupied with other matters, Yu takes the king's own sword and kills herself. All of us could readily relate to the position of the concubine and were impressed by her resoluteness. We were also pleasantly surprised to find this cultural commonality between the Japanese and Chinese, this willingness to sacrifice all for love and lord. Some years later, when our nation and I would be facing our own moment of inevitable defeat, the scenes of this opera would vividly come back to me.

The second opera, *When Dragons Die,* was also a tale of love and war. While *Farewell* was from the classical repertoire of the Beijing Opera, Mr. Liu had explained that *Dragons* was of more recent composition. The story concerned a small island kingdom that invades a large continental kingdom. Through conspiracy and intrigue, the small kingdom manages to place traitors in key positions in the large kingdom, leading to a series of victories on the battlefield for the small kingdom. Later, however, through the heroic— and ultimately fatal— efforts of one of the concubines in the court of the large kingdom, the armies of the small kingdom are vanquished and sent in undignified retreat back to their islands. The climax of the opera is a dance in which a cobra-like dragon swallows an elephant, with the elephant then later bursting out in dramatic fashion and stomping the dragon to death. Hoshi and I speculated as to whether there might be some hidden message in this piece— as, for example, the larger will always eventually triumph— but in the end we decided it was meant as pure entertainment.

After the Chinese troupe finished the scenes from these two operas, we came on and performed several of our own numbers. When we were done, there was an intermission, and during the intermission Taibo entertained the crowd by putting on an exhibition of sumo wrestling with four wrestlers from Mongolia. The grand champion demonstrated a number of holds, tossing the Mongolians on to the floor and out of the quickly rigged ring from a variety of creative angles. For his finale, Taibo took on the two strongest Mongolians at the same time in a simulated bout and easily bested both of them. The crowd loved it.

"It's good for the morale of the troops," Mr. Wakinuma

said from the wings, giving all of us a broad wink.

In the second half of the show, both we and the Chinese troupe performed more numbers, and then when the show was done there was a brief chance for the press to ask questions. As in Tianjin, most of the questions went to Taibo and me. The next day, the headlines in all of the local papers said the same thing:

Grand Champion and Maiden Maiko Create Sensation

Our other four performances in Beijing were also all sold out and all were reviewed in similarly glowing terms.

"Wait until you see the papers in Japan," Mr. Wakinuma said, tooting his own horn. "You'll be even more famous when you get home."

We stayed on in Beijing two more days after our final performance, and with this extra time we were able to do some sightseeing and shopping. The first day we went to the Imperial Palace, the Temple of Heaven, and the Summer Palace.

"I still can't believe they let us into the Imperial Palace," Hoshi said as we walked the same courtyards once trodden by royalty and thousands of eunuchs.

"It seems such a waste," Mangetsu said after Mr. Wakinuma explained what a eunuch was.

"Really," Koyo agreed, "I can't believe a man would voluntarily have his essential equipment removed just to get a job."

"It must have been a very tough job market," Mangetsu concluded.

"Indeed," Koyo said, tilting her head for emphasis.

The second day we went by car out to the Great Wall, with the press boys coming along as well. Mr. Wakinuma wanted them to get some photos of us standing on top of this well-known symbol of China.

"Right up there would be fine," Mr. Wakinuma said, indicating where he wanted us to stand.

First we did a group shot, with the four of us and the Madame and Taibo and Ummu all in it, and then we did a few shots just with the four of us, and then the press boys asked for us to do a shot with Taibo holding me in one arm and Hoshi in the other. Everyone was very pleased with this last shot.

"There's your cover shot, boys," Mr. Wakinuma said, self-satisfied.

Then, just as we were starting to get off the wall, Taibo suddenly reached down and picked up a startled Ummu, raising him over his head.

"How's this, gentlemen?" Taibo shouted.

The press boys scurried to get back in position to take more photos.

"A little to the left," one cried out.

"And now a little more to the right," another yelled.

"Hold it right there," a third said.

When they were done with their photos, Taibo gently put Ummu back down.

"When one is held over the head of a giant," the Sensei declared, somewhat shaken, "one longs for the ground to be underneath one's feet."

Later that day Mr. Wakinuma took us four girls and the Madame to one of his favorite shopping haunts. Mr. Ma came along to interpret and bargain down the prices. Mangetsu and Koyo each bought a fur hat and a leather handbag, while the Madame bought herself a nice fur coat. Hoshi and I stood back, knowing it was not yet our place to buy anything.

"Pick out a fur hat for yourselves," Mr. Wakinuma said to us.

We both looked at the Madame.

"I'll pay for it," Mr. Wakinuma added. "You've both earned at least a fur hat."

"Well, just this once," the Madame said. "Go ahead."

"Thank you, Mr. Wakinuma," we said in unison.

And we both picked out a hat, after first modeling several each. It was a fun way to finish up our time in Beijing, I thought to myself.

But it is rare indeed that one gets something for nothing in this life, and that night Mr. Wakinuma came around to collect on his payment. I awoke from a deep sleep to find him standing over the edge of my bed, his hand on my mouth.

"This is what you've wanted all along, isn't it?" he whispered. "I apologize for not having paid you a visit earlier."

I made a quick look to see if Hoshi was there, but she was gone— one of the nights she was visiting Taibo.

"We'll find out now about this maidenhood claim you've been making," my depraved intruder declared.

"Yes, we will," I whispered loudly, and then I quickly jumped out of bed and grabbed his wrist in an aikido hold and held him there while he writhed in pain.

"What do you think?" I asked. "Would you like to conduct your examination from this position?"

"No," he screamed.

"Or maybe from this position?" I asked, twisting his wrist and rolling him to one side.

"No," he screamed again.

"Or maybe this position," I asked, flipping him over.

"No, no, no," he screamed one last time. "I've had enough!"

"Fine," I said, releasing him, "but we can always play more another time if you like."

He picked up his hat, which had fallen off during our

scuffle, and gave me a withering look of contempt.

"I suggest we both just forget this little incident," he said, before turning and walking out of the room.

The arrogance of the man— to come into a young lady's boudoir in the middle of the night and try to seduce her. And while wearing his hat!

20

It was a long and mostly quiet train ride from Beijing to Shijiazhuang, where we transferred for the second leg of our trip to Taiyuan. Step by step, I was getting closer to seeing my Lieutenant again. You may not recall this, but the Colonel had mentioned Shijiazhuang in his first letter. He had told me to find the city on the map, going south from Beijing, and then going west from there until I found Taiyuan. As we pulled into the station, I remember being happy that I recognized the name of the city and had some idea of where we were.

During our short layover I felt uneasy, listening distractedly as the other girls talked. At the time I thought it was due to Mr. Wakinuma, who was sitting not far from me, but as I look back on it now, I think I may have had some premonition of what was to come. Then about an hour into our journey to Taiyuan it happened— the train came to an abrupt stop, and for the first time I came face to face with one of the more disturbing aspects of fame.

"You'd better get away from those windows," Taibo cautioned.

And then suddenly four men with rifles burst into our

railcar. "Who is the Maiden Maiko!" one of the men shouted in crude Japanese.

There were screams and then silence.

"Who is the Maiden Maiko!" the man repeated.

"There is no Maiden Maiko here," Taibo said defiantly, standing up and towering over the Chinese.

All four men pointed their rifles at the Yokozuna, screaming at him, motioning excitedly for him to sit back down. After a tense moment, Taibo complied, sitting down while repeating his insistence that there was no Maiden Maiko. Then while the other three kept their rifles trained on Taibo, their apparent leader came closer to us four girls and inspected each of us. He seemed to quickly come to the conclusion that Koyo and Mangetsu were too old, and then he gestured for Hoshi and me to step forward.

"There is no Maiden Maiko here!" the Madame screamed.

The man ignored the Madame, pulling first me and then Hoshi out into the aisle. Then the words just seemed to fly out of my mouth, as though they were being spoken by someone else. I must assure you there was no intent of bravery.

"I am the Maiden Maiko," I said quietly.

"Suzu!" the Madame gasped.

The man took a newspaper clipping out of his shirt pocket and carefully compared me to the photo. Then he motioned for Mr. Ma to also step out into the aisle, and started speaking to him harshly in their common language. At this point, Ummu Sensei suddenly stood up and jumped out into the aisle.

"There is no need," the Sensei said calmly, "for any man to hold up the sky."

At this, one of the other men whacked Ummu in the face with the butt of his rifle, sending the Sensei sprawling to the floor, and then Taibo stood and tried to grab the man's rifle and a shot rang out, hitting the Yokozuna in the shoulder and sending him to the floor as well. There was considerable screaming and a general sense of chaos, and in the midst of all of this, Mr. Ma and I were roughly hustled off the train.

"Suzu! Suzu!" I heard the Madame and the other girls cry out.

"Help me!" I screamed back.

"Suzu! Suzu!"

Outside, there were four horses tethered to the train, and the leader and one of the men got up on the horses, and then the other two handed me up to the leader and I was thrown across his horse in front of him like a bag of rice. Mr. Ma was then hoisted up on the other horse, and then the two remaining men mounted their horses and we were off, galloping down the incline from the train tracks and off across a field and up into the nearby foothills. After we'd gone maybe two or three kilometers we came to a halt, and I was taken down off the horse.

"You will not be hurt," Mr. Ma said, interpreting for the leader, "if you cooperate."

I wanted to cry, but there was no time to, as I was soon back up on the horse, this time straddling it with the leader holding on to me from behind— a most unladylike position in which to find oneself. We then set off at a slower pace, climbing farther up into the mountains on a narrow path. After about two hours, we came to a small valley, and at the end of the valley there was a village. As we rode in, the people of the village came out and gathered around us, yelling excitedly, obviously pleased that their men had not only returned home unscathed but had two captives with them as well. The leader waved his hands at the people and they quieted down, and then pointing at me, he began to speak. I managed to pick up a word or two of the Chinese being spoken, but anything beyond that was impossible. Mr. Ma interpreted, saying the leader had told his people that I was the famous Maiden Maiko, the same Maiden Maiko who was a god in Japan. They must make sure no harm came to me, as I was very valuable and could bring a good deal of wealth to the village. A god? Now I was a god? I was in too much shock at this point to give this latest designation much thought. The leader motioned to a couple of his men, and we were led away to a small hut and left there with a single guard outside our door.

"I think they intend to ask for a ransom," Mr. Ma said as soon as we were settled in our new, primitive surroundings.

"Do they really think anyone is going to pay money for me?"

"I think you underestimate your worth, Miss Suzukaze. You are indeed the Maiden Maiko, after all."

At this point I did begin to cry. How had I gotten myself into this? If only I had confessed to the Madame when I should have. To be so near to seeing the Lieutenant again, and now for this to happen. Is this what the gods had intended? To lure me here to be kidnapped? Was this the punishment they had in store for me? Mr. Ma came closer then and put his arm around me.

"Everything's going to be all right," he said, rubbing my back, "everything's going to be all right."

"How can you say that?" I said, continuing to cry.

I must have fallen asleep, exhausted from the terror and anxiety of the day, and when I awoke it was late afternoon. Mr. Ma was standing over me.

"Miss Suzukaze," he said, "we've got to go."

I looked over to the door of the hut and saw our guard and another man standing there.

"We've got to go," Mr. Ma said again.

I stood up, still feeling surprisingly exhausted and weak, and I grabbed ahold of Mr. Ma's arm and we went with the men across the village to another hut, somewhat larger than the one in which we were being held. The leader was waiting for us there together with a woman. The leader motioned for the other men to leave, and the two men went outside, and then he gestured for us to sit down on the straw mat that covered one section of the dirt floor. He was tall and thin, his face unshaven and scarred in at least two places. I guessed him to be in his mid thirties. The woman looked to be about the same age, of average height, a slender figure, with a broad face that was attractive in its own way. The man said his name was Chen. The woman's name was Bai. She was his wife. The were both members of the Communist Party, he said. He asked if I had heard of the Communists, and I thought back to what the Colonel had written in his letters— about the Communists hiding in the mountains and attacking the railroads— and I said, yes, I had heard of them. The kidnapping all made a little more sense now. Then he asked where I was from, and what my father did for a living, and how it was that I had become the Maiden Maiko. I momentarily hesitated, not certain which version of my life to recite, but then I decided that— at least in this case— it was best to tell the truth. I think I somehow sensed my humble origins would play better to this audience. And so I said I was from the backward fishing village of Kujirahe, not Kagoshima, and that I was the daughter of a carpenter, not the daughter of a samurai family, and that I'd been taken to Tokyo by my relatives when my mother died, and that those relatives had forced me to work as a servant and later sold me to the House of Sugutatsu. The man named Chen listened closely as Mr. Ma translated, showing no reaction, and then he asked again how it was that I had become the

Maiden Maiko. It was not possible in answering this specific question, of course, to tell the entire truth— certainly no mention could be made of the Lieutenant— but I did talk about the Minister of Public Enlightenment and how I had met him the night of my debut and how it was he who had decided I would become the Maiden Maiko. When Mr. Ma was finished with the translation, Chen nodded, as though he had reached some sort of conclusion, and then he and his wife began a lengthy conversation with Mr. Ma that Mr. Ma didn't bother to translate.

I was still very tense, and the smoke from the small fire in one corner of the hut was making it even more difficult to breathe. I tried to calm myself, taking short, regular breaths, but the more I thought about my predicament, the worse my breathing got. By now, Hoshi and the others would have arrived in Taiyuan, and the Japanese forces there would know I'd been kidnapped. Would they pay a ransom like Mr. Ma thought they would? But what about this man sitting across from me, Chen? Would he exchange me for money? Or had he just said I was valuable so the local men wouldn't haul me away to a nearby field and ravish me? Didn't he intend to keep me for himself? What if my own side wouldn't do a deal? Was it a decision the Colonel could make? And what about the Lieutenant? He, too, would have learned by now that the Maiden Maiko had been kidnapped. His entire camp would be abuzz with the news. He'd want to lead a rescue party, leave immediately. But they'd suspect something, his superior officers. Why was the Lieutenant so passionate about rescuing the Maiden Maiko? Was he that much of a patriot? Wasn't there something between the two of us? They'd suspect something. And if that was the case, wouldn't it be better that the Maiden Maiko become a martyr, her soul sent to Yasukuni? Could the Colonel stop them? Would he want to stop them if he knew about me and the Lieutenant? Oh, my mind was spinning a million miles a minute and I couldn't breathe and I felt like I was going to pass out and—

"Miss Suzukaze..."

Mr. Ma was touching my arm. Our captors had evidently finished their conversation with him, and now they wanted to talk to me again.

"You seem like a nice enough young lady," Mr. Ma translated for Chen, "and yet you support this war against us. Why?"

This was not a question I had expected, but still the answer seemed straight-forward. I was grateful Ummu Sensei had schooled us so well. I told him we were there to liberate him from the Westerners. Chen laughed when he heard me say this, and he picked up a stick and drew a circle in the dirt floor— not a circle with any apparent meaning— and then he looked back at me again and asked if I really believed this. I was silent. Of course I believed it. That's what I'd been taught.

"Maiden Maiko," he continued, "aren't you Japanese the same as the Westerners?"

This was very confusing indeed. How could we be the same as the Westerners? Wasn't it obvious we were different?

"Are you aware of how many thousands of Chinese your armies have killed?"

I am ashamed to admit that, up until this point, I really hadn't given this much thought. I really hadn't connected the deaths of people with the liberation of the country. I know this sounds foolish. There had been all those reports in the newspapers, and the Colonel had written about the large battles we'd had with the Chinese, and certainly that must have meant that many men had been killed, but somehow it hadn't seemed to be connected to the liberation of the country. Chinese were being killed in their own liberation. There had to be some good explanation. I wished Ummu Sensei was there. He would have been able to tell me why it all made sense.

"Maiden Maiko...

I tried to focus again on Mr. Ma's translation.

"Do you understand you are a symbol of Japanese imperialism?"

Now I was a symbol? A symbol of what? What in the world did he mean by "imperialism?"

"You are being used by the capitalist overlords of your society."

Capitalist overlords? Even Mr. Ma seemed to be struggling to find the right words in Japanese.

"Your armies are not here to liberate us. They are here to make more money for their capitalist masters back in Japan. Yes, they want to drive out the Westerners— so they can make more money for themselves."

Is that what this war was about? Making more money? But why would young men die to make more money for others? This, too, just didn't make any sense. There had to be some greater purpose.

"It's actually easy to understand, Maiden Maiko, how a young person like yourself could be caught up in the fables and falsehoods promoted by your government."

Fables? Falsehoods?

"But what you must understand is that the real war is not between China and Japan. No, the real war is between the bourgeoisie and the proletariat."

The bourge... what? And the prole... what? Who were they?

"And you are a member of the proletariat— a daughter of a carpenter, a daughter of the working class... a daughter of the proletariat. You are one of us."

I was?

"And so that means we are allies, not enemies."

This was an awful lot to digest at one time, I must say. At least we weren't enemies. I am certain you can understand my great relief upon learning this, given the circumstances. Unfortunately, my relief was to be short-lived.

"Are you hungry?" Chen asked.

I nodded in the affirmative, even though I didn't think I'd be able to eat anything, and he reached across to the fire and picked up some pieces of chicken and put them on a plate and handed them to me. Then he told Mr. Ma to take some chicken for himself, and as he was doing so, the woman named Bai poured out some hot wheat tea for us. But there was a grudging nature in her offering of the tea, and when she was done, she asked me a most peculiar question.

"Are you really a god in Japan?"

Even though Chen had earlier made reference to this same allegation, I was still surprised at the question. Where would she have heard such a thing? I told her, no, that was certainly not the case. She said all the Chinese newspapers had said I was a god in Japan, and I understood then that the Chinese also made "small adjustments" in pursuit of their "greater truth." I reassured her again that I was not a god in Japan— or anywhere else, for that matter— but she looked skeptical, and asked if I had volunteered to be the Maiden Maiko. It seemed she might not think of me as an ally in the same way her husband did. I told her I had most certainly not volunteered to be the Maiden Maiko. It had been forced on me, I said— a slight exaggeration, but I of course couldn't tell her all the particulars of how I had come to be in this position. Wasn't it true, she went on, that I wasn't even a maiden? The Chinese knew very well what a geisha was. How could it be expected that I would be a maiden? The Japanese people might believe something like that— they might even believe I was a god— but the Chinese people were not that gullible. It showed just how primitive and superstitious the Japanese were, that they would believe something like this. I didn't know what to say to all these accusations. What could I say? Mr. Ma tried to be as gentle as possible in his translation— I'm certain the original Chinese was even harsher— but still there was no avoiding the raw sting of this woman's words, and I could feel myself shaking now, and my breathing once again became uneven and labored. Chen looked silently off into the fire while his wife conducted her attack on me, showing no reaction, and when she was done, he called the two guards from outside and they came in and took us away, motioning for us to take our uneaten chicken with us. As we left, I turned and looked at Chen one last time, hoping he might have some further words of encouragement, but he said nothing. Nothing at all.

21

Back in our hut, I started to cry again. I was ashamed I was so weak, but I couldn't help myself.

"What's to become of me?" I asked Mr. Ma.

Chen had said we were allies, but then his wife had been so hateful. Who would decide my fate? I'd heard Chinese women were very strong. Wouldn't the wife make the decision? Wouldn't she see to it that I was executed? She seemed very displeased that I was a god in Japan— even though this was an outright lie. Wouldn't she want to execute the Japanese god?

"She was just jealous," Mr. Ma said, sitting closer and rubbing my back again, as he had done earlier. "There's nothing to worry about."

"But what if our side won't pay a ransom? What then?"

"What then?" Mr. Ma echoed.

The guards had left us some of the wheat tea, and now Mr. Ma poured some for both of us. As he poured the tea, he said again that there was nothing to worry about. The Chinese would ask for the ransom, and the Japanese would pay it. I was silent, wiping the tears from my face with the sleeve of my kimono.

"You haven't eaten your chicken," he said, trying to distract me.

I shook my head, and Mr. Ma smiled. He said I reminded him of a girl he knew in Japan. She'd been her most beautiful when she'd cried. I smiled sheepishly, wiping away my tears again. He'd stayed with a family when he was a student, he said, in a house in Atago, near Shiba Park. It had been near enough the university, near enough Keio, for him to walk. They'd had a daughter. They'd also had three sons. The father had worked in the government, in the Foreign Ministry. He'd hoped his children would learn Chinese from Mr. Ma. The eldest son had been the same age, the daughter a year younger. I knew he was telling his story to make me feel better, to get my mind off the horrible state of affairs in which we found ourselves, and I was grateful. I realized then, too, how self-centered I'd been, how inconsiderate of Mr. Ma's feelings. I wasn't the only one who had been kidnapped, after all.

"And the daughter was most beautiful when she cried?"

"Yes..."

He picked up his chicken and started to eat it, and he motioned for me to eat mine as well. Hesitantly, I took a bite and then a sip of my tea.

"Were you in love with her?"

"In love..."

Mr. Ma paused a long moment, and I thought maybe he wasn't going to answer my question.

"You're still young, Miss Suzukaze," he finally said. "Have you ever been in love?"

I so wanted to talk to him about the Lieutenant. I hadn't been able to tell my story to anyone, not even to Tomo. This might be my last chance. Who knew what would happen? In a day or two, I might be sent to the next world. But I couldn't bring myself to do it, to talk about the Lieutenant.

"As geisha," I said instead, "we're not supposed to fall in love."

Mr. Ma raised his eyebrows. "That must be very difficult."

"I wouldn't know, being so young..."

He nodded, and then took a sip of his tea. "Yes, I was in love with her..."

I looked into his eyes, and I could see him thinking back to those days when he'd been a student and he'd lived in the same house with the girl he loved.

"Did she love you?"

"I think she did..."

"Why didn't you get married?"

There was another long pause, and then he said, "I think she was sorry she fell in love with me."

"Sorry?"

"She wasn't supposed to fall in love with me. She was a girl with plans. She was supposed to marry a businessman or a doctor or a diplomat, not a Chinese student."

"Is that what her parents decided?"

"No... that's what she decided."

The light was growing faint by then. We talked about

other things, about why his parents had decided to send him to Japan, and about the girl he had married when he got back to China, and about the Japanese trading company he worked for in Tianjin. At some point I asked about the long conversation he'd had with Chen and Bai. What had they talked about? He said they'd asked about his family background, in the same way they'd asked about my family background. He'd lied, he said. He'd told them his father owned a small drug store in Tianjin, when he actually was a landowner in Shandong. He wasn't sure if they'd believed him. Being a small shop owner wasn't good, but being a landowner was worse. It would have been better if his father had been a carpenter, like mine, but a carpenter sending his son to Japan to study was too unlikely a story. He'd had to tell them about studying in Japan. He'd had to explain why his Japanese was so good. They wouldn't like it, but there was nothing he could do about it. Just before I fell asleep, I asked him again about the Japanese girl he'd been in love with. When had he seen her cry? It had been just the one time, he said. It was when she told him she didn't love him and couldn't marry him. That's when she'd cried. That's when she'd been her most beautiful. That's when he'd known for certain that she loved him.

We went to sleep thinking the next day would be uneventful as we waited for word on the negotiations for our release, but we were awoken early by our guards and told to get ourselves ready to leave the village.

"It seems your compatriots have sent a rescue party after you," Chen said when he saw us. "We're going to have to move."

As we left our hut, the woman named Bai appeared, looking at me with disdain. She was undoubtedly upset that her husband and other men from the village would be putting their lives at risk because of me, and she would have likely just as soon had me executed right then and there. I could see it clearly in her face.

Chen nodded at his wife one last time, and then we were off. There were no horses this time. Instead we took off at a rapid pace on foot, heading farther up into the hills behind the village. I tucked my kimono up above my knees so as to be able to keep up with the others— no time to be standing on the finer points of etiquette. In addition to Chen, there were three more men with us, the same three who had taken part in the kidnapping. Two were younger, probably only three or four years older than I, while the third was a much older man, much older even than Chen. None of the men was very friendly. Despite what Chen had said about us being allies, they couldn't have been pleased to find themselves being chased by a unit of the Japanese Imperial Army on account of my presence. After climbing for what seemed to be about an hour, we started down, winding our way along a well-worn path until we came to a small river, and then as the sun rose higher in the sky through the rest of the morning, we followed the river, keeping up a steady pace.

"Aren't you tired?" Chen asked at one point, turning around as he continued to walk. "You seem to be in remarkably good shape for a geisha."

I didn't tell him about our martial arts training. It didn't seem worth the bother at that particular moment. Mr. Ma, unfortunately, was not in as good shape as the rest of us. By late morning he was visibly struggling, and Chen shouted at him more than once to pick up the pace. I couldn't understand the exact language used, of course, but later— in a private moment— Mr. Ma told me that he had been called an "effete intellectual." I said that didn't seem a good thing to be called, and Mr. Ma agreed— it was not a good thing to be called, and he repeated his concern that Chen and Bai might not believe what he had told them about his family history.

Sometime about noon we stopped for a quick lunch. Chen, fearful that we might be spotted by the enemy— the enemy as he defined the enemy, of course— moved us away from the river into a small grove of trees. There wasn't much food, but Chen saw to it that Mr. Ma and I got as much as the others. I was quite hungry by then, and more than a little grateful for this thoughtful act. Soon after resuming our hike, we came to a point where the river narrowed and bluffs rose up on either side. The path continued alongside the river, but Chen chose not to take this way and instead climbed another path that took us up towards the bluff. As we made our turn, he said something about not being able to escape if we were caught along the river. Our surroundings became much more heavily wooded as we climbed, with the river only visible at certain points as we came to small clearings. And then at one such point, Chen, who was in the lead, suddenly fell to the ground and motioned for the rest of us to do likewise.

"Look there, Japanese troops," Mr. Ma whispered to me.

I looked down, and indeed there below, still at somewhat of a distance, was a unit of men dressed in the familiar uniform of our Imperial Army. My heart leapt into my throat. Was that my Lieutenant at their head? They were still too far away. I couldn't tell. It might be him. He was tall enough, and the way he carried himself looked similar. But he was too far away. I wanted to cry out, to alert him. Chen glared at me, warning me silently not to shout out to my fellow Japanese. The troops came ever closer. I still couldn't tell if it was the Lieutenant. Chen and the others had their rifles trained on him. Would they shoot me instead if I shouted? They were too close. I had to— And then a shot rang out.

Followed quickly by the sound of someone yelling

in Chinese. I buried my head in my arms and hugged the ground, and then after a long moment I heard Chen shout something back. There were further exchanges in Chinese, and then I slowly lifted my head. The voice from the other side was coming from behind us, not from below.

"They're saying we're surrounded," Mr. Ma whispered to me. "They want us to hand over the Maiden Maiko."

I was shaking violently, gasping for breath. How could this be happening? How could they be fighting over me? Couldn't they see how senseless it was?

"If they attack, Chen says he will kill the Maiden Maiko."

Kill me? How could...

"I'm certain he doesn't mean it," Mr. Ma added apologetically.

Then another shot rang out, and the older man, the man much older even than Chen, slumped over, blood pouring from his head. I screamed. Why had the Japanese troops fired on us? Hadn't Chen said he would kill me if they did? Did they think he was bluffing? Were they willing to gamble my life to find out? I knew then the officer at the head of the Japanese troops could not be my Lieutenant. He would have never given the order to shoot. Chen and his two younger comrades now returned fire, shooting rapidly in the direction of the voice behind us and then directing their aim at the men below. The Japanese troops had advanced to a position almost directly underneath us and as I watched, a soldier in the front of their column fell, hit by a bullet. Then Chen grabbed my hand and we were off running, running back down the path we had just come up. There were no thoughts of trying to stay behind or flee to the Japanese side. I simply ran, ran like a wild animal escaping its pursuers. Part way back down the path, Chen cut off on another trail that went off the back side of the bluff, away from the river.

We sprinted down, dodging trees and brush. Several times I thought I would fall, but Chen caught me, still holding on to my hand. Mr. Ma and the two others were right behind us. We ran this way for what seemed a long time, continuing to duck and dodge, and then suddenly Chen stopped and looked about, and then he got down on his hands and knees and squeezed into a narrow opening, pulling me with him, and Mr. Ma and the two others came in behind us. Inside it was very dark and damp, and the space only large enough to barely hold the five of us. Outside we could hear the Japanese troops searching for us, shouting to each other. Chen put his hand over my mouth, but he needn't have— I knew that crying out would only bring more shooting and killing. After a while the voices faded away, but we stayed where we were, very still and quiet, and we stayed there for a very long time. At some point I fell asleep, and when I awoke, Mr. Ma was gently shaking me.

"We're going to go now," he said.

"Are they gone?"

"Yes, they're gone."

Night had fallen and it was difficult to see, but Chen seemed to know his way. We walked for two, maybe three hours, and we finally came to a village, and we were fed, and then we slept the sleep of the dead.

Over the next several days I tried not to think too much about what lay ahead. Now that a rescue attempt had failed, it seemed any ransom talks could only be a distant possibility. I had gotten so near to seeing the Lieutenant again, only to now find myself in what seemed a hopeless situation. Would we stay here in the mountains, or would Chen try to move us? Would Mr. Ma stay with me? Would I be in Chinese hands the rest of the war?

Would I even survive the war?

22

In the end, despite all that had happened, I was only with my Chinese captors another two weeks before being returned to the custody of the Imperial Army. The Colonel himself came out from Taiyuan with a small troop of soldiers to meet Chen and his band at the designated point of exchange. As our men got out of their trucks, I urgently scanned their ranks for the Lieutenant, carefully looking up and down the line once and then twice, but he wasn't to be seen.

I immediately panicked. Had he been killed or wounded? Had he been transferred to another location? But of course there was no reason why he had to be with this particular group of men on this particular assignment— even if he in fact was still in Taiyuan.

While the rest of us waited, Chen and the Colonel walked off with Mr. Ma some distance and had a discussion. Mr. Ma would be staying behind with his fellow countrymen. If not for me, he would not have been kidnapped. Now he might never see his wife and children again, and as I watched him translating for Chen and the Colonel, I once more rued the day I had decided not to confess to the Madame and instead chosen to become the Maiden Maiko.

When the men were done with their discussions, the exchange was officially completed and we got into our trucks, while the Chinese got back up on their horses.

"Goodbye, Miss Suzukaze," Mr. Ma said.

"Take care of yourself," I shouted, waving back.

He nodded, and then as he and the other Chinese turned away and rode off, tears filled my eyes. I would later often think of Mr. Ma and his family, and hope all of them had survived the war and the civil war that followed and all the other unrest that seemed to overwhelm China without end.

The Colonel was sitting next to me in the truck. I knew he could sense the intensity of my many emotions as we drove off— the relief of being back with my fellow Japanese, the guilt and sadness at leaving Mr. Ma behind, the sheer exhaustion caused by the extreme stress of my captivity— but he didn't turn to me or say anything. In front of his men, he couldn't allow himself any familiarity. At one point, however, when the other men had nodded off, he did reach over and squeeze my wrist, and I must say I felt very comforted by this small gesture. He told me later that another unit based in Shijiazhuang had at first been put in charge of my case. Rather than negotiate a deal, they had tried to rescue me. The "stupidity" of the other commander had needlessly put my life at risk, he said. When we arrived at army headquarters in Taiyuan after our long ride, the Colonel tried to secretly rush me into the building, but the press nonetheless managed to catch us.

"Are you still a maiden?" was the first question they threw at me.

I could see the Colonel was angered by the bad manners of the questioner, but he controlled himself and allowed me to answer.

"Yes, of course," I said.

The pressmen didn't look convinced.

"Are you certain?" another of them asked. "You were in enemy hands for two weeks, and you're saying they didn't touch you?"

"How can you say that?" yet another yelled.

At this the Colonel did lose his composure, slapping the last offending inquisitor on the side of the head. "You heard the young lady," he growled. "She's still a maiden."

There were a couple of more questions, much more polite in tone, and then the pressmen dispersed. Thereafter there were always rumors that I had been deflowered by the enemy, but the official line maintained by the government, the army, and the press was that I had fiercely protected my maidenhood, as only a daughter of Yamato could, despite numerous savage attempts on my citadel by my captors.

Once we got inside the building I was met by the Madame and my sisters and Taibo and Ummu Sensei. There were tears all around, even in the eyes of the grand champion and the honorable Sensei. When I had been taken from the train, all of us had no doubt been fearful that we might never see each other again.

"Oh, it's so good to have you back," the Madame said, and then she and Hoshi and Mangetsu and Koyo all hugged me at once as the two men looked on.

There was still a welt on the face of Ummu where he had been struck by the rifle butt, and Taibo's arm was in a sling—it seems his wound had not been serious and he would make a full recovery, although there was no telling how it might affect his wrestling skills. Everyone was sorry to hear about Mr. Ma's fate.

"In war," Ummu declared, "one must choose one's side carefully."

After we had talked for a few minutes and our emotions had settled down, we went to our nearby hotel and the Madame had Hoshi take me upstairs. The two of us would be sharing a room. There was still no sign of the Lieutenant. I had thought he might be with the pressmen, hanging on the edge of the crowd, or that he might be waiting inside the headquarters building, in the lobby or one of the hallways, or that at least there might be a message for me upon my arrival at the hotel. But he was nowhere to be seen, no messages either, and my earlier worries were heightened. Had he been killed or wounded? Had he been transferred? Then again, I told myself, he was just being careful. The risks were enormous for both of us. He would find a way to see me when it made most sense. The gods would not have brought me this far only to keep us apart.

"I can't imagine what it must have been like," Hoshi said as soon as she'd closed the door to our room.

It was a spacious Western-style room, with high ceilings, large windows, a beautiful bureau, an exquisite writing desk, and two lovely single beds. I walked over to one of the beds and flopped down, closing my eyes.

"Poor thing. You must be exhausted."

"Yes, a little tired…"

"I'll draw a bath. That will help you relax."

"Oh, that would be wonderful."

Soon I could hear the sound of running water. I lay there for another minute or two, and then I forced myself to get up and get undressed, and I went into the bathroom, where Hoshi was waiting. She asked if I'd like to wash my hair, and I said I would, and she undid my hair and let it down, and then she had me stand over the sink and she poured a bucket of water over my head and gently shampooed my hair. When she was done, she motioned for me to get in the bath. I stuck a toe in and quickly pulled it out, and she added cold water, and then I tried again, slowly easing myself into the tub. Oh, it felt so good. After letting me soak for a while, Hoshi handed me a cloth she had soaped up, and I slowly began to wash the grime of the last two weeks from my body. I was still not used to the idea of washing myself in the tub, as the

Westerners did, but any bath was very welcome at that point.

"Want me to wash your back?"

"Oh, that would be so nice."

I knew Hoshi wanted to talk about my time in captivity, but she thoughtfully refrained. We could talk about that some other time, when I was more rested and had had a chance to recover from my tribulations. Instead, as she rubbed away at my back, she started to talk about what she and the other girls had been up to while I'd been away. They'd continued to rehearse almost daily, she said, and they'd also had to entertain at private events four or five nights. The Colonel was the one who arranged the evening functions. He was very apologetic, Hoshi said, feeling it wasn't quite appropriate that people would be partying while the Maiden Maiko was held in captivity, but there was nothing he could do about it, as his commanding officer, a General Asano, had ordered him to make the arrangements. It seems General Asano knew the Colonel had known the Madame for many years, and he, General Asano, wanted to use that relationship to his advantage. As I finished up my bath and dried off and dressed myself in a simple yukata, Hoshi continued on with her story. She emphasized that none of them had enjoyed themselves at these functions, with my plight constantly on their minds, and that the Colonel in particular had appeared distraught throughout my absence. I should not think badly of him because of his attendance at these evenings of entertainment. He was only doing his duty, as were they all. It had been a trying time for Koyo in other ways, she said. Evidently General Asano had taken a liking to Koyo, and he had been quite aggressive in pursuing her, ordering her to go home with him at the end of one night of entertainment. It seemed the usual conventions did not apply when at the front lines. The Madame had protested,

Hoshi said, but there was nothing to be done about it and rather than make a scene, Koyo had left with the general. The next day Koyo had been indignant that she would be treated as no more than a common call girl, but she said she had had the last laugh, as the general had been too drunk to perform his manly duties— although the next morning she had been certain to tell him how wonderful he'd been, knowing he wouldn't remember a thing. Recently, Hoshi said, it seemed Koyo had been unlucky with men. After the incident with the general, she had confided that things had also not been going well with Mr. Fukunaga— her patron, as you will recall. Evidently his munitions business was so profitable that he had become the patron of a second well-known geisha, O-Tama of Akasaka. It wasn't so much that Koyo was jealous, Hoshi said, but it was humiliating that a geisha of her stature would have to compete with another geisha for the attention of this man. It was likely Koyo would break off the relationship when we got back to Tokyo. She would certainly have no trouble finding another patron.

"I suppose that's what men are like..."

"Like what?" I asked, lying down on my bed.

"Always wandering off..."

"I guess we'll find out..."

"I guess so..."

Hoshi left then for a rehearsal session with Koyo and Mangetsu. I protested that I should go with her, but she insisted that I rest. She said the Madame had given her strict orders to make sure that I lie down for a while. I thought again how lucky I was to have a sister like Hoshi. It is rare indeed to have someone nearby who is so caring and protective, whether that person be of the same blood or not.

Later that afternoon the Madame asked me to meet her in the courtyard of the hotel. There was a small coffee shop there, and we sat in a corner where no one else would be able to hear our conversation. She had the waitress come over and she ordered some tea, and then she asked if I'd like to have some Chinese pastries. She had tried them herself and they were very good. I told her that would be nice, that I'd never had Chinese pastries before.

"You've been through such a trial, Suzu" she said after the waitress left.

I looked down and nodded.

"We were all so worried..."

Unlike Hoshi, I did feel as though I should tell the Madame in some detail about my time with my captors. She was the head of our troupe, after all, and I was one of her charges. So I told her about riding on the horses up into the mountains, and I told her about the conversation with Chen and Bai and how they said the Japanese people believed I was a god, and I told her about the rescue mission that had come after me. She cringed when I got to the part about the older man being shot in the head.

"Oh, Suzu, I just can't imagine..."

"No, it was..."

I told her, too, about the Japanese soldier being shot and how badly I felt about men risking their lives for me.

"All," I concluded, "for the Maiden Maiko."

The Madame pursed her lips and looked away. She didn't say anything. She didn't need to. We both knew she felt responsible for having put me in this position, and we both also knew there was nothing to be done about it. The pastries came out, one for each of us, and I quickly ate mine.

"Suzu," the Madame said as I finished, "there is something else I need to talk to you about. It's a little difficult to bring up... but it's something we do need to discuss..."

I knew immediately that she wanted to know whether

or not I had been defiled by my captors, and I reassured her that I had not.

She nodded and then leaned forward, putting her face closer to mine. "As one woman to another," she said softly but insistently, "you should not feel embarrassed to talk to me about such matters. Whatever happened, it certainly wasn't your fault."

I must confess that at this point it actually did occur to me that perhaps I should tell her that I had been violated. In one fell swoop I could be freed of my duties as the Maiden Maiko as well as any expectations that, in fact, I was still a maiden. But it didn't seem such an easy thing to say. What about the expectations of the Minister? What about my duty to my country? What about the honor of the House of Sugutatsu? And then there was the Lieutenant— would he think I'd actually been had by my captors if such a story were to get out? Even if I later told him the truth? Yes, he should believe me, of course, but...

I told her again that nothing had happened.

"That's good to hear," she said, apparently convinced and clearly relieved.

I took a sip of my tea, and there was a long pause.

"Because if something had happened..."

I shifted forward in my seat.

"...it would have been a breach of national security... and we would have had to report it to the relevant authorities."

The state of my maidenhood had now been raised to a matter of national security? I reassured the Madame again that nothing had happened, all the while being very aware of the narrow grounds upon which I was making my claim. Nothing had happened while I was a captive, but what about before then? National security? How had things reached this point? Was there really such a big difference? It had only been that one time. My heart was still pure like a maiden. Wasn't that enough?

"That's good to hear," the Madame said again.

Having been reassured about this first critical point, the Madame went on to say the rest of the troupe were prepared to go home, if that is what I wanted to do. It would certainly be understandable, given what I had been through, but if I did want to go on with the tour, the other members were also willing to do that. It was up to me. I didn't think long before giving the Madame an answer— I'd like to finish up the trip. I suppose it was the old motto— the show must go on. We'd come this far. Why not see what the rest of China had to offer?

Taking all due precautions, of course.

23

By noon of the next day I had still heard nothing from the Lieutenant, and I was beginning to think he might no longer be in Taiyuan. He might no longer even be in this world, of course, being a soldier in an active war zone, but I chose not to believe that possibility. He might indeed have been transferred, or perhaps he was away on an urgent assignment. It was still possible, too, that he was in Taiyuan and just hadn't had the chance to approach me yet. We would be in Taiyuan for another four or five days. I might still see him here, I told myself. I had to stay strong, whatever the eventuality.

Late that afternoon I did see the Colonel again. One of his aides came and asked that I follow him to another room in the hotel. There, the Colonel was waiting for me.

"It's so good to finally be alone with you," he said as soon as the aide had left.

I smiled, and he walked over and stood very close to me and inhaled deeply, as though he were taking in the scent of a deliciously fragrant flower.

"Yes, so good..."

I smiled again and bowed low. He motioned to a chair and asked me to sit.

"How are you feeling?"

"Better... I was able to rest yesterday."

"It was a terrible ordeal, wasn't it?"

"Yes..."

"Would you like some tea?"

"Allow me," I said, standing to reach for the tea pot on the table in front of us, but the Colonel insisted on serving both of us.

"This is actually quite good tea, specially shipped in from Guangdong."

"You shouldn't be wasting it on me."

"On the contrary."

He then slowly looked me over again, seemingly appreciating once more the beauty of my youth. "I'm sorry you had to see combat."

"It was horrific..."

As I had with the Madame, I told him about the Chinese soldier who had been shot in the head right in front of my very own eyes, and I told him, too, about the Japanese soldier who had fallen. Did he have any word about that soldier? Had he survived? Unfortunately not, the Colonel said, and at the thought of these men dying for the Maiden Maiko, tears once more came to my eyes.

"I'm sorry...," he said again.

He stood then and pulled out his handkerchief and handed it to me, and I wiped the tears from my face.

"One never knows when one's time will be up..."

I handed his handkerchief back, and he carefully folded it and put it in his pocket, and then he walked to the window and looked out towards the mountains in the distance. He talked about the Communists then, as he had in his letter, about how they hid in the mountains and attacked trains and ambushed his troops. And then he asked me about Chen. What sort of a man was he? He'd been kind enough in many ways, I said, but he had also threatened to shoot me.

"Yes," the Colonel said, "I suppose it's not fair to ask about a man's character in the middle of a war."

He wanted to know how many men Chen had had with him and what their fortifications looked like, and I told him I really didn't know. There had been only the four men with me. That's all I'd seen. I did also tell him about Bai, Chen's wife. The Colonel said he was familiar with her. She was actually quite a high-ranking official in their party. I told him what she had said about the Japanese people believing I was a god.

"Yes, I'm certain they fed you a lot of propaganda, a lot of talk about the proletariat and the bourgeoisie."

"Yes," I said, "Chen even told me I was a member of the proletariat."

The Colonel smiled when I said this, and then I told him what Chen had said about our armies being in China to make money for the capitalists, and how I had told him we were actually there to liberate him from the Westerners. The Colonel laughed at that.

"That's very good. You told him that right to his face?"

"Yes, I did," I said somewhat boastfully.

The Colonel laughed again, and then he said how all war

was complicated and how sometimes it had to be simplified so the common people could more easily understand.

"In any event," he said, "it's all about protecting our national interests."

He was right, of course. It had been so much simpler when I'd only thought we were in China to liberate the Chinese from the Westerners. Then Chen had told me we were there to make money for these people called the capitalists. Now the Colonel was telling me we were there to protect our national interests. I asked him what was meant by national interests.

"Ah, that's the beauty," he said, "a national interest can be anything."

Anything? This did not help to clarify my confusion. And what about all the Chinese who were being killed during the course of their liberation? I hesitated a moment, but then put this question to the Colonel as well.

"Ah, yes," he said, "the unfortunate realities of war and politics."

Unfortunate realities? What could these realities possibly be? I expected he would go on to tell me what they were, to give me more of an explanation, but instead he walked over and sat down and pulled his chair very close to mine.

"I'm wondering," he said, "if you wouldn't mind sleeping with me tonight." I must have looked startled, for he was quick to add, "Nothing will happen, I can assure you. I just..." and his voice trailed off.

"We will talk to the Madame, of course," he added.

I was speechless, at a loss to fathom this strange request.

"We will talk to the Madame," he said again.

The Colonel did talk to the Madame, and afterwards she spoke with me. It was indeed a strange request, she acknowledged, but she had known the Colonel for a long time and she was confident we could trust his word. To make certain, however, she herself would also sleep in the same room. It was a little difficult to explain, she went on, but the Colonel had told her he was in a rather depressed state of mind. He had a feeling this war was never going to end, and this feeling never left him. I said he had written the same thing to me in his first letter. Again, the Madame said, it was a strange request, but maybe our spending the night with him would somehow comfort him— and there would be no detriment to either of us.

That night neither Hoshi nor I slept in our room, she going to Taibo's while I went to the Colonel's. The room was dark, a night light in one corner allowing me to barely make out the figures of the Colonel and the Madame. They were already lying in their separate futons, the Colonel in the middle, the Madame to one side of him. I bowed politely, and then quietly lay down in the remaining futon. I was there for what seemed a very long time without a word being said, and I thought that's the way it would be— that we would not talk— but then the Colonel spoke up.

"It's a dirty business, this war," he said, "a very dirty business."

There was another long silence.

"Suzu," he went on, "humans are such degenerate beings... I sometimes wonder if we aren't the lowest form of life... I so wanted something pure and innocent... Maybe you can't understand that, but..."

I could hear the Colonel's muffled breathing as he searched for the right words.

"And that... that's why..."

There was another long pause.

"That's why... I've asked you to allow me to write letters to you, and asked for you to write to me... and asked you to come here tonight... I've asked all of this of you... for the sake of my... sanity... for my sanity... Can you understand that? Can you?"

I could, in that moment I could understand it. I could feel his sadness and his loneliness, and I wanted to touch him, and I extended my hand and I felt his hand there in the dark and I grabbed it in mine and squeezed it, and he squeezed my hand back. And we lay there like that for some time before I let go.

And the next morning I got up early, not saying a word, and I left him and the Madame lying there asleep.

24

By the morning of our departure from Taiyuan I had still not heard from the Lieutenant. It was a bitter disappointment, as I had been certain I would be able to see him. Despite my admonitions to myself to stay strong, I felt as though a gaping hole had been opened in my heart, and I once more began to have doubts about the Lieutenant's declarations of love. He had to have known I was there in Taiyuan, and yet he had not even left a message. Wasn't I just making excuses for him when I said he might have been wounded or killed or transferred? Hadn't he simply chosen not to see me? Oh, I'd been such a fool to fall in love.

As we drove to the airfield, Mangetsu could see I was out of sorts and she tried to cheer me up. I'm certain she could hardly have imagined my melancholy had anything to do with love, and most certainly thought I was still suffering from the aftereffects of my captivity.

"Suzu," she said, "we'll be in Wuhan just a few days, and then it's on to Shanghai. There will be so much to do there."

Koyo was sitting to my other side in the back seat, and she was quick to also try to raise my spirits. "They say there's some very nice nightclubs. We should go to one. Have someone serve us for a change."

Mangetsu laughed. "Yes, that's the idea."

"Maybe do a little shopping too," Koyo added. "What do you think, Suzu?"

I tried to smile politely. "I don't know..."

"But you do have to be careful of fakes," Mangetsu cautioned.

"Don't worry," Koyo said with a grin, "I've got a good eye."

"That you do."

Both girls laughed and looked at me expectantly, but I could manage no more than another polite smile, and I was certain again that they attributed my poor mood to the repercussions of my prolonged stay in the mountains. I thought it likely they even believed I had been had by the Chinese. Neither of them had asked me about it directly, as the Madame had, and even though the Madame had probably told both of them about my assurance that nothing had happened, I still had the feeling they strongly suspected that something had. It was the nature of men to partake of what was in their reach, and it was not probable that a delectable morsel like myself would have been passed over. But unlike the Colonel and the Master, perhaps even unlike the Madame, Mangetsu and Koyo were well aware the role I was playing was strictly theatrical in nature, and they were content to not let minor contradictions get in the way.

We had managed to do two shows in Taiyuan, and now we would be flying on to Wuhan. Train service between the two cities was unreliable, and there was no desire to replicate the experience we had had in getting to Taiyuan in the first place. The Colonel came to the airfield to see us off. He couldn't make any special farewell to me, but he did nod in my direction and I nodded back. My affection for the Colonel would never be anything similar to the feelings I held for the Lieutenant, but I did have a special place in my heart for him— especially after the night we spent together in Taiyuan We would continue to correspond on a regular basis over the next few years as he finished up his assignment in Taiyuan and moved on to Singapore, and then Burma— where he would make his military name.

None of us had ever flown before, and the prospect of getting up in the air in a plane was extremely daunting.

"You have nothing to worry about," Mr. Wakinuma said with a broad wave of his hand. "Heavier than air flight has been a fact of life for almost forty years now." But his reassurances weren't very convincing, particularly with Taibo being one of our fellow passengers.

"We should be fine," the pilot said, coming back to inspect our seating, "just so long as we balance the grand champion with enough people on the other side."

"Are you certain?" the Madame asked skeptically.

We calculated it would take five of us— the four girls and the Madame— to offset the grand champion, and then we added Ummu Sensei and Mr. Hu— our new interpreter— to one side and Mr. Wakinuma to the other. This didn't make for an exact balance, but it was close enough, according to the pilot. We took off, the whole plane shaking, all of us girls screaming as we headed straight for a small building at the end of the runway, and then just at the last millisecond, when we were all certain we had breathed our last, the plane rose off the ground and strained up, up, up into the air. The pilot banked to the left, continuing to rise, and then we roared back over the airfield south towards Wuhan.

"When death is near, one's heart races," Ummu declared, his face pale.

Little did I know then that I myself would be piloting a plane some five years later, albeit with a very different objective.

It was wonderful being up so high looking down on everything. The great plain was brown and dusty and seemed to stretch endlessly to our west, and to our east were the mountains— the mountains where Chen and his comrades were hiding out— and the mountains were brown and dusty, and we followed the edge of the mountains for a long while until we came to a large river, and Mr. Hu told us this was the Yellow River, and we crossed the river and started to come down out of the mountains, and the land became flatter and greener. I imagined this was probably how the gods looked at the world, and it made sense to me then that they would be so much wiser. They could see the mountains and they could see the rivers and they could see the fields and they could see the forests, and from up here it would be so much easier to put things in order. Poor humans, I thought, down below in our unruly rat race, never able to see the forest for the trees— what chance did we have of ever making sense of anything?

As we got closer to Wuhan we could see evidence of the major battle that had occurred there. Large parts of the countryside were scarred with craters, and there were still numerous burnt-out tanks and trucks and cars scattered about. Vast numbers of homes had also been leveled. During my captivity I had seen a small portion of the war, but this was the first time to see its destructive effects on this scale. Overwhelmed by the scene that stretched out below us, the plane grew very quiet. As we circled in over the Yangze

River and approached the airfield, we could see the level of destruction was dramatically less in the city proper. It seemed the Chinese forces had chosen not to contest Wuhan itself, and had instead withdrawn their army to the west. But clearly a large number of people had been killed in this enormous battle, and I seriously wondered again if there wasn't a better way to conduct this liberation— or making of money, or protecting of national interests, or whatever it was.

It seemed there had to be.

25

And then came the moment for which I had all but given up hope.

There was a message waiting for me when I checked in at the hotel. The clerk said the gentleman had explained that he was my brother, and he was hoping to meet me in the lobby of the hotel at eleven o'clock the next morning. He hadn't left a phone number, but he would be calling in to the clerk later to see if that time would be convenient for me. I told the clerk it would. It was the Lieutenant! As I walked away from the desk, I felt weak in the knees and thought I might faint. The Madame and my sisters were in the middle of the lobby sorting out their luggage, and as I approached them Mangetsu called out to me.

"What's the matter, Suzu?"

What should I say? They knew I had received a message. I couldn't very well say it was nothing. And he would be coming tomorrow.

"It's my brother," I said.

Hoshi put her hand over her mouth. "Your brother?"

"Did you know he was here?" the Madame asked.

"No… we haven't seen each other for a number of years."

Everyone was very excited for me. I explained how my family had been split up when my mother had died. This was my eldest brother. Again, I said, I hadn't seen him for years. I'd get the full story on what had happened to him when I saw him tomorrow.

"How many brothers do you have?" Hoshi asked when we got upstairs to our room.

"Three."

"So your brother Tomo in Tokyo and two other brothers…"

"Yes…"

"You didn't know he was in China?"

"I didn't even know he was in the army…"

"It really is incredible, isn't it?"

If only she knew. That night I didn't sleep at all. I could hardly believe I was finally going to see him again. He had come back to me. He still did love me. Why had I doubted his affections for even a moment? And yet I was still very nervous. Would he be disappointed? Would he wonder what it was that he had first seen in me? And now there was this further complication of our supposed relationship as brother and sister. The Madame and Mangetsu and Koyo and Hoshi had all asked to be introduced to him. They were curious about this brother that none of them had known about. Oh, why did everything have to be so difficult? Why was I being forced into another "small adjustment" of the truth?

"Will you be going out with your brother?" the Madame asked at breakfast.

"I really don't know…"

"We have a rehearsal at one o'clock, but you shouldn't

feel that you need to be back."

"No, no, I'll be back," I protested.

But the Madame insisted I stay with my "brother" as long as needed. "When our fighting men have a chance to see a family member," she said, "we must make sure they make the most of it."

And then it was eleven o'clock. I waited in the lobby by myself while the minute hand on the large clock on the wall opposite me slowly ticked forward. One minute after, two minutes after, three minutes after, seven minutes after, ten minutes after. And then there he was, walking through the door. Our eyes met immediately. He looked the same— the same ramrod straight posture, the same jaunty tilt to his cap. Perhaps a tinge thinner. I did notice that.

"Suzu..."

I smiled and bowed.

"You're even more beautiful than I remember."

I blushed, and it all came flooding back to me, that evening at Nagabashiya and then that late afternoon in Jinbocho. It was as though no time at all had passed.

"I was so happy to get your message. I wasn't sure if..."

"Yes, I know."

The Madame and my sisters were waiting in the lobby coffee shop. I told him I'd promised to introduce him. He wanted to take me for a ride along the bund, he said. There was a nice Japanese restaurant he knew. We could have lunch there. I nodded, and he reached out and briefly touched my hand, and then we went to the coffee shop.

"It's so nice to meet you," the Madame said, standing.

"The pleasure is mine," the Lieutenant replied, bowing.

And Mangetsu and Koyo and Hoshi all stood as well and bowed.

"Can you join us for a cup of tea or coffee?" the Madame

asked.

"I'm afraid not. There are a few things I want to show Suzu, and we don't have much time."

"That's a shame, but we certainly understand. You must have a lot to catch up on."

"Yes... I'm very sorry..."

And with that we politely made our farewell. Outside, the Lieutenant signaled for a rickshaw. The puller brought his vehicle forward and we got in, and the Lieutenant gave him directions, and then we were off. He reached across and grabbed my hand and smiled, and I smiled back, the two of us sharing our relief that we had managed to spend so little time with the Madame and my sisters.

The hotel in which we were staying was in the Hankou section of the city along the river. It seems Wuhan was actually made up of three smaller cities— Hanyang south of the river, and Wuchang and Hankou north of the river. Hankou was another of the "treaty ports," similar to Tianjin, and as we rolled along in our rickshaw I once more felt as though I were in Europe instead of China, with the broad boulevards and the large Western-style buildings. After a ride of seven or eight minutes we came to our destination, the restaurant. It was a very charming establishment, a two-storied building in the traditional Japanese style facing the Yangze. The proprietress greeted us warmly at the entrance— it was evident the Lieutenant was a frequent customer— and then we were shown to a private, tatami-matted room on the second floor. We walked over to the window, looking out on the river, and behind us the proprietress, a stylish middle-aged Japanese woman in an elegant kimono, knelt down and put her hands out in front of her on the tatami and bowed low.

"Please enjoy a leisurely lunch," she said. "We're not

expecting any other customers for this room. Ring me when you need something."

And she bowed low one more time, and then left, sliding the door closed behind her.

"What a wonderful view," I said.

"Yes, a lot of traffic, some of it coming all the way up from Shanghai."

He was standing close behind me now, and I could feel his warm breath on the back of my neck and sense the quiet rising and falling of his broad chest.

"Can you see the ferries?"

"Where?"

"Those boats there. Those are ferries going back and forth between Hankou and Hanyang."

That late afternoon in Jinbocho… walking down the hill, him standing there on the corner, stopping at the bookstore, drinking our beer, the students singing…

"And out there, that's an Imperial Navy patrol ship. Probably headed farther upriver. More action going on up there."

…him leaning across and taking my hand, looking deeply into my eyes…

"The Chinese junks are beautiful, aren't they? Those large square sails billowing in the breeze…"

"Yes…"

…leaving then and going down the alley, to that boarding house and the small room upstairs, his friend not there, and…

"Oh, Suzu…"

And he reached forward and put his arms around me and held me tight.

"Suzu…"

I could feel myself going to him. Did he intend to…

here... Oh, I so wanted him to hold me, but... But then he gently released me, and turned me around, and smiled and gestured to the low-lying table. We sat down, he on one side and I on the other, and I took a long, deep breath.

"Who would have ever thought," he said, "the two of us meeting here in Wuhan..."

"No, I..."

"Oh, Suzu..."

He apologized for not seeing me in Taiyuan. He'd been sent to Wuhan suddenly on a "special assignment," and he had thought it safer not to leave a message. I wondered what the assignment could have been, but was not bold enough to ask.

"The gods arranged it," I said.

"Only something the Maiden Maiko could request?"

"Perhaps..."

He asked if I was all right, if I'd recovered from my time in captivity, and I said I had. I was quick to add that the Chinese had treated me well— intimating that nothing untoward had happened without coming right out and saying it— and the Lieutenant didn't ask any more questions about the subject.

"Colonel Yamanaka told me he had to pay some money," I said.

"I wouldn't know about that," the Lieutenant replied. "Above my pay grade."

I couldn't control my curiosity at that point, and asked if he and the Colonel were in the same unit.

"Yes," he said, "he would be our commanding officer."

So, it was indeed as I had speculated. I thought momentarily of telling him about my correspondence with the Colonel, but then thought better of it. What was to be gained by that? And there was certainly no need to tell him about the night we had spent together. He might needlessly suspect there was something of more significance going on between the two of us than there was.

"For the safety of such an important person as the Maiden Maiko," the Lieutenant went on, "it's only to be expected that a large sum of money would be offered."

I had had no intention of talking about the Maiden Maiko so soon, but now that it had come up, it seemed I didn't have a choice. I hoped he didn't think I had volunteered for the position, I said. It had been forced on me. I hadn't had a choice. Sugutatsu had traditionally had a close relationship with the ruling class, I said— borrowing from the official line— and that is why the Ministry of Public Enlightenment had requested a girl from our house. Knowing what he did about me, I hoped he wouldn't think I was a girl of no morals— willing to play the role of the maiden when, as he knew, I wasn't a maiden, but I just hadn't had a choice. He was quick to tell me it didn't matter, that as soon as he had seen the news he had assumed it had been forced on me. And then, for the first time since that night, he again told me how much he loved me. He loved me, and that was all that mattered.

He asked then if I was hungry, and I said I was, and he rang the bell, and one of the waitresses of the house appeared and took our order. She came back not long after with a large bottle of beer and two glasses, and the Lieutenant poured for us, and I drank my first cup rather quickly and soon felt light-headed, just as I had that earlier time. He unbuttoned the top of his uniform, and I saw the scar again that ran from his collar bone down, and I was reminded once more of how uncertain was the life he led. This would be our only chance to see each other, he said. He had to take a flight back to Taiyuan late in the afternoon. He had hoped we'd be able to spend more time together, but... The lunch came out, a delicately done breaded pork dish, and we ate, and when we were done he asked about my duties as the Maiden Maiko. I told him about the interviews and the frequent evenings of entertainment that were expected in my new role. And I told him, too, about my visit to Yasukuni, and how that had been difficult for me, standing there before the spirits of all those fallen men, playing the role of the Maiden Maiko when I was not in fact a maiden. And as soon as I said it, I wished I hadn't, as I was certain I could see the guilt he felt for having put me in that position. I quickly reassured him I had no regrets. Didn't he think the spirits of the soldiers would understand our love for each other? He smiled, and said he thought they would. Yes, they would.

"It's not an excuse," he said, turning very serious, "but I wasn't sane at the time. You drove me mad, Suzu. You drove me mad."

There was some pride, I must admit, in knowing I had driven a man mad.

And then I asked him about the letters. I had hoped I would have some letters from him. I had so wanted to write to him, but I didn't have an address to write to because I had never gotten a letter from him. He looked surprised. He had sent two letters, he said. Hadn't I received them? No, I said, I hadn't. Unfortunately, the mail was notoriously unreliable, he said. He promised to write more letters. Hopefully they would get through in the future. I asked him for his address. He said he didn't know it off the top of his head, but he'd send me a letter and then I'd have it. I felt bad about pressing him further, and said no more about the letter writing.

He rang the bell then, and when the waitress came in to clear away the dishes he asked her to make sure we weren't disturbed. And then he came to my side of the table and sat with me, putting his arm around me, and I snuggled up against his broad chest.

"Oh, Suzu," he said.

And I could feel myself going to him again. Did he intend to... here... But we couldn't, we couldn't... But it made no sense— he had already had me. What difference did it make, one time or two? We were deeply in love. We only had this brief time together, this very brief time... His hand started to move up and... But we couldn't... I was the Maiden Maiko now and... It made no sense, but...

"Oh, Suzu," he said again.

And I took his hand and pulled it away and sat up.

"No, we can't," I said more emphatically than I had intended. "We can't."

And he smiled in a pleading way and once more tried to pull me closer, but I pushed him back.

"No, we can't," I said again.

And he paused, seemingly calculating the net balance of his passion versus the constrictions now placed on us by my position, and then he let out a sigh.

"Suzu," he said, "I understand... I understand..."

And I moved closer to him again and once more nestled up against his chest. We were both silent then. I felt bad, but there was nothing to be done about it. The war would be over one day, I said to myself, and he would no longer be a soldier and I would no longer be the Maiden Maiko, and he would come home and we would be together then forever. The gods would see to it, of that I was sure. And I looked up at his soft and inviting eyes, and I was so certain all would be right in the end.

26

When I got back to the hotel, the Madame and all of my sisters were waiting for me in the lobby.

"Your brother is so handsome," Mangetsu said.

"And so polite," the Madame added.

"Has he always been so quiet?" Koyo asked.

"You thought he was quiet?"

"Well, he just seemed rather..."

"I've never thought of him as quiet," I said, laughing.

They wanted to know what had happened to him after the family had been split up, and I realized the Lieutenant and I had forgotten to invent a story for that, and so I told them he'd been adopted by a well-off family in Oita. The father of the family had been an army officer, and my brother had followed in his adopted father's footsteps.

"He's been very fortunate," the Madame said.

"And so handsome," Mangetsu said again.

With the repeated comments about the Lieutenant's good looks, I began to worry that my sisters suspected this man was something more than a brother, but there was nothing I could do about that now other than act as normal as possible.

"It was good to see him after such a long time," I said.

The Madame nodded her head vigorously. "Yes, I'm certain it was. The gods must have made special arrangements for you to see him so far from home."

We only gave one performance while we were in Wuhan,

but it was to a very large audience, several thousand soldiers sitting outside in a park. There were a number of other acts besides ourselves— singers and dancers and comedians. Taibo was to have put on another exhibition of his wrestling skills, but that was not possible now with his wound, and he was instead simply honored by those present for the valor he had displayed in trying to defend the Maiden Maiko. From Wuhan we flew on to Shanghai, where we would spend one final week and do four more shows. It had been a long trip, and by that point we were all more than ready to get back to Japan.

"When one has eaten too much duck," Ummu declared, "one longs for home."

Shanghai was a huge city, like Tokyo, and similar to Tianjin and Hankou, it was a treaty port and had its Western sections along with its Chinese. We had to perform most nights, but our last day we were free and we went out to a night club, just as Koyo had wanted. Mr. Hu accompanied us, while the rest of the men were on their own, with Mr. Wakinuma taking Taibo on his own night tour of the city and Ummu Sensei remaining in his room meditating. It was a beautiful evening, warm with a slight breeze, and Mr. Hu suggested we take a walk before going on to the night club. We were staying at the Astor Hotel, just north of Suzhou Creek, and it was only a short distance to the bund of the Huangpu by way of the Garden Bridge. We'd heard there had been a large battle in and around Shanghai early in the war, but we saw no evidence of it now as we walked along the embankment of the river surrounded by the magnificent buildings the Westerners had built— the Customs House, and the Cathay Hotel, and the Palace Hotel, and the Hong Kong & Shanghai Bank, and many others. As we came to the end of this part of the bund, Mr. Hu hailed a taxi and we drove to what he said was the French section of the city.

I'd never been in a night club before. It was quite exciting, actually, to be on the receiving end of female hospitality for a change, as the Chinese, Russian, and French hostesses got us drinks and food and entertained us with witty chatter, as translated by Mr. Hu. Two Frenchmen even came to our table and asked to dance with Koyo and Mangetsu. The Madame nodded her approval, and our two older sisters were whisked away. Later, after she'd had a few drinks, the Madame asked one of the Frenchmen if he wouldn't mind dancing with her. She said she had never tried Western dancing before, and she might never again have the chance. The Frenchman, through Mr. Hu, replied that it would be his great pleasure. The Madame looked quite content as the tall and dashing Frenchman pulled her close to his chest and slowly guided her around the dance floor. We lived in such different worlds, I thought— I could hardly imagine the Madame dancing with the Master in similar fashion.

The next day we bid farewell to China, getting on a ship and setting out to sea for Japan. Mr. Wakinuma and Mr. Hu came down to the pier to see us off. I must admit that as I waved goodbye to Mr. Hu all I could think of was Mr. Ma. Was he even then still alive? As for Mr. Wakinuma, we heard sometime in the summer of 1942 that he had died in a car accident in Shanghai. That's what we were told, but there were also rumors of a black market deal gone awry.

I'm afraid the news of his death did not stir any sorrow in my heart.

27

When we returned home we found that the Master had fallen off the wagon— he was drinking again. It was the first time I had seen the Madame get that angry. She was furious. From my room on the second floor all the way at the other end of the house, I could hear her screaming. It was then I realized just how much she still cared for this man. It wasn't about him jeopardizing his role as the Master of Sugutatsu— I was certain that was not it. No, she was outraged because this man whom she still loved had once more fallen into the gutter. She had loved him, then lost him to drink, and then thought she had him back only to lose him again. The next couple of weeks were touch and go before the Master finally started to get himself back on track. In the end, it was once more Unmu Sensei who provided the spiritual tonic necessary for recovery. The Master began attending our morning sessions again, and day by day I could see his condition improving. It was clear that however strong the Madame's love might have been, it was only the Sensei who could effect a cure. I think this must have been quite vexing to the Madame, to understand her love alone was not enough, that she would have to share the Master's affections with the Sensei— not romantically, of course, but ultimately in a devotion that was just as meaningful. And not only would she have to share those affections, but if the person with whom she was sharing those affections, the Sensei, were to leave, the very life of her true love would be in peril. It was a very complicated situation, and I could fully understand why the Madame might have been confused in her feelings towards both the Master and the Sensei.

As events would have it, over the next several months I, too— despite my earlier faith in the gods— would have to come to grips with a harsh reality concerning my own true love.

Soon after getting back to Sugutatsu, I sent my first letter to the Lieutenant. There had been no letters from him and so I didn't have an address, but I assumed it must be the same as the Colonel's. I am ashamed to say I hadn't thought to ask what his bottom name was, but surely there wouldn't be more than one Lieutenant Nogi in the Colonel's unit. So I sent off the letter confident it would reach its destination and that I would soon have a letter back. But several weeks passed, and there were no letters. I continued to write from my end— restraining myself as much as possible from sending too many and thereby arousing suspicion— but there were no letters coming back from his end. Weeks passed, and then months, and still there were no letters. Once again I was forced to confront the possible reasons why. Had the address I used not worked? Had he been transferred to another unit? Had the letters he sent been lost due to the "notoriously unreliable" mail? Had he been wounded or killed? Had he simply chosen not to write me?

Once again, day after day, these various scenarios played out in my head until I was finally forced to conclude— in a shocking moment of clarity— that he must be dead. Even today, as I think back to that moment, I can feel the cold and nauseating impulse that shuddered through my body at the sudden realization. It literally knocked me to the ground. I'd been out for a walk by myself, near the river, and a passer-by came to my assistance, offering me a helping hand to a nearby bench. I managed to thank the kind stranger and tell her I was fine, and then I was once again left alone with my thoughts. He was dead. There was clearly no other conclusion. If he were alive, he would have written me. The mail may have been unreliable, but I had continued to receive letters on a regular basis from the Colonel, and there was no reason why at least one letter wouldn't have gotten through from the Lieutenant. It didn't matter if none of my letters had gotten through to him. He had expected to write to me first before receiving any back. He had promised to write, and I was certain he would have— if he were alive.

I was devastated. And the devastation was compounded many fold by the fact I could talk to no one about my loss. I did my best to carry out my duties, putting on a brave face when entertaining or attending official functions, but there was no hiding my grieving state from my sisters or the Madame. There was clearly something wrong with me, and each of them in her own way tried to be helpful, but I couldn't open up to any of them about the cause of my unhappiness. I did briefly consider using the "brother" card again, but that would have raised expectations for funeral arrangements and other matters, and I was in no mood for more deceit and subterfuge. No, I would have to keep this to myself. I did find some comfort in prayer. I prayed to the gods many times a day for the soul of my beloved. I prayed it hadn't been too painful a death. I prayed he had thought of me in his final moments and found solace in my love for him. And I prayed for the day we would be together again, when I too would be sent to the next world. One day that fall, the fall of 1940, I even made my own special pilgrimage to Yasukuni, where the souls of all our martyrs lay, and I offered up sticks of incense and prayers for my Lieutenant.

Looking back on it now, I realize of course it was easier

to think of him as dead than to admit he might not have written. He might indeed have been dead, or he might have been wounded, or he might simply have chosen not to write, but I had decided to put him among the dead— knowing in the deepest recesses of my heart that he might still be alive.

28

During the summer and fall of 1941 the Colonel sent me several letters in which he expressed his growing fear of a war with the United States. It seemed the Americans wanted Japan to get out of China. I thought we had gone into China in the first place to liberate the Chinese from the Americans and the other Westerners, but now it seemed the Americans wanted to liberate the Chinese from us. But America was so far away. Why were they so concerned about what was going on in China? Did it perhaps have something to do with making money for the capitalists? They must have capitalists in America too, I thought. Or perhaps it had something to do with national interests. As to what national interests, I couldn't say.

Then in December of that year, December 8th to be exact, I was awoken early in the day by a large commotion on the street outside our house. I jumped out of my futon and threw open the shutters. Down below there was a crowd of about ten or fifteen people.

"It's a great victory for our navy," I heard one of them say.

"Where?" another asked.

"Hawaii," the first man replied.

"Hawaii?" the second man said with surprise. "Our navy

went all the way to Hawaii?"

"Yes," the first man confirmed, "they went all the way to Hawaii and they gave the Americans a good thrashing."

I ran downstairs to the living room, and found the Madame there listening to the radio.

"Oh, this is horrible," she said.

"Horrible?"

"Yes, horrible. We don't need more war."

Our tour of China had perhaps given the Madame a sense of all the tragedy this new war might bring us at home in Japan. In any event, she was nearly the only person I knew at the time who wasn't excited about the events that occurred at this place known as Pearl Harbor.

"They're saying on the radio that our troops have also landed in Malaya."

"Malaya? And where is that?"

"Somewhere in Southeast Asia, south of China."

"South of China?"

"Yes, south of China."

Later that same day I saw Tomo.

"They're going to take everyone now," he said. "My draft notice is probably already in the mail."

"Don't they have a deferment for comedians?"

"Not for apprentice comedians, I'm afraid."

"It's a shame, isn't it, to have to give up your career."

"Not to worry. This war will soon be over, and I'll be back on the boards again."

"How can you say that?" I asked, keeping in mind what the Colonel had said about the war in China.

"Do you really expect the Americans to come all the way across the ocean and fight in the jungles of the South Pacific?" he exclaimed, as though the answer were as clear as day.

"They might," I quietly replied.

"How can you say that," he insisted, "when you know they don't have the fighting spirit of we Japanese?"

It was a difficult point to argue at the time— although we would of course find before long that the Americans were indeed quite willing to fight in the jungles of the South Pacific. Tomo was right about one thing— he was soon drafted. He was drafted that February, the February of 1942, and after a period of training sent to the Philippines. And there he would remain for the duration of the war.

It was only towards the end of that same month that I learned in a letter from the Colonel that he had been with the troops that landed in Malaya. The letter arrived not long after the surrender of the British forces in Singapore. There had been much celebration in Tokyo at the time of the surrender— loud newspaper headlines and dancing in the streets— but the tone of the Colonel's words was much less optimistic.

February 27, 1942

My dear Suzu,

I am writing to you from Singapore. Please look at a map and see where this is. As I've written before, I want you to know where I am. This is important to me. First find Tokyo and then take your finger and move southwest until you hit Taiwan, and then continue southwest from there until you find the coast of Indochina, and then go on from there until you run into the coast of Malaya. It was there, on the east coast of Malaya, that I landed with my troops on December 8th.

General Yamashita has been proclaimed a national hero by the newspapers and given the nom de guerre of "Tiger of Malaya" for our victory over the British here, but you must not read too much into this. The general was, in fact, set up to fail in this mission. It is only by a very peculiar quirk of events that he did not. No one would admit to this, of course, but if one looks at the situation with an objective eye the truth is more than clear. It was all part of a larger strategy by the general command in Tokyo to bring the war in China to an end. The plan was to simultaneously attack across an impossibly large swath of territory, giving us absolutely no chance at success; when these attacks failed, as the nitwit general command were utterly confident they would, then the nation would have the necessary face to sue for a negotiated settlement in China— or so the thinking went.

Why else this insanity of our tiny nation, already bogged down in a huge war in China, simultaneously attacking half the rest of the world? With failure assured, they made certain to choose a man outside their own faction, General Yamashita, to lead the attack on Malaya. As for the attack on Pearl Harbor, any naval man would have done— as they were all adversaries to the army— but that being the case, why not choose the navy's most dynamic leader, Admiral Yamamoto, for the inevitable humiliation? So Yamashita was sent on his suicide mission to Malaya, while Yamamoto was put in charge of the impending disaster in Hawaii. How else could these two outrageous missions be viewed? On the one hand, 70,000 of our troops would be sent on bicycles through the jungle to attack a combined British force of 140,000 in Malaya and on the impregnable island fortress of Singapore; on the other hand, a carrier force would be sent 7,500 kilometers across the Pacific to attack a superior American fleet in the comfort of its own home port. I think it is safe to say that in the annals of military history there are few cases of inferior forces waging successful campaigns by bicycle— maybe chariot, or horse, or tank, but not bicycle! And what chance would a large carrier force have, in this day and age, of traveling 7,500 kilometers across the Pacific without being detected? And once detected, what chance would that carrier force have of surviving a combined attack by the American fleet and its land-based air forces?

The only miscalculation the general command made was in the level of incompetence of the opposing commanders for the British and Americans. In this, I must admit, the enemy have outdone themselves, performing well below any reasonable expectations. And so now we have a situation where— due to the failure of our success— Yamashita and Yamamoto have become national heroes, despite the best intentions of the general command, and instead of being able to sue for peace in China we are forced to defend an absurdly large area of territory stretching from the North Pole to the equator on one axis and from the mid Pacific to Thailand on the other.

The one place where the strategy of the general command has met with at least partial success— due to its failure to date— is the Philippines. Here again an inferior force of 130,000 men has been put up against a larger force of 150,000 men commanded by the Americans' supposedly most brilliant general, MacArthur. But MacArthur, too, has somehow managed to squander his advantage and is now cornered, and I'm afraid the ultimate success— in other words, failure— of our campaign there is not in question.

As I've said before, my dear Suzu, the army is full of jealousies and rivalries. Being a member of General Yamashita's faction, I was sent here with him; and now I am sure it will not be too long before we are made to pay for our victory. I have even heard rumors that next we will be sent to attack India. Can you imagine that? Is the earth's most populous nation not enough? Must we attack the second most populous as well?

You must forgive my rambling on, my dear, but as I've said before, you are the only one in whom I can confide.... And the only one who can still inspire me to believe there is some hope for the human race. I often recall with great fondness our night together in Taiyuan, the electricity of our emotions coursing through our linked hands, your purity preserved for yet another day. It is only these memories that keep me going now.

I'm afraid I didn't follow much of what was written in this letter from the Colonel. I have never much been one for military strategies. I am certain, however, that there will be readers who are interested in such insights, and so I have included the full body of the letter here as part of the historical record.

In those early months after Pearl Harbor there was a change in the country. The war in China had been dragging on for four years and would continue to drag on for several more, but somehow, with all those victories in the Pacific and a map that now showed Japan controlling half the world, the somber mood that had been hanging over the nation seemed to lift— at least for a while. As for our own fortunes at Sugutatsu, business continued to boom. There were numerous military officers with large spending accounts and businessmen who were making good money off the war. Many of these men liked to relax in the evening with the company of geisha, and our house continued to get more than our fair share of the market for such services.

In March of that year, 1942, Hoshi was promoted from *maiko* to full-fledged geisha. We were both now eighteen and had both been apprenticed for five years. I should have been promoted as well, but because of my peculiar status as the Maiden Maiko, I was passed over. The Madame had been ready to go ahead with the promotion, and had even called me in to make plans for it, but at the last minute I was told those plans had been canceled. The Minister had apparently gotten wind of the promotion and intervened.

"The Minister feels it is critical for the war effort that your status remain unchanged," the Madame said, giving me the news.

"Couldn't I be the 'Maiden Geisha?'" I asked.

"He doesn't feel that would have the same impact as 'Maiden Maiko.'"

I was of course disappointed I was not promoted, but there was nothing to be done about it, and not long after this conversation I was summoned to Kasumigaseki together with the Madame and the Master to see the Minister himself.

"Your trip to China helped to raise morale immeasurably," the Minister said, "while also building cultural bridges between Japan and China."

"It is most kind of you to say so," the Madame replied, bowing low.

Also present was Captain Mushitani, perspiring heavily as usual.

"I hear the performances with the Beijing Opera were particularly well received," he said enthusiastically.

"We would like you to undertake another tour," the Minister continued, "this one to the western region of the country."

"We would be most honored," the Master said, stepping forward.

"Ah, yes, the Master of Sugutatsu," the Minister exclaimed, clapping the Master on the shoulder. "And a baron nonetheless... an inspired choice, if I do say so myself... a choice we have not made enough of..."

I could see the Captain melt even further in size at the sound of these words.

"Mushitani!"

"Yes, sir!"

"Why is it that the Master did not go on the tour of China?"

"National security, sir."

"National security? What idiot made that determination?"

"It was in the regulations, sir."

"What idiot drew up the regulations?"

"I did, sir."

"Idiot!"

"Yes, sir."

"Idiot!"

The Minister continued to dress down the Captain for

several more minutes, but the upshot of our meeting was that both the Master and the Madame would be making this next trip. The proposed itinerary would start in Kyoto and then move on to Hiroshima. From Hiroshima we would board a ferry, crossing the Inland Sea to Matsuyama in Shikoku, before crossing one more time to Beppu and Oita in Kyushu. Oita would be our final stop, and then we would make our way back to Tokyo. At the mention of Oita, I let out an involuntary gasp of excitement, as we would be very near my hometown of Kujirahe, which I hadn't seen since leaving when I was nine. Despite the tongue lashing he had taken, the Captain would, unfortunately, be leading our tour this time around, and Unmu Sensei would once again accompany us. The Sensei's spiritual guidance would be more necessary than ever, the Minister emphasized, especially during the Maiden Maiko's visits to the Fushimi Inari Shrine in Kyoto and the Usa Jingu Shrine in Usa, not far from Beppu. The Madame asked if Yokozuna Taibo would again be traveling with us as well, but the Minister said he would not. He had recovered from his wound and returned to competition the previous autumn, but "other commitments" would prevent the grand champion from joining us this time. Mangetsu, Koyo, and Hoshi would also once more be traveling with us, and I was of course greatly reassured by this. As we left our meeting, I could see the relief on the face of the Madame— she would not have to worry about leaving the Master on his own again for an extended period. And the Sensei— despite the mixed feelings the Madame might have about him— would also be with us. As for the Master, I could see his chest swelling with pride as we exited the Ministry's building. This time not only would he be traveling with the Maiden Maiko as she made her next grand tour, he would be doing so as the Master of the House of Sugutatsu and chief associate of Unmu Sensei, a Grand Master of All Things Japanese.

Although the Madame had to be relieved the Master would be going with us, it was also apparent she wasn't particularly happy about making the trip itself. "They have their own agenda" is all she said to me on the way home, but I knew the fee the Ministry would be paying the house would be no where near what we could make on our own over the same period of time. The Madame had told us this following the China trip. But perhaps more importantly, I think the Madame had growing doubts by this point about Sugutatsu continuing to participate in such projects. It wasn't that she had become opposed to the objectives of this war, or thought it a bad war, or a war that our nation shouldn't fight. It was simply that she had come too close to war in China, and she wanted to put the death and destruction she knew came with war out of her mind and have nothing to do with it. And as I noted earlier, I think too that she could foresee the devastation this new war would bring to Japan itself, and perhaps she thought if we had less to do with the war, it would somehow go away and not touch us. And if we had more to do with the war, perhaps that would only invite it to come ever closer.

But the choice was not ours to make.

29

In the second week of April we were met at Tokyo Station by Captain Mushitani.

"You would think they could have found a more substantial man," Mangetsu whispered as the train left the station.

"All the substantial men are at the front," Koyo replied.

"I suppose so..."

"Nothing to be done about it..."

"I suppose not, but still..."

The Captain had arranged for the journalists who had covered my *mizuage*— Messrs. Wada, Tada, and Yada— to accompany us on our trip. The Captain and the journalists sat together in one compartment, while the Master and the Sensei sat in another, and my sisters and I, together with the Madame, occupied yet a third. This first leg of our journey, which would take us to Kyoto, was an all-day affair, taking nearly seven hours, but there was plenty to eat and drink and more than enough entertaining conversation. Koyo was the only one of us who had been to Kyoto before, and we all had questions for her. She was able to answer our many inquiries about the food in considerable detail, testimony to the strong impression the local cuisine must have left with her. She had less luck fielding our questions about the sights of the city. She had gone to several well-known temples, she said, but now the names seemed to run together and she wasn't certain whether she had actually been to a particular temple or just read about it in her guidebook. Being aware of the circumstances of her visit, it was easy to understand how she could have been unclear on this point.

It seems, you see, that she had made her earlier trip with Mr. Kawano, the patron I previously mentioned, the man with whom she'd been deeply in love. She'd been seventeen or eighteen at the time. She didn't bring up Mr. Kawano by name, but I knew she had gone with him because Hoshi had once told me about it. It must have been so romantic, to spend four or five days alone with the man she loved in such a beautiful city as Kyoto. I wondered if she had ever had thoughts of marrying Mr. Kawano. It was not unheard of, after all, for a patron to buy out a geisha's debt and take her home and marry her as his proper wife. She'd been so young when she'd met him. It wouldn't have been surprising at all if she had had such thoughts. But his company had gone bankrupt, and she'd had to stop seeing him, and she must have felt so cheated to have to give up the man she loved. And who knew what kind of a man fortune would choose to send her next? As for Mr. Fukunaga, she had indeed broken things off with him after we'd gotten back from China. A girl has her pride, after all. If the man had been subtle about his new relationship with O-Tama of Akasaka that would have been one thing, but to be trumpeting news of his conquest about town as he had, that was entirely another. Certainly Koyo could not put up with that. Recently she'd been seeing a Mr. Yazawa. He was the chairman of a utility company, and I think she was actually quite fond of him. But I didn't think she would ever again give her heart to anyone like she had to Mr. Kawano.

As we rolled down the Tokaido, skirting the eastern shoreline, my musings about Koyo and her lost love turned my thoughts to my own Lieutenant and I was suddenly overcome with emotion. I had to turn away from the others and dab at my tears with the sleeve of my kimono, and then I abruptly got up and left our compartment and walked to the end of the car and stood there by an open window. By then it had already been two years since I'd last seen him in Wuhan, and more than a year and a half since that horrible day I'd realized he must be dead, but he never left me, and from time to time I would still have moments like this.

"Are you all right?"

It was Hoshi. She had followed me down to the end of the car.

"Yes… I just needed to get up for a second."

"You're sure?"

"Yes, I'll be fine."

"You're sure?"

"Yes..."

Hoshi hesitated, and then she nodded and went back towards our compartment. Oh, I so wished I could have talked to her about my Lieutenant, I so wished I could have. But of course I couldn't, and I stood there for several more minutes, listening to the click-clack of the train running over the track, lost in my gloomy thoughts.

We arrived in Kyoto late that afternoon and checked into our inn, and then early the next morning we went to one of the more famous temples in the city, Kinkakuji. Captain Mushitani had arranged the visit, as he wished to have the journalists take some photos and write up our impressions of the temple. I must say I rather enjoyed the excursion. The rustic beauty of Kinkakuji, its three-storied frame reflected in the waters of its pond, was quite moving. Some years later, after the war, it was burned down by a deranged monk and then rebuilt completely in new gold leaf. But at the time we saw it, its gold covering had been faded by many centuries of weather and it was coarser and perhaps less pretentious, and I think I liked it better that way. It was just a short outing, but it relaxed me and helped me to recover from my melancholy of the day before.

That afternoon the Captain, Unmu Sensei, the Master and I went to the Fushimi Inari Shrine together with the journalists. The Madame and the other girls didn't go. The Maiden Maiko would be offering prayers to the gods of the mountain, the Captain explained, and it would not be necessary for the other women to attend. No one said anything further to me about this, but plainly going forward there would be an effort to raise the Maiden Maiko ever higher on her own pedestal. We were met at the magnificent main gate of the shrine by an entourage of priests and acolytes, and also by a number of local pressmen. The acolytes were young girls about the same age as I, all dressed in red *hakama*— long, pleated skirts— and white *haori*, kimono jackets. The girls were *miko*, shrine maidens, and I had no doubt they had all been especially chosen for this assignment. Meanwhile, I was dressed in the same simple white robe I wore while in training with Ummu Sensei. As part of the day's ceremonies, I would be taking a considerable hike up the mountain, making the light cotton robe the appropriate attire.

Once assembled at the main gate, our procession was led into the grounds of the shrine by the high priest and the Sensei. I followed immediately behind, with the Master, the other priests and the acolytes trailing after. We proceeded to the main hall, and then the high priest, the Master, the Sensei and I alone went on to the inner sanctum, where certain of the gods and their artifacts were housed. While I bowed my head low, the high priest and the Sensei shouted out their incantations to the spirits of the dead, exhorting them to go in peace to the next world, and when they were done with their ceremonies we returned to the courtyard of the main hall. There, I was sat down in a place of honor and the shrine maidens then performed a ritual dance, beseeching the gods of the mountain to come down and dance with us in support of our holy war. And when they were done with their dance, the Sensei stood and stripped down to his loin cloth, and then he and I set off up the mountain, passing through the hundreds of *torii* gates that lined the route to the top. Most people would take two hours to traverse the course, but the Sensei kept up a very rapid pace and we did it in half the time. At the summit I was somewhat winded, but not terribly so, and for the first time ever it seemed that perhaps a physical challenge of this sort had taken more out of the Sensei than it had out of me. He took a few moments to gather himself, and then he clutched me by the arm and walked me over to the edge of a nearby cliff and had me kneel down, and there he shouted out more entreaties to the gods. I must admit I could not understand all that he said— some of the phrases being of more ancient origin— but I did catch certain words such as "this girl" and "pure" and "cleanse" and "the impurities of our nation," and what Koyo had once said to me about maidens being sacrificed now came tumbling back into my mind, and I grew fearful that I was about to be tossed over the side. But then the Sensei stopped his supplications and took me by the arm and raised me up and said:

"Go down from this mountain and spread the spirit of the gods, for only you are the pure and perfect Maiden Maiko."

And with that, we started our trek back down. By then the sun had fallen low towards the horizon, its rays piercing the forest here and there in divinely beautiful patterns, and I felt a sudden and appreciable peace, brought on no doubt by the setting but more so by the relief that my young life would continue for at least some time longer.

Once back at the main hall, in an apparent effort to follow the Minister's directive to "make more of the baron's status," the Captain handed the Master an ancient scroll and motioned for him to step forward. Then the press gathered around. At first the Master looked lost, unsure what to do, but then he hesitantly began to read, slowly picking up the pace and the intensity of his words as he went along until a truly noticeable change came over him. His eyes grew large and cloudy and his voice took on an other worldly tone, and I quite unexpectedly found myself being taken back to the time when my father lost his mind after my mother died. It was only a brief inkling, a fleeting sense, but it was an image

I thereafter had difficulty getting out of my mind whenever I saw the Master speak at one of these events.

30

The following day we made two public relations appearances related to the selling of war bonds, and then that night we had the first of two joint engagements with Kyoto geisha. Hoshi seemed to be intimidated by the thought of entertaining on the "home grounds of the geisha," as she put it, but Mangetsu and Koyo were both quick to dismiss such talk. There was assuredly no reason, they said, for the geisha from the proud House of Sugutatsu to lower their heads in awe upon arrival in the ancient former capital.

Three rickshaws came to pick us up at our inn and take us the short distance to Gion. I was riding with Mangetsu, while Hoshi rode with Koyo, and the Madame with the Master. Captain Mushitani had already gone on ahead on his own, walking over to the upscale restaurant where the evening's entertainment would be held.

"It's too bad we don't have Yokozuna Taibo with us on this trip," Mangetsu said out of the blue.

"Yes, it is, isn't it... I'm sure Hoshi is even more disappointed."

Hoshi didn't talk much about her relationship with the grand champion, but I knew she hadn't been seeing him as often as she used to. With a patron such as the Yokozuna, a girl never knew how these things might play out. You might see him frequently for a time and then not much for a while, and then the whole thing might just end one day. The

Minister had said the Yokozuna wouldn't be able to travel with us because of "other commitments," but I was also aware that it hadn't been the best of times for him. He had had his unbeaten streak broken after coming back from China, and then just this last tournament he had had to drop out due to injury. There was even some speculation in the newspapers that he might soon have to retire. His income must be down, I was told, and it would drop even further when his career was done. I wondered if this had affected the frequency of his assignations with Hoshi. There was no doubt about his love for Hoshi, but in the world of the geisha love is not free.

"It's such a beautiful night," Mangetsu said, making a sweeping motion with her hand at the scenery gliding past us.

"Indeed..."

"Such a beautiful night..."

And indeed it was— a mere hint of crispness in the air now that the sun had gone down, the quaint restaurants and drinking establishments with their tasteful facades and glowing lanterns, the narrow canal running alongside, the path crowded with revelers out for the night. The rickshaw puller was a talkative type with a heavy Kyoto accent, and I could only catch every third or fourth word. He was excited to learn we were from Asakusa. He'd heard there was an amusement park there, and he wanted to visit it. There was a small crowd gathered in front of the restaurant when we arrived. The word must have gotten around that geisha from the House of Sugutatsu, including the Maiden Maiko, were to be there that evening.

"That must be her," an old woman in the crowd said, pointing at me.

"Yes, that's her," another old woman standing next to her agreed.

It would have been easy to identify me as the *maiko*, as I would have been the only one wearing the fancier attire of an apprentice.

"I hear His Highness the Emperor chose her himself from thousands of young girls."

"Is that so?"

"Yes, it's thanks to her that our armies have won so many victories against overwhelming odds."

This was the first time I had heard such talk and it was quite frightening, to say the least. There had been many articles in the press, of course, about the "sacrifice" I was making "for the good of the nation," but there had certainly been no references to His Highness, or to victories won on the field of battle due to my efforts. It was unnerving indeed to see how the misinformation planted in the press in good faith could be so twisted by the imaginations of our citizens.

"Welcome, welcome," a fawning little bald man said, coming out of the crowd.

He looked very much like the fawning little bald man who had greeted us on the night of my debut as a *maiko*, and it brought back flashes of memories from that eventful occasion. He motioned for us to follow him, and we did, in through the gate and along a stone path that took us over a series of small bridges through a lovely water-laced garden. I'm sure we made an impressive sight, even for the staff of an establishment so used to seeing geisha. Proceeding down a series of corridors we eventually came to the large room where the evening's festivities were being hosted. There the Master and the Madame stepped to the side, and the fawning little man proceeded to announce each one of us girls, starting with Koyo. As my turn came and I entered the room, I could see that it was a large crowd of businessmen and army officers, and that a good number of geisha had already been seated.

"She must be the Maiden Maiko," I heard one of the men say as I swished by.

"How can you be certain?" the man next to him asked.

"What do you mean?"

"I hear there are several 'shadow Maiden Maiko'— to lessen the chance of assassination by enemy agents."

I almost stopped dead in my tracks— perhaps an unfortunate choice of words— but it was an extreme shock, as I'm sure you can imagine. Had these rumors of my influence on the outcome of battles spread so far that they had even reached the ears of the enemy? And were these rumors so credible that even the enemy would believe them? I recalled my time in captivity and how that despicable woman Bai had doubted I was a maiden and accused me of pretending to be a god.

"Just there would be fine," I heard a voice from across the room say.

I looked up to see one of the Kyoto geisha pointing to the cushion in front of me. Nodding politely, I took my seat, and then I made my greetings to the gentleman to my right.

"It's a pleasure indeed," he said, "to make the acquaintance of such a devoted patriot."

He was middle-aged, rather handsome and sophisticated looking. I gave him a modestly coquettish smile, but said nothing. What was there to say? There is no way to respond to such a comment without appearing vain or simpleminded.

"The chairman has taken the words from my mouth," the gentleman to my left now said. I turned to him, and he went on, "yes, a pleasure indeed to meet someone who has done so much for our country."

He was an army officer— also handsome, although in a more rugged way— and appeared to be about the same age as the first gentleman.

"Let me offer you some *sake*," the officer said.

"No, no, it is I who should be serving you," I demurred.

"Not at all," the officer insisted.

He turned more fully towards me to pour the *sake*, and it was then I saw that the other side of his face was severely scarred and that he was missing part of his left arm. I'm afraid I momentarily revealed my— I would not say revulsion but rather surprise— and the officer paused for an instant, looking ill-at-ease, before continuing with his pouring. I drank up my *sake*, and then poured some for the officer in return, and then the gentleman who had been referred to as "the chairman" spoke up again, perhaps trying to defuse the awkward moment.

"I would not protest if you were to offer me some *sake* too," he said.

"Oh, I'm so sorry," I said, turning in my seat once more and gently picking up the *sake* jar.

"Is this your first time to Kyoto?" he asked, lifting his cup.

"Yes, yes, it is."

"Then you will not have seen our Kyoto geisha perform before."

"No," I said, looking around the room, "I have not previously been so fortunate."

"It should be quite interesting— the Kyoto style versus the Tokyo style."

"Yes, I'm certain it will be," I agreed, lightly fanning myself.

Looking around one more time, my sight landed on a young geisha, perhaps about the same age as myself, a bit of a roly-poly girl with dull-looking eyes. She was staring right back at me and seemed to be very upset about something. I then realized she was jealous. She was in love with the chairman, and she was jealous that he was so obviously enchanted by me. How unprofessional, I thought to myself—before recalling the wayward movement of my own heart the night I had met the Lieutenant. Had anyone noticed my feelings in a similar way?

"Let's start the entertainment," one of the senior officers shouted out.

"Yes, on with the entertainment!" another officer loudly agreed.

One of the Kyoto geisha stepped forward and bowed very low in a comic manner. "Of course, of course, honored gentlemen, let us proceed with tonight's humble offerings. First, from Kyoto, the geisha Momoe performing 'Love Suicide at Arashiyama.'"

"Ah, the great Momoe," the chairman whispered, leaning in close to me. "You will enjoy this."

I nodded politely, raising my fan and giving it a few quick flicks of the wrist.

The "great Momoe" then stood and elegantly made her way to the front of the room and the samisen player, another geisha, then started to play and the singer, yet another geisha, began to vocalize the lyrics. It was quite common in Tokyo to begin an evening's lineup with a love suicide number, and it was interesting to see that they did the same in Kyoto— at least on this occasion. The chairman was right— Momoe's performance was indeed impressive, her exquisite movements expressing in mesmerizing fashion the deep emotions of the heroine, the daughter of a bank manager. In the story, the young woman falls in love with a much older, failed novelist. Her parents forbid their marriage, and her lover suggests they go to Arashiyama and die together by jumping off the bridge there. However, the leap is only three meters and the depth of the water only one meter, and their suicide attempt is a failure. The woman laments the failed attempt, vowing to find a smarter lover. The lyrics went as follows:

> *Such passion,*
> *Such devotion,*
> *Such love.*
> *Such naiveté,*
> *Such pain,*
> *Such humiliation.*
> *You may think my existence*
> *merely an overdraft on your account,*
> *But how can one not know the leap*
> *from Togetsu Bridge is only three meters*
> *while that of Kiyomizu is twelve?*

Momoe's number was followed by Mangetsu's performance of "Love Suicide at Shinbashi." Koyo and Hoshi sang, while I played the samisen in accompaniment. When we were done, the scarred officer to my left leaned in and whispered to me.

"Very impressive," he said.

And then, looking almost disappointed, the chairman leaned in from the other side and concurred. "Yes," he said, "very impressive indeed."

The night was still young, but the tone had been set. The opening number for the Kyoto side had been technically accomplished, but the choice of material had been poor. It was curious indeed that our Kyoto sisters had selected such an uninspiring story. To use the daughter of a bank manager as the heroine and to then have the love suicide itself fail— in Tokyo we could never imagine employing such a narrative. Granted, one might give points for originality, but the lack of drama— not to mention lack of poetry— was simply devastating. As the evening progressed, the Kyoto side continued to produce one insipid story after another. I began to wonder if there were simply no good stories in Kyoto, or if perhaps it was a cultural difference— a case of the bland and banal being valued over the poignant and captivating. After all, Kyoto was an older culture than Tokyo, and it was possible that over the centuries their renowned penchant for the understated and subtle had slid into a preference for the hackneyed and clichéd.

"I'm stunned," the chairman said to me at the end of the evening. "I just had no idea..."

"No idea?"

"I just had no idea how consummately skilled the Tokyo geisha were."

I cast my eyes down so as not to appear arrogant in victory, but we both knew the contest had not even been close.

"It's true," the scarred officer said, "I too am stunned. I'm afraid we may be in the midst of a cultural crisis of faith here in Kyoto."

It must have been the alcohol— by this point I had consumed quite a bit— but I found myself suddenly talking to the chairman about the roly-poly geisha I had observed earlier in the evening.

"It seems you have a secret admirer," I said.

"Ah, you mean the roly-poly one," he said, motioning with his head towards the other side of the room.

"Yes..."

I looked over at the young lady in question, and found her again glaring back at me.

"Yes, she's been chasing me for quite some time," the chairman continued, taking two cigars out of his pocket and offering one to the scarred officer. "Would you like one?"

"No, thank you," the scarred officer said, waving his good hand.

"You know," the chairman said, lighting up his cigar, "this is just the type of girl who will write a book later and put all of us in it. And guess who will have a very flattering self-portrait?"

"You're probably right," the scarred officer said, shaking his head.[*]

The ride back to our inn in the rickshaw was very pleasant. It was a clear night and looking up at the sky, I could see millions of stars. I closed my eyes and took a deep breath, and the rush of the cool air on my face, still hot from the alcohol, felt invigorating and refreshing. The next day we would perform one more time in Kyoto, and then the day after that we would take the train to Hiroshima. There was still much to look forward to on this trip.

31

We got into Hiroshima in the early evening and checked into our hotel, which was downtown near the Hall for Industrial Promotion. Of course at the time we had no idea that this building— a large three-storied structure with a

---

[*] The author is likely referring here to Tashiro Yukiko, who did indeed write a highly informative and entertaining book about her life entitled *On the Wrong Side of the Canal: Tales of a Gion Geisha* (Kyoto: Nisedo Press, 1997). Photos in the book show a stylish and slim Tashiro, and other sources confirm she was actually quite a beauty as well as being very popular with the other geisha in the district. Unfortunately, it appears the author's jealousy has gotten the better of her in this account of Ms. Tashiro.

dome on the top— would become the symbol of the atomic blast that would devastate the city some three and a half years later. Mr. Yada said he knew an excellent seafood place, and after we had had a chance to freshen up a bit, we met in the lobby and headed out for dinner with him and Messrs. Wada and Tada. When we had a night off during the trip, we ladies often dined with the three journalists, who, as it turns out, were very good dinner company. The Captain rarely chose to eat with us unless it was an official event on our itinerary, and that was just fine with us. As for the Master and the Sensei, they often met on these off nights with priests and other persons affiliated with the local shrines or temples of the city we were visiting. The Master had continued to be drawn ever closer to the Sensei, and on this trip that closeness was more evident than ever. I never saw them exchange many words— as I've said, the Sensei was a man of few words— but they always sat together in the trains or cars or ferries we used during our tour, and they always sat together for meals, and they always did their meditation together in the morning— even when I, the Maiden Maiko herself, might occasionally miss such a session. As I've earlier noted, this had to be a difficult situation for the Madame, but she never once revealed any jealousy— even on this trip, where we were all in close quarters for long periods of time. She must have by then, I felt, reached an accommodation in her own heart.

That evening we went by streetcar to our dinner, on the way crossing over two of the five rivers of the delta that make up the city. The streets were crowded with housewives and businessmen and students, and I saw more than a few men in uniform as well. The restaurant was a small place, already full, but Mr. Yada had had the hotel call ahead and hold a table for us.

"The best seafood in western Japan," he said, self-satisfied, as we sat down. "You've got to try the octopus— absolutely superb."

The octopus was in fact superb, and we had several other very good seafood dishes as well— assorted sashimi and grilled squid and prawns and fried flatfish— and some vegetable dishes to go along with everything. The *sake* was also excellent. We finished the first two jars, and then we started in on a third and a fourth, and they all went down very smoothly. I had criticized Hoshi for drinking too much when we were younger, but I'm afraid by this time in my life I was also drinking quite a bit. Mangetsu of course also liked her drink, and that evening even Koyo and the Madame drank more than they usually did. I don't know what it was— the *sake* itself, or the atmosphere, or maybe just the added stress we were feeling then from the pressures of the trip— but all of us, including all the journalists, did indulge quite a bit that night. When we were all pretty much "done up," an old man from the table next to us— who looked to be in a similar state— offered some of his own *sake* to Mangetsu, who just happened to be the one sitting closest to him. Mangetsu accepted the offer, and from there we proceeded to exchange several more cups of *sake* with the old man and his companion. He was quite a loquacious character, telling us tales of the many businesses he had started and the women he had conquered. We didn't believe much of what he told us, but I do have to admit he was entertaining, and it left us with a distinctive memory of our one night in Hiroshima.

The following day at noon there was a ceremony on the steps of city hall in which, following several speeches promoting patriotic sentiment and the sale of war bonds, I was awarded the keys to the city by the mayor himself. It was embarrassing indeed to continue to be singled out in such fashion in front of my sisters, but there was nothing to be done about it. My citation in part read: "For dedication to our country, and extreme discipline above and beyond the call of duty, you are hereby..."

Following the ceremony, we headed for the port, and there we boarded a ferry for Matsuyama. It was a magnificent afternoon, the sun shining brightly as it gradually dipped towards the horizon over the course of our journey. The sea was idyllic, dotted with little islands, and between the islands, and in their coves and bays, numerous fishing boats and trawlers and other smaller boats crisscrossed about. At one point, in the warmth of the spring day, I was just about to nod off when a squadron of Zero fighters flew over, one of them tipping his wings to the ferry— a sharp reminder that elsewhere there still was a war in progress.

In Matsuyama we stayed at an inn downtown, just across from the central park. It was a quiet evening, as we ate right there at the inn and turned in early. The afternoon of the next day we got on a streetcar and headed off to Dogo Spa, which was about twenty minutes away, nestled at the foot of a hill. Mr. Tada said the spa was one of the oldest in Japan, not to be missed, and so we went and had a relaxing bath, and then that night we entertained at a spot not far from our inn. It was probably because of the extended travel and the variety of locations at which we had had to entertain over such a short period of time, but in any case it proved to be a dull evening, with none of our performances "reaching the heights," if you will.

The following day there was a ceremony at Matsuyama Castle at which I was presented a seventeenth-century samurai sword and proclaimed the "Maiden Defender of the Nation." Apparently Captain Mushitani was originally from Matsuyama, and that is why Matsuyama had been put on the itinerary, even though it wouldn't necessarily be the first city one would think of for such a tour. The Captain was good friends with the mayor, and it seemed it was the mayor who had come up with the idea of the sword and the "Maiden Defender" tag. The Captain was thrilled with the whole idea, and even arranged for photos afterwards of me wearing a full complement of armor, my sword in hand. It was one of these photos which later appeared on the cover of a number of magazines and was subsequently widely distributed throughout the country. It became what I think is known as an "iconic photo" of the period.

After the ceremony we were taken from the castle to the port and put on an Imperial Navy patrol boat for the trip to Beppu. It seems there was no regular ferry service between Matsuyama and Beppu, and the Captain had had to use his connections to arrange for the transportation. This evidently had not been difficult, given the fact that the Maiden Maiko— or as I was also now known, the "Maiden Defender"— would be one of the passengers. I must say it was very awkward when the sailors on board saluted me getting on and getting off. We stayed that evening at one of the inns well known for its hot spring, and then the following morning I was put in a car with the Master and Ummu Sensei and Captain Mushitani, and we were driven to the Usa Jingu Shrine. Once more neither the Madame nor my sisters were allowed to accompany me. The ceremonies at the shrine were similar to those that had been conducted at Fushimi in Kyoto— a procession of priests and acolytes into the shrine, incantations to the gods shouted out by Ummu Sensei and the high priest in the inner sanctum, and a ritual dance performed by the shrine maidens beseeching the gods to come and dance with us in support of our holy war. This time, however, there was no hike to the top of the mountain.

Instead, after the completion of the dance, I was knelt down in the middle of the courtyard and doused with buckets of water by the shrine maidens while Ummu again shouted out entreaties to the gods in the ancient tongue of our nation. And once more, while not able to understand much, I was able to catch certain words here and there such as "this girl" and "pure" and "cleanse" and "the impurities of our nation."

When the ceremonies were finished, I quickly changed into a dry kimono, and then we made our way back to Beppu. Once back at our inn, the Madame insisted on me warming myself in the hot spring, and then our entire group boarded a private bus for the trip to Oita. I had heard from Mangetsu that Oita had been put on the itinerary for the same reason as Matsuyama— another special request from the Captain.

The particular reason Oita was on the itinerary made no difference to me, but the fact that we were in Oita was of course personally significant. As I earlier noted, I had not been back to my home area of Kyushu since I had left after my mother's death, some nine years before. My emotions were mixed, to say the least. I was tempted to ask the Madame for permission to make the short trip to Kujirahe. If I left early the next morning, I would be able to take the train there and get back again to Oita by mid afternoon, with still plenty of time before our engagement that night. On the other hand, there was part of me that had no desire to make the trip. Kujirahe was another lifetime ago, and although I had many wonderful memories of those days with my parents and siblings, I had also spent many years building a wall against the trauma of having been wrenched away from that life.

As it was, even though in the end I decided not to go, I still came face to face with my past. It happened in this way. Early on the morning of our second day in Oita, I was awakened by a knock on my door. It was a bellboy, telling me I had a visitor downstairs in the lobby. I asked him who it was— as by this time, due to my fairly considerable fame, it was not unusual for crackpots to try to make contact with me— but he said the young woman had not given him a name, only claiming to be a "family member." I would have asked for more verification if we had been in any other city, but since we were so close to Kujirahe, I decided I had better go down and see who it was. When I met the young lady, I could not at first recognize her, but once she said her name I could immediately see the resemblance. It was Hanako, my sister, the number four sibling, just a year older than Tomo and three years older than I. She was living in Oita then, and had heard about my visit and decided to try to see me. My eyes filled with tears as soon as I knew it was Hanako, and a flood of emotions quickly overwhelmed me, indeed as though a hole had been punched in the wall I had built.

"It's difficult to believe," she said, "that our little Panko has become such a beautiful and well-known geisha," and tears filled her eyes as well.

I pointed out that I was still a *maiko*, but the distinction didn't seem to be of much importance to her.

"Such a beautiful and well-known geisha," she said again.

We talked for more than an hour there in the lobby. She asked after Tomo, and I told her about his budding career as a comedian and his current status as a drafted soldier in the Philippines. And then I asked her about our other siblings, and she gave me an update on each of them. She began by reporting the death of our eldest brother, saying that he had enlisted in the army and had then died in the early fighting in China, leaving a wife and a son[†] behind. Our second brother, who had yet to marry, had been drafted and was in

---

[†] It was this son, Funabashi Jinbei, who would take care of the author in her old age and later pass on her notebooks to me.

Manchuria. As for our elder sister, she was living with her husband's family in Fukuoka and had two children, a boy and a girl.

"So I'm an aunt," I said.

"Yes, you're an aunt. Isn't it nice to find that out?"

"Yes, yes it is."

As for herself, she said, she was still single. She hoped she would be able to make a good match, but with so many men gone to the war, it would not be easy.

"No, I imagine not," I said.

"I wish we had been born in another time."

"Yes, but that was not our fate..."

"No, I suppose not... Nothing to be done about it..."

I thought I might be able to see Hanako again the following day, but at the last minute I got a message that she would not be able to come, and then early on the day after that we began our trip back to Tokyo. It had been good to see her, however briefly, and on the train I thought about how nice it would be to get all of us— our brother in Manchuria and Tomo in the Philippines and our sister in Fukuoka and Hanako in Oita— together again in Kujirahe.

But it would be many years before I would be able to return to Kujirahe, and in those intervening years much would happen that would change everything for all of us.

32

In April of that same year, 1942, there had been reports in the newspapers of our troops liberating Burma from British rule, and the heroic exploits of my own Colonel were given considerable play. The press reports were unstinting in their praise, saying his bravery had been unmatched in leading his unit on a forced three-day march over terrible terrain in order to cut off the enemy's retreat. At the point of attack, it was said, he had been at the forefront of his troops, pistol in hand. The Colonel gave a much more modest version of these events in a letter I received in late June. Below I quote that letter in its entirety:

June 4, 1942

My dear Suzu,

It's early morning in Rangoon, and it's raining. Down here in the coastal region it's been raining for several weeks already and I'm told it will continue to rain until the end of October. By comparison, our "rainy season" back home in Japan is a passing afternoon shower. Usually I'm in Mandalay, up in the central part of the country, but I had to come to Rangoon for some meetings and I'll be here for a week. There will be no campaigning during the monsoon, and now that we've driven the British and Chinese from Burma, I doubt we'll see any signs of them when the weather gets drier either.

As I've requested in the past, I would ask one more time that you get out a map and locate where I am now. As I've said before, it is important to me that you know that. First find Tokyo and then take your finger and move southwest until you hit Taiwan, and then cross over to Hong Kong, and from there go almost due West across southern China and the northern reaches of Indochina until you come to Burma, and almost right in the center of Burma you'll find Mandalay, and then from there go south until you hit the coast and Rangoon.

This campaign has been presented as our effort to shut off the so-called "Burma Road" and end the shipment of supplies to the Chinese by their Western allies, but our Western friends are flattering themselves to think that what they've been sending has somehow been propping up Chiang Kai-shek. Any supplies that have come in have most certainly been sold off for the personal gain of the generalissimo and his cronies, and have assuredly had no effect on the military situation. In actuality— as in all of our other military actions since December of last year— the objective of our campaign was simply to continue to overextend ourselves and bring about a few well-chosen defeats. As I noted in an earlier letter, our dimwit general command feel that a few such defeats will give us the proper pretext to negotiate a settlement in China.

Once again, however, by reason of our success, we have failed. And once again the primary cause of that success— that failure— was the ineptitude of the enemy commanders. Our unit was shipped out from Singapore to Rangoon in mid March, and then in early April we started up the Irrawaddy River Valley against the British forces. The British commander was named "Slim." I thought it a very odd name and double checked it to see if I had gotten it wrong, but no, that was actually his name. It didn't seem a name that would inspire confidence, especially among his men when discussing their prospects for success. I wondered if his second in command was named "None." (That's a joke, my dear.) I think it is likely that the British never have been much of a military race, and have built their empire primarily by pitting one tea merchant against another. You may have read about my unit's exploits in the newspapers and magazines back home. I am told that I am now known as the "Viper of Burma" or some other such nonsense. It's amazing the claptrap the press can come up with. In point of fact, our actions were nothing more than what might be expected of any Imperial Army unit— or for that matter any well-led and motivated unit in any army. But that's the precise problem for the British forces here— they are neither well-led nor motivated. In the main they are composed of Indian and Burmese troops, most of whom, not surprisingly, have no interest in saving the British Empire. In the particular series of engagements for which I received my ridiculous nom de guerre, we simply outflanked and trapped the enemy near the Yenangyaung oil fields. In a humiliating turn of events, the British had to call on Chinese units to rescue them. I see that the Chinese have now declared this to be some sort of a "great victory," despite the fact that both they and the British were shortly thereafter completely driven out of Burma.

You must remember, my dear Suzu, that all of history is a myth, a fable, simply the telling of a tale, and what is passed down always depends on who is doing the telling.

So here I am today in Rangoon, looking out from the wooden hut where they have given me a small office, listening to the rain pounding down on the tin roof, thinking about where this war is going. We have made every effort to be defeated, and yet have failed, and now our only hope, it seems, is India. I'm certain it won't be long before we attack there as well. Given that country's huge population and immense size, surely we will finally find our defeat— that is, victory— there. But will that be enough? We have won too many battles and stretched our empire too far. Peace will not come in one defeat or two, I'm afraid.

You must forgive me for running on about all of these military matters, but it's all I know. Recently I've tried my hand at calligraphy and water painting and have even tried writing a little poetry, but nothing seems to interest me for long. I've been drinking too much sake and watching too much rain fall. A colleague of mine suggested I take up Zen meditation. I tried it, but the rain was still there when I was done. I don't know that I will live to see the end of all this. I somehow feel that I am fated to pass on to the next world while here in Burma.

Forgive me for sharing such thoughts with you, but in the interest of full honesty between us I feel I must. Not an hour passes when I am not thinking of you, my dear Suzu— not even when in battle, not even when sleeping. You are still young, and have a long life in front of you, hopefully a life full of many good things. But at the very least, I want you to know this— you have brought meaning to this one man's existence.

Knowing the Colonel the way I did, however sporadically and briefly, his courage did not surprise me. I was concerned, however, by the consistent "black tone" of his missives. His mention of the possibility of his own death in particular was quite unsettling.

Throughout that year of 1942, and on into early 1943, the war was still in a relatively distant place for those of us on the home front. Out in the Pacific, there were battles at places with names like "Midway" and "Guadalcanal," but the maps we saw still showed Japan controlling half the world and there was a sense that the Americans would soon enough have to pack up and go home.

As for the Maiden Maiko, I continued to keep up a busy schedule throughout this period, entertaining several nights a week as customary, as well as making an increasing number of visits to shrines throughout the Tokyo area and elsewhere around the country. Captain Mushitani, Ummu Sensei, and the Master invariably accompanied me on these excursions, but never the Madame or any of my sisters. As you might well imagine, these sorties to the shrines were not pleasant, trapped as I was for endless hours with the irritating bond salesman, the taciturn monk, and the Master— who had continued to be drawn ever closer to his mentor. But there was nothing to be done about it.

I would just have to persevere as best I could.

33

As 1943 progressed, there were fewer outright victories for our brave men in the field and the war appeared to be settling into a stalemate. This perception was contradicted somewhat in the spring of 1944, when there were reports of our forces making new advances in India and China, but then in July Saipan fell, and there was a general feeling the war was coming much closer to home.

In August of that year we made a retreat to Nikko, just as we had continued to do every summer. The day of our departure was hot and sunny, very similar to the day we had first set out for Unmu's temple five years before. And just as on that earlier day, we must have created quite a sight, all the ladies with our parasols up, people stopping on the street to watch us as we paraded by. We arrived at the temple late in the morning, and that afternoon we hiked up the mountain, Ummu leading just as he always did. The Madame stayed back at the temple, but the Master came with us, as was his custom in more recent years. Ummu couldn't keep up the pace of his younger self, but he was still very impressive for a man of his age. I myself was still in peak shape, and all of the other girls were also much improved compared to our first visit. After the hike, as was our usual routine, we washed up in the pool of the nearby river, and then in the evening we sat down to a dinner of roots, twigs, various plants, and dried fish. After dinner that night there was a lecture by Ummu— a review of the creation of the nation— and then the next morning we worked on our martial arts as well as our singing and dancing and samisen skills. That afternoon we went on another hike, and then that night there was one more lecture, an outline of the merits of the Greater East Asia Co-Prosperity Sphere— as the half of the world which Japan oversaw was now known. The third day we followed the same routine, and then that night we gathered around again, expecting a final lecture from the Sensei, but instead there was a talk by the Master. I don't think the talk was prearranged by Ummu and the Master. In fact, my guess is that it wasn't. Rather, as we were sitting there, waiting to see what the Sensei had to say, it seemed the Master simply felt the need to talk and proceeded to do so. The Madame looked startled, but said nothing.

"My father, Sugutatsu Tatsuzo, was a very quiet man," the Master began.

And then he went on to talk about the history of the House of Sugutatsu, about its founder, the great Sugeimon, about the association of the house from its early days with the shogunate, and in brief about each of the ten intervening masters between himself and the founder. He emphasized how each of his predecessors had contributed something unique to the glory of the house— from one who had initiated kendo training, to another who had designed the house crest, to his father, who had introduced modern methods of scheduling.

"As for myself," the Master said in conclusion, "I feel I can point to only one accomplishment— the recruiting of the Maiden Maiko."

From the look in his eyes and the tone of his voice, it was clear the Master deeply believed every single word he had spoken— and yet we all knew the entire history of the House of Sugutatsu had been invented. It was one of the "small adjustments" that had been made as part of our holy war to liberate our fellow Asians from the West. We understood that such "small adjustments" were necessary "in pursuit of the greater truth," but as professional performers we also understood this was not real. Just as we as geisha created a fantasy world for our customers, so had the Ministry created the Maiden Maiko and the House of Sugutatsu for the necessary enlightenment of the public. But somewhere in the Master's mind the fantasy and the reality had become blurred. He thought he actually was the twelfth in an uninterrupted line of Masters of the House of Sugutatsu, and he thought he actually had recruited the Maiden Maiko. And once again, as it often had in recent years, the image of my deranged father involuntarily flashed through my mind.

A mere three weeks later the Master was dead, having taken his own life by jumping into the Sumida River from the Azuma Bridge.

"I wonder if the Master took his life in sympathy with those who died in Saipan?" Koyo mused one day not long after the funeral.

"It's certainly a possibility, isn't it?" Mangetsu said.

As earlier mentioned, Saipan had fallen in July, and for the first time there had been reports of numerous Japanese civilian casualties.

"The Master was such a patriot after all, and the news about Saipan had to be disheartening."

There was no way of knowing, of course. Had he in fact been insane? Had the very act of taking his own life been proof of his insanity? Perhaps, but as I look back on it now, many years later, I tend to think it may have actually been the opposite— a sudden recall to reality, a sudden realization that everything he so desperately believed in was in danger of collapse. Maybe the fall of Saipan had indeed been the trigger.

The Master's death was devastating for all of us, but most particularly of course for the Madame. I saw her cry only once, the day of the funeral, but the color was gone from her cheeks, and her eyes were sunken in her face, and she stayed in her own room most of the time, talking to no one. It didn't help that our house was shortly thereafter shut down— along with all other geisha houses and places of entertainment. The government evidently had decided eliminating amusement would help us to steel ourselves for more trying times. Instead of headlines proclaiming glorious victories, we were suddenly being admonished to "let no heart be faint." Over the next few months food rationing was increased, consumer goods of every description became scarcer, and gas and charcoal for heating began to disappear. Sunday holidays were even eliminated.

There had been a dramatic change in our circumstances, to say the least.

34

"Life is no fun anymore," Hoshi said. Indeed, life was not what it had once been. In Hoshi's case, I knew she was also talking about her relationship with Taibo. He had had to retire that spring, and his income must have decreased considerably. He was no longer calling on Hoshi.

"Were you in love with him?" I asked indiscreetly one day.

"You know that's against house rules," she replied evasively.

"Yes, I know," I said, "but a woman's heart doesn't always follow rules."

"No, I suppose not..."

I didn't press her any further. I knew she'd been seeing the sleazy doctor recently— the one who had bid unsuccessfully on her *mizuage*— and she couldn't have been happy about that. Our house was officially closed down, but certain entertainment continued to go on "behind the scenes." There was still plenty of money out there in the hands of some individuals— the doctor was one of those individuals, and as soon as Taibo had dropped out, he had started sniffing around.

"Business is business," is all Hoshi would say.

As for myself, there were still regular payments coming in from the Ministry. There was never any pressure on me to bring in extra income. I was the Maiden Maiko, and that was enough. Then one day in early December of that year the Madame called me into her room. She was still not looking well, although there did seem to be a renewed determination in her eyes that I had not seen since the death of the Master.

"I have something of great importance to talk to you about," she said.

These were the exact same words she had used when she had first talked to me about the Minister's *mizuage* proposal.

"As you know," she continued, "our nation is facing difficult times."

"Yes," I nodded.

The Madame shifted in her seat, looking down at her hands and then back up at me again. "Last week I had a visit from a Rear-Admiral Nishida of the Imperial Navy."

"A gentleman from the navy?"

"Yes, the navy... It seems they've formed a new combat unit down in Kyushu."

I couldn't imagine what that might have to do with me, but I had a bad feeling about where the conversation might be headed.

"Yes, some sort of a 'special attack force.'"

"I see..."

The Madame looked down at her hands again. "Suzu... I want you to know that you are not obligated to... do what it is that I am about to ask you to do."

What could it possibly be?

"The rear-admiral would like you to join this unit."

I sat up in my seat. "They want me to join the navy?"

"Well... yes, sort of..."

"Sort of?"

"Yes, it would be mostly a public relations job..."

"A public relations job?"

"Yes, not much different from what you're doing now."

"And what does this new unit do?"

"Do?"

"Yes, what is so special about it?"

The Madame looked down at her hands again, and then over to the other side of the room to the scroll that hung there, and then out the window at the garden.

"What they do," she finally said, "is fly planes into enemy ships."

I thought I had misheard the Madame. "You mean they fly planes over enemy ships and bomb them."

"No," the Madame said, using her two hands to demonstrate what she meant, "they fly planes into ships."

"And what is the purpose of that?"

"The purpose is to sink the ship."

I took a moment to digest this. I had to be missing something.

"Wouldn't it make more sense to drop bombs? I mean, if the pilot flies his plane into the ship, doesn't that mean the pilot will be dead?"

The Madame sighed deeply. "Yes, probably..."

"Probably?"

"I'm just telling you what they told me," the Madame said, her lips trembling.

I reached over and touched the sleeve of the Madame's kimono.

"I'm sorry... it's just that..."

"Yes... Oh, Suzu..."

The Madame broke down then, tears streaming down her cheeks. It had to have been a very difficult discussion for her, given the Master's recent death by his own hand.

"Maybe we could do with a drink," the Madame said, wiping away her tears with the sleeve of her kimono, and she called for Takako and asked her to bring us some *sake*.

"Oh, this war is a horrible thing," Takako said as she set down the *sake* in front of us.

"Stay and have some with us," the Madame said to Takako.

"But Madame..."

"No," the Madame said, gesturing to the cushion next to her, "it's not a time to stand on ceremony."

Takako sat down, and then the Madame picked up the *sake* jar and poured some for Takako and me and herself.

"I can remember the day Suzu came to live with us," Takako said, sipping on her *sake*. "A little scruff of a girl... And now look at her— all grown-up and such a beauty."

The Madame smiled wanly.

"And to think that now she's going to be sent off to the war. Isn't it enough that they send our young men?"

It was evident that Takako had been listening in on our conversation. I thought for a moment that the Madame might scold her, but she didn't, instead picking up her *sake* cup and taking another drink.

"Oh, this war is a horrible thing," Takako said again.

"Yes...," the Madame concurred, shaking her head.

The next day the rear-admiral himself came to see me, and before I had a chance to say anything, he congratulated me on my decision to join the special unit in Kyushu. Despite what the Madame had said, it was clear I would not have the option of opting out of this assignment. The rear-admiral also made it clear, however, that this would be "primarily" a public relations job, just as the Madame had told me it would be.

"We can't be putting the 'Kamikaze Geisha' at risk," he said.

This was the first time I had heard the term "Kamikaze Geisha." I pointed out to the rear-admiral that I was still a *maiko*.

"Young lady, you're getting a promotion," the rear-admiral said, looking over at the Madame for confirmation.

"Yes, I'm afraid I forgot to tell you yesterday," the Madame said.

I was not familiar with the term "kamikaze," and I asked the rear-admiral what it meant. He said it meant "divine wind," and that it had first been used back in the thirteenth century in reference to the typhoon that had destroyed the invasion fleet of the Mongolians. In similar fashion, the pilots of the unit I was joining would destroy the invasion fleet of the Americans.

"Your induction ceremony is scheduled for next week," the rear-admiral said on the way out. "A tailor will be coming by tomorrow to measure you."

After the rear-admiral was gone, Koyo and Mangetsu and Hoshi and Takako came into the room. It seemed they had all been listening just outside.

"Does this really mean you're going to Kyushu?" Hoshi asked.

"It looks that way, doesn't it?"

"It's just so sudden," Mangetsu said. "Can't they put it off for a while?"

"I don't think so."

"You can't postpone a war," Koyo added glumly.

One by one we sat down on the tatami floor in a circle, all of us looking downcast and despondent.

"It just doesn't seem fair," Hoshi said, holding back tears. "What's going to become of all of us?"

There was silence, no one attempting an answer to Hoshi's question.

"First the Master dies," Hoshi went on, "and then our house is shut down, and now Suzu is being sent to Kyushu as a so-called 'kamikaze.'"

There was more silence, and Hoshi's eyes welled up, and then a single large tear fell and ran down her cheek. I thought this is where the Madame, or perhaps Koyo or Mangetsu, might speak up and say some encouraging words about the fighting spirit of the House of Sugutatsu, and how we had never been ones to give up easily, and how everything would work out in the end. But there were no such words from any of them. No, there was simply more silence, and a deep feeling of dread, and a sense that the House of Sugutatsu would never again be the same.

35

As planned, the tailor came the next day. I was to be outfitted for three uniforms— an officer's whites, an officer's blues, and a naval aviator's jumpsuit. There had never before been a female officer in the Imperial Navy, necessitating the special fitting.

"It just seems so strange," Takako said, supervising the tailor as he made his measurements.

"What do you mean?" I asked.

"We should be fitting you out for your new kimono as a geisha, and instead we have this character here measuring you for uniforms."

The little man doing the measurements gave Takako a contemptuous look, and Takako stared right back at him and stuck out her tongue. She wanted to take out her anger on someone, and the little man was the only person available.

"I would be more careful with your language," the little man said. "Your patriotic sentiments might be questioned."

"By whom?" Takako said with a laugh. "You? Just keep your mind on the measurements and let others worry about the 'patriotic sentiments,' okay?"

The little man appeared to want to say something more, but then he looked at Takako again and thought better of it. She truly did look scary right at that moment.

The night before my induction to the navy, we had a brief *erikae* ceremony at the house to commemorate my promotion from *maiko* to geisha. What should have been a joyous occasion was all very sad, really. Where we should have been marking the change of my collar from the red of a *maiko* to the white of a geisha, we were instead marking the change to the white of a navy officer. Mangetsu read a poem she had written:

> *Deep in the darkness of the night*
> *in the shimmer of the shimmering light,*
> *where once I saw*
> *the nape of your neck so white,*
> *now will I see*
> *there before me*
> *only the stiff collar*
> *of a navy officer.*

Mangetsu had written her poem out on the delicate

surface of a piece of rice paper, and now as she folded the paper and put it into its envelope and handed it to me, there wasn't a dry eye in the house.

"When you come back," the Madame said, "we'll give you a proper ceremony with a proper new kimono."

But none of us thought we would see such a day anytime soon— if ever.

Early the next morning the Madame and Takako and I went down to the navy recruiting station in Shinbashi. We had been told to be there at eight-thirty. Captain Mushitani and numerous members of the fourth estate were already at the entrance, waiting for us.

"Is it true that you're being promoted to geisha?" one of the press boys shouted at me.

"I'm afraid I can't comment now," I shouted back.

"What about your status as a maiden?" another yelled.

I looked at the Madame.

"There will be an announcement after the induction," she said, gently grabbing me by the shoulder and pushing me through the door.

Inside we were immediately met by Rear-Admiral Nishida and a bevy of navy officials— officers and clerks and doctors and nurses.

"We thank you for your service to the nation," the rear-admiral said with a curt bow.

With that I was led into a small room and asked to remove my clothes down to my most inner layer of kimono undergarment. My height (158 centimeters) and weight (45 kilos) were taken by one of the nurses, and then a doctor came in and conducted his exam, looking at my eyes and down my throat and into my ears, before pressing his cold stethoscope against various spots on my back and chest, including two presses precariously close to the most accented points of my modestly accented bosom.

"Everything appears to be in order," the doctor said.

Next I was taken into another room by one of the clerks and asked to fill out several forms. I took my time in completing the task, being careful with my calligraphy. It wouldn't do to bring shame on the House of Sugutatsu by exhibiting poor penmanship. When I was finished I was taken to yet another room, where a hairdresser was waiting for me.

"In order to wear your aviator headgear," she said, "I'm afraid we will have to modify your hairstyle."

"I understand," I said cooperatively.

Then my hair was let down and washed and cut. No longer would I wear the *fukumage* style of the *maiko*, or even the *shimada* style common among most geisha. No, henceforth I would wear the unique *katana-kiri*, "sword cutting," style of the Kamikaze Geisha.

"Perfect," the hairdresser said when she had finished dressing my hair.

Then I was taken to yet one more room, where this time a young female attendant was waiting for me. Hanging on the wall was an aviator's jumpsuit. I removed the last inner layer of my kimono undergarments and then, with the help of the young lady, first put on the underwear she handed me— not standard navy issue, I was told— and then a simple set of grey trousers and shirt, and finally the jumpsuit itself.

"Just one more touch," the young lady said.

And then from a box that was sitting on a table in the room, she took out my aviator's headgear. She fluffed it up, just like you might see an actress do with a fashionable hat in one of those American movies, and then she handed it to me. There was a mirror in the room, and I stood in front of it and fiddled with the hat until I had it on just right, my newly styled hair peeking out nicely from both sides.

"Oh, you look wonderful," the young lady said when I turned around. "Only as one might expect of the Kamikaze Geisha."

I thanked the young lady, and then she took me back out to see the rear-admiral. "Stunning," the rear-admiral said, "simply stunning."

Then the rear-admiral called the press in, and the boys swarmed all around me, and the rear-admiral read a statement:

> *Facing grave circumstances in our holy war to liberate East Asia from the West, it is necessary that all of the resources of our great nation be brought to bear. Each of us— no matter how high or low in station, no matter how rich or poor, no matter how brilliant or dimwitted— must make our contribution. In this regard, I am delighted to announce today that Miss Funabashi Suzukaze of the House of Sugutatsu, well known as the "Maiden Maiko," has volunteered to join our newly formed Special Attack Force based at Kikuna Naval Air Station in Kagoshima Prefecture. Miss Funabashi has been inducted into the Imperial Navy this morning as an officer with the rank of kamikaze geisha, junior grade. She will retain her status as a maiden while on duty in her new role.*
>
> *Rear-Admiral Nishida Hajime,*
> *Imperial Navy*

"Okay, boys, that's it," the rear-admiral said when he was done reading the statement. "You can take a few photos now."

With that, the flashes started flashing, one after another, and shouts came for me to strike this pose or that.

"Tip your head this way," one said.

"Put the earflaps up," said another.

"Earflaps down," said yet one more.

It was all over before I knew it. The pressmen were gone, and I had changed back into my kimono, and I was leaving the recruiting station with the Madame and Takako.

"It all seems a little surreal," I said.

"Yes, it does, doesn't it?" the Madame agreed, nodding her head in resignation.

Over the next week, photos of me in my jumpsuit were in newspapers and magazines all across the country.

Maiden Maiko Volunteers as Kamikaze Geisha

was a common headline. Many of the accompanying articles were quite long, often putting special emphasis on my Kagoshima roots. ("What else would one expect of a young lady following in the tradition of Saigo Takamori and the other fierce warriors of Satsuma?")

As it happened, I didn't have to report to the air station in Kikuna until after New Year's. I spent that time making the rounds of clients and others who had been so kind to me over the years, and then the night before I was to leave the Madame and my sisters hosted a farewell party for me.

"You'll never guess who's coming tonight," Mangetsu said.

"Who?"

"I can't tell you. It's a surprise!"

And indeed, it was quite a surprise— Taibo himself. He came accompanied by two other sumo wrestlers and four young ladies— who, by the look of them, were also of the willow trade but no where near the grade of our house.

"I hope you don't mind," the former grand champion said to the Madame, "but I thought maybe you girls could use some cheering up and..."

The Madame smiled. "What a novel idea."

It was maybe the first genuine smile I had seen from the Madame since the death of the Master.

"Don't worry about the extra people," Taibo said, smiling back. "We've brought a few things with us. I still do have some connections."

He then motioned to the other two wrestlers, and from outside they brought in boxes of sushi and fresh whole fish and bottle after bottle of *sake*.

"Oh my," the Madame said, "you didn't need to..."

I just happened to look at Hoshi then and caught her exchanging glances with Taibo. It was evident that although they had not been seeing each other recently, their hearts were still one, and this made me very happy. It was truly moving to have the Yokozuna show up for my farewell party, and my eyes filled with tears.

"Isn't it wonderful," Mangetsu said, "to have the old gang together?"

"To our lovely Suzu," the Madame said, raising her cup."

"Cheers!" everyone said in unison, and we all drank up, emptying our *sake* cups.

As I sat there, looking around at our little group, I thought back on our trip to China. It seemed like ages ago. What a crazy world it was. The entire globe was at war, and here I was going off to Kyushu to join a special unit that flew planes into ships. There was nothing for it but to get drunk. It seemed everyone else was in a similar frame of mind that night, as the passing of the *sake* jar was fast and furious, and we were all soon thoroughly in our cups.

"We've prepared some entertainment," Taibo said, standing up.

Then he motioned to the young ladies he had brought

with him, and they got up and went to the front of the room and began their performance. Two of the girls danced, while one sang and the other crudely played the samisen. There were three dances, all variations on the theme of tragic love. Without going into detail, let me simply say the portrayal of the love aspect of each story was quite graphic— quite graphic indeed— and evidently humorous as well for everyone except myself. I'm afraid I still lacked the requisite experience at this time of my life to appreciate such humor.

"Make sure the 'Maiden Maiko' covers her eyes," Taibo shouted out.

"She's not a *maiko* anymore," Mangetsu shouted back.

"No, but she's still a maiden."

Everyone got a good laugh out of that— except me, of course. But I was a good sport about it. This was my family, after all, and I was going to miss all of them— miss all of them very much.

Over the rest of the night there were more dances and games and a good time was had by all, but as the sky grew red with the coming of the morning we were forced to face the reality of the end of our time together. Each of my sisters came forward and exchanged a final cup of *sake* with me.

"Never forget," Koyo said, sitting with me first, "to seek comfort in your roots whenever facing difficulties."

"And never forget, either," Mangetsu said with a smile, sitting with me next, "to drink only the best *sake*. Remember, only the best in *sake*... and the best in men."

Everyone laughed, and then Hoshi came forward. "Oh, Suzu, we're going to miss you so much," she said, her voice choking.

"And I, all of you," I said, tears coming to my eyes again.

And then finally the Madame came and sat with me and looked deeply into my eyes for several long moments, gently shaking my hands as she did so. "Oh, our little Suzu," she said at last, "always remember you've got a home here."

And then Taibo came over and picked me up in his arms and held me over his head and twirled me around, and all the girls laughed and applauded.

36

On January 4th I took the train from Tokyo as far as the Kure Navy Base, near Hiroshima. Kure was the home port of the battleship Yamato, I was told by the sailor who met me at the train station and escorted me to the base. The ship was back in port then after having participated in a battle in the Philippines. The mention of the Philippines made me think of Tomo. I hadn't heard from him since the start of the fighting in Luzon in late October, and I was worried. So far he'd had a free pass. He hadn't had to face the trials the Lieutenant or the Colonel had, but I was fearful he might now be right in the middle of harm's way.

From Kure I boarded an Imperial Navy patrol boat for Kagoshima. As we started out into the Inland Sea, I recalled our trip some two and a half years earlier when we had crossed over from Hiroshima to Matsuyama, and then from Matsuyama to Oita. The weather had been beautiful on those two crossings, warm and sunny spring days, but it was far different this time, drizzling with a cold, biting wind. I stayed below deck most of the trip, rocking with the thump thump thump of the boat hitting the waves, watching the spray rise high in the air and then fall back down again, thinking about what had already passed in my life and what was yet to come.

I would be lying if I were to say I wasn't lonely. I'd only been gone a day and already I missed the Madame and the girls from Sugutatsu. It was far too much like when I'd been taken from my first family and sent to Tokyo. What lay in front of me then was completely unknown, and it was the same now. It was a very unsettling feeling.

The rear-admiral had told me I would only be doing public relations work, but still the thought of serving with men who would be flying planes into ships was quite disorienting. In the course of my career as an apprentice geisha, I had often been confronted with self-sacrifice in the context of love, but never in the context of war. It would take some getting used to. And I must admit, too, that somewhere in the back of my mind I had doubts about the rear-admiral's promise that my duties would be confined to public relations. At some point, wouldn't they want to send me aloft with the others? What would the situation be when I got to Kikuna? How would I react? It was all quite overwhelming. Along the way, one of the sailors let me know we were passing my hometown of Kujirahe, but when I went up on deck I could see only a vague outline of the shore in the distance, the visibility being poor with the bad weather, and that only made me feel all the more depressed. It seemed as though all the familiar reference points in my life had been removed, that I'd been put on a ghost ship to nowhere.

Down below deck again, I took out the latest letter I'd received from the Colonel. By then it had been almost five years since I had last seen the Lieutenant in Wuhan, but he was still always in my heart, and in a certain way I felt I could connect with him through the Colonel's letters. He was no longer in this world. I was convinced of that at the time. But what if he were? There was that remote possibility. What if he were alive and still in the Colonel's unit? Sometimes, especially as the years passed, I did allow myself these thoughts. And if that were so, then all the Colonel wrote about— the combat and the rain, and the high tension and the monotony, and the exotic plants and animals and smells of the jungle— all of this the Lieutenant was also experiencing. And in these moments, when I did allow myself these thoughts, I also sometimes wondered if the two of them had ever spoken about me. They were in the same unit, after all. It would not have been out of the question. Might the Colonel's dark moods have pushed him one day to open up to the Lieutenant, to talk about his "pure and perfect" maiden? Oh, how shocked the Lieutenant would have been. What would have been running through his mind then, knowing he had deflowered not only the nation's Maiden Maiko but his commanding officer's treasured correspondent? And would he have thought me unfaithful to him? Why had I never spoken to him about the Colonel? Would these thoughts have occurred to him as well? And sometimes, when these fantasies were swirling about in my head, I wondered if one day the Lieutenant, driven over the edge himself, might confess he knew the young lady. And if he went that far, wasn't it possible, he might go even further and confess he not only knew the young lady but had had intimate relations with her? And then what? Wouldn't the Colonel, in a fit of rage— having discovered his "pure and perfect" maiden was in fact not a maiden, and that the despicable deed had been done by his own subordinate officer— wouldn't he draw his pistol and shoot the Lieutenant on the spot? And if the Colonel somehow instead managed to control himself, wasn't it probable the Lieutenant would nonetheless be arrested and charged with treason? And wouldn't the Kamikaze Geisha be charged with him? And wouldn't we then be found guilty and executed, the only question being the method employed— hanging or beheading?

Yes, I would sometimes have all these thoughts. And then I would remind myself he was already dead, already in the next world. None of this could possibly happen. And I would put it all out of my mind.

Below deck, reading over the Colonel's latest letter once more, the persistent darkness of his mood was well evident. The letter read as follows:

October 22, 1944

My dear Suzu,

The monsoon should be ending in another two weeks or so, and when it does we expect a renewed attack from the British forces. Our incursion into India in the spring was a disaster— perhaps the disaster the general command was looking for all along, but it has come too late. We have inflicted too much pain and humiliation on our Western enemies, and there will be little chance for negotiations now.

Saipan has been taken and the Americans will now seek to capture islands even closer to the home islands— Iwo Jima is a probable target. They will use these islands as "fixed aircraft carriers" to bomb the home islands into submission. The irony of this whole war is that the vast majority of our forces, more than 3.5 million men, remain in good fighting shape on the mainland of East Asia, stretching from here in Burma down through Indochina and across through China to Manchuria and Korea. The capability of these men to go on fighting on the continent is virtually without limit. As you may be aware, there is even an offensive currently underway— the so-called "Ichi-go Campaign"— that aims to link up our troops in China with those in Indochina. The thinking is that even if the Americans control the air and seas of the Pacific, our forces will still be able to support one another on the continent. The only problem with this thinking, of course, is that while we are protecting one another on the continent, our home islands will have been sunk to the bottom of the ocean by the Americans. If you are a chess player, my dear, it's a little like holding on to all of your pieces except the king. For some army men here in Burma, however— and elsewhere on the continent, I'm sure— this appears to be a relatively small problem. For them, their own survival is all that remains. The idea of Japan as a nation has long ago dissipated in the fog of war.

Recently I often find myself thinking of my younger days in Aizu, up in the mountains. In the summer I would go on long hikes with other boys from the village, hunting for beetles and butterflies. Over the years I was able to put together quite a collection. It might still be there in the old family home, hidden away somewhere in a closet. I hope someone finds it and takes it out and shows it around. Many of the boys I grew up with are still there in the same village. They never left. It might remind them of me and the fine times we had when we were young. It's odd how these random thoughts come to me now, here in this foreign country so far from home.

Suzu, it may very well be quite dangerous for all of

you on the home front as this war winds down. You must do everything you can to save yourself. Do not think of this as being selfish. You are still young and have too much to live for. If I can only know that you will survive this war, I will die a happy man.

Given the date of the letter, the Colonel hadn't yet learned of my promotion to Kamikaze Geisha— unless, that is, he had had previous knowledge of this development through his own back channels. That is a possibility, of course— and his admonition to "save myself" may have been an indication that he was indeed aware— but I would never know, as this was to be the last letter I would receive from him. Thereafter circumstances worsened to the point where letters from the front simply were not getting through to anyone.

By this time I had become resigned to the Colonel's death. He had mentioned it often in his letters— this premonition that he would not survive his time in Burma— and I had come to believe it as well. I hope you will not consider me unfeeling or cold, but in truth notions of the Colonel's impending death seemed to add a bittersweet poignancy to our relationship that greatly deepened my affection for him. For those of you who did not live through the war, or who have not experienced the nearness of death in some other way, my feelings may be difficult to understand. But for the many who lived through the war in similar circumstances, I am certain you are familiar with the emotions I describe here.

37

Commander Kimura was in charge of the unit to which I was assigned. He was a tall, thin man, and always seemed very sad. Now since his job was to send young men off to die for Emperor and country, you might think it would only be natural he would always have a sad look about him, but I think he was born that way. I think he was born that way and I think he stayed that way. If pressed, I have no good reason to give for this assertion. It was just a feeling I had.

"Be seated," the Commander said when I entered his office the first time and saluted.

"Yes, sir," I said, sitting down.

"I just want to let you know up front," he said immediately, "that I think this whole thing is ridiculous."

I was caught off-guard and didn't know what to say. "I'm sorry, sir, but..."

"This whole thing about being the 'Kamikaze Geisha.' For heaven's *sake*, they've even given you a rank— kamikaze geisha, junior grade."

I could feel my face turning a bright red.

"What do you have to say about that?"

"I hadn't really..."

"You hadn't really what?"

"Thought about it."

"Well, don't you think you should?"

"Yes, sir."

The Commander stood up and lit a cigarette and started

pacing about the room. "I hear you're from Kyushu, here in Kagoshima as a matter of fact."

"That's not exactly true, sir."

The Commander stopped his pacing. "What do you mean?"

"Well, I am from Kyushu, but uh... not Kagoshima..."

"Good lord, where are you from?"

"Kujirahe."

"Where in the world is that?"

"Just south of Oita."

The Commander started his pacing again. "But you are related to Saigo Takamori, right?"

"The great samurai?"

He stopped again and gave me a long and penetrating look. "Who else would I be talking about?"

"Yes, sir, of course... Well, not exactly... You see..."

"Is there anything about you that is factual? I suppose the next thing you'll be telling me is you're not even a maiden."

For one short moment I did consider telling him just exactly that. I needn't tell the whole truth, implicating the Lieutenant. I could tell him the Chinese had had me. But then I quickly realized it was far too late for such a confession. If the Chinese had had me, why had I waited so long to tell the authorities, allowing countless shrines to be contaminated by my presence? In this scenario as well, charges of treason would no doubt be brought. No, there was no turning back now.

"I am a maiden," I said resolutely. "There is no question about that."

Seemingly taken aback by the adamant tone of my voice, the Commander walked back behind his desk and sat down again. "What do you think your role here will be?"

"I was told I would be in public relations."

The Commander lit up another cigarette and gazed up at the ceiling. "Does this look like a public relations outfit to you?"

"No, sir."

"No, it doesn't, does it? Look, we're sending young men off to fly planes into ships. This is serious business. You understand?"

"Yes, sir."

"If headquarters wants to send reporters down here to take photos of you in some ludicrous outfit and then write up fairy tale stories, there's nothing I can do about that."

"Yes, sir."

"But while you're under my command, I will expect you to participate in all of the training just like all of the other recruits. Is that crystal clear?"

"Yes, sir."

"Even if you are here just as some sort of a publicity stunt... Good heavens— 'kamikaze geisha, junior grade.'"

And with that, I was dismissed.

Following general assembly that morning, I was taken aside by an aide to the Commander and introduced to the three other members of my section— Naito, Muto, and Saito. Since the second Chinese character of the top name of each man was the character for *fuji*, "wisteria," we would be known as the "Fuji Team."

"We are very happy to have you join us," Naito said, stepping forward.

Muto spoke up next. "You could have been assigned to any section. We are most fortunate it was ours."

I waited for Saito to say something as well, but when he didn't, I bowed deeply to all three of them, saying, "I will do my best. Your forbearance of my inadequacies would be most appreciated."

I was to find Saito was a man of very few words.

"Let's move it out," an officer said now, rushing by and motioning for us to head in the direction of the athletics field.

My three new companions started to run after the officer, and I followed closely behind. The field wasn't far away, and when we got there we were formed into ranks, and then the calisthenics instructor started to put us through various exercises— stretching, and sit-ups, and push-ups, and things of that nature. I could see already that Naito was not much of an athlete. He was of slight build, small and thin, and he was having trouble keeping up with the repetitions.

"You're in very good shape for a geisha," he said, exhausted after we had finished our push-ups.

I waved my hand in modest disagreement.

"No, you really are," Muto insisted vigorously.

Muto was much bigger than Naito, tall and muscular, and he had easily completed all of the exercises. I would later learn he had been a judo champion at university. As for Saito, he was of average build, but by no means that much stronger than Naito that a meaningful distinction could have been made. After the calisthenics, we moved on to martial arts training. This, of course, was an area of particular strength for me. I was to find, in fact, that all of the training we received at Kikuna was remarkably similar to the training I had undergone at Sugutatsu. The only significant difference was flight training being substituted for training in the performing arts. That said, the time spent on genuine flight training would in reality be quite small, gasoline supplies being very low throughout the nation. We started with drills in kendo, and then we moved on to judo. For the judo I was matched with Naito. I tried not to hurt him, but I'm afraid two or three times I was a little too aggressive in my throws, resulting in him crying out in pain as he hit the ground. Each time I was quick to apologize, and each time Naito was quick to tell me he was all right, trying to put a brave face on things. I shouldn't back off, he said.

"Why do you know so much about martial arts?" Muto asked during our lunch break.

Using the "company line," if you will, I explained how our founder, Sugeimon, had been appointed to his position as Master of the House of Sugutatsu by Shogun Yoshimune, with the directive to promote the principles of bushido in addition to the traditional skills of singing and dancing. For added effect, I went on to to detail the contributions of the ten succeeding masters right down to Tatsuzo, the Master's father, who— as you may recall— had introduced modern methods of scheduling. For obvious reasons, I did not talk about what the Master had perceived as his contribution.

"I'm afraid," Muto confessed, "that I had some very wrong preconceptions."

I reemphasized the fact that Sugutatsu was like no other geisha house. Nonetheless, it would not be surprising if he had had some "wrong preconceptions," as he put it. "There are many mistaken stereotypes about geisha," I added. "We're used to it."

"Are you really the Kamikaze Geisha?" I heard a voice say.

I looked up to see that a small crowd had by then gathered around. My participation in the workouts had created quite a stir.

"Yes..." I said softly.

"That's so special," one of the others said, "to have the Kamikaze Geisha herself right here with us."

"I've heard," another said, "that she was chosen by His Highness himself to sanctify our missions."

I lowered my head and said nothing, feeling once more a

deep sense of disquiet and inadequacy, just as I had the day of my first visit to Yasukuni and on so many other occasions since. This sense was all the more intensified as I came to grips with the fact that all of these young men around me would soon also be interred at the national shrine.

By the end of that first day, I was exhausted both physically and emotionally. It was an awful lot to take in, as I am certain you can well imagine. But I did feel, in a certain sense, that I was now "one of the boys"— even, of course, if I wasn't.

38

Although I would indeed participate in all of the training just like the other recruits, the Commander did take my gender into account when arranging for my billeting. There was a small house on the base where one of the cooks lived, and I was given a room there. The cook's name was Yoshiko. She was a heavy-set woman from the local area, perhaps in her mid to late thirties, and she had a very strong southern Kyushu accent. The Kujirahe accent was slightly different but close enough that listening to this woman made me feel very much at home.

After I'd been at Yoshiko's place for a week, she asked if I'd like to invite the other members of my section over for dinner. Of course we usually all ate dinner at the mess hall, and Yoshiko herself had to be there to help prepare the meals, but this coming Saturday was her night off and she'd received special permission from the Commander to have dinner with the Fuji Team at her place, if that was something she'd like to do. I told her I didn't want her to have to work on her day off, but she insisted that would not be a problem and encouraged me to have the boys over. I think she was worried about my adjustment to my new life, and I think the Commander, despite his initial tough stance towards me, had had similar concerns.

"Kamikaze Geisha, you look very beautiful," Muto said when I greeted the boys at the door.

I'd brought a kimono with me from Tokyo, not one of my finer ones but still something somewhat special, and I'd decided to wear it for this occasion. I'd also applied a little make-up, nothing near what I would wear when entertaining but still more than enough to catch the attention of any man.

"Please don't be so formal," I said, putting my hand up. "Call me Suzu. I will simply be your geisha tonight— not the Kamikaze Geisha."

Muto looked at me very seriously. "Are you sure that's all right?"

I laughed lightly. "Very sure. Now come on in."

There were only two rooms in the house, one of six tatami mats and the other of eight, and there was also a tiny kitchen. The three boys sat in the larger room with their legs snuggly tucked into the *kotatsu* table, the coals below keeping their feet warm, while Yoshiko and I prepared the simple meal. Those who have never been to Kyushu tend to think it has a tropical climate, but the winters can actually be quite cold, and the *kotatsu* in Yoshiko's house was something for which I was especially grateful that particular winter. We served the boys some *sake* first, and then when the stew of fish and vegetables was ready, we took it in to them and ladled it out into their dishes. Then we too sat down in the *kotatsu*.

"Nice and cozy," Yoshiko said.

"Just right," I agreed.

"Yes, very nice," Muto said, raising his *sake* cup. "To the Fuji Team!"

"To the Fuji Team!" we all shouted, emptying our cups.

This was the first chance we had really had to talk to each other in a more relaxed setting, and as the *sake* flowed, I got to know more about the personal histories of each of my comrades. It seems they were all college students, and all the same age— twenty, actually the same age I was at the time. Naito had been drafted out of Keio, where he had studied civil engineering, while Muto had studied business at the Tokyo College of Commerce. Saito said he had been at Waseda, but was vague about what he had studied. Naito mentioned something about "medieval history" by way of explanation. I would come to find that Saito spent most of his free time copying Buddhist sutras or meditating. I never knew if this had anything to do with his study of "medieval history."

When we were done eating, I stepped out of the room to fetch my samisen. Besides my kimono and the Colonel's letters, it was the only other thing I'd brought with me from Tokyo. I'd felt it would help to keep my ties with Sugutatsu and the other girls.

"Are you really going to play for us?" Naito asked when I returned.

"Of course," I said.

"It's quite a treat," Muto interjected.

"Yes," Yoshiko added, "quite a treat indeed. You boys are very lucky. I don't know of any other unit that's got its own geisha."

"Yes, that must be true," Naito agreed, smiling.

The song I played was "One Night in Asakusa." The tone was lighter than most of the more traditional numbers in the Sugutatsu repertoire, being a love story in which a young couple successfully elope. Given our setting, I felt that only something of this nature would be appropriate.

"It must be quite the thing to be a geisha in Tokyo," Yoshiko said when I had finished singing my last note.

"Oh, I don't know about that," I replied modestly.

"But you must have met some famous men."

I avoided a direct answer, saying I'd been fortunate to meet many people and see many places.

"You've been overseas then?"

I told her I'd been to China, and I listed the cities I'd visited— Tianjin, Beijing, Taiyuan, Wuhan, and Shanghai. I didn't talk about the detour I'd been forced into because of my kidnapping.

"Isn't that something," she said. "I suppose it was part of your duties as the Maiden Maiko?"

I told her that, yes, that was the case. I'd gone with some other geisha from the House of Sugutatsu to entertain the troops and build cultural bridges with the Chinese. I even impressed myself with how nice the words "build cultural bridges" sounded coming off my tongue.

"Isn't that something," she said again. "I've never even been outside of Kyushu. I did go to Nagasaki once. My late husband took me."

I told her I was sorry about her husband, and the others expressed their sympathy as well. As though reading my mind, she said he hadn't died in the war. It had been appendicitis. He'd had a pain in his stomach and he'd thought it was something he'd eaten, and by the time he'd been seen by a doctor it had been too late. It had happened many years ago. They'd only been married five years. I told her again I was sorry.

"You never know how you're going to go," she said, and then she caught herself, looking around the room at the boys.

They knew how they would go. They even knew when they would go— not precisely, but sometime soon.

"Oh, my," she said, covering her mouth with her hand.

"Not to worry," Muto said, reaching across and gently touching Yoshiko on the arm. "Each of us has his own fate to follow."

I picked up the *sake* jar and poured another round for everyone, and quickly the conversation turned to other topics and the mood rose again. But in my own mind I couldn't get away from the sad thought that these boys would soon die, and I momentarily latched on to the idea that all of us— not just myself— had been gathered here to enact a grand charade for publicity purposes. Everyone would play his part, each and everyone of us— even the Commander, who had maintained so convincingly that this had nothing at all to do with publicity. We would be trained, and the boys would be sent off in their planes, and it would be reported that they'd rained down death on scores of enemy ships, and they would be properly mourned. And then we would learn one day that none of them had died, that they had all flown to a safe haven somewhere, and stayed there untouched until this horrible war had somehow miraculously ended. It was absolutely too crazy to contemplate any other scenario.

But in my heart I knew it was the craziness that was true.

39

Of the three boys, it was Naito whom I got to know the best. That's just the way it worked out, I suppose. Saito, of course, didn't speak much anyway, and although Muto could be quite talkative, what he said seemed to float right by me. It's odd how that can happen with some people. Sometimes I would think back on what Muto had said and feel I should have been more interested. But I wasn't. He was a very nice boy. There was no doubt about that. And sincere, too. But our conversations never lasted more than a few minutes. It was different with Naito. I could talk with him about even the most mundane of subjects and never get bored. I wondered if I might be a little in love with him. Not in anyway like my love for the Lieutenant— I want to make that very clear— but there was a special attachment to this boy, I must admit. I was worried he might sense these feelings I had for him and perhaps build up some expectations, but I needn't have worried. He had his own girl at home. One day he wanted to take a walk, and he asked me to come along. We had no particular route in mind, starting out near the mess hall and wandering along the outer fence of the airfield until we came to the far edge of the runway. There was a long, thick log there, and we sat down on it, and then for some reason I started talking about my kidnapping.

"You must have been very frightened," he said when I'd finished.

I said that, yes, I'd been frightened, especially when they'd first taken me and then again when the Imperial Army forces attempted their rescue. He wanted to know more about Mr. Ma, and I told him about how he'd come to Japan to study, and how he'd stayed with a Japanese family. And then I told him about the daughter of the family and how he'd fallen in love with her, and how she'd cried when she said she didn't love him.

"That's a very moving story," he said.

"Yes... Sometimes I think of how different his life would have been if he'd married her. Maybe he would have stayed in Japan..."

"Or maybe she would have gone to China..."

"Yes..."

And then he asked what it was like to see a man die. The Chinese soldier had been shot in the head right in front of my own eyes. I'd told him about that, and now he wanted to know what it was like. There wasn't much I could say. What could I say? It was shocking, yes, it was shocking. That's all I could say. He looked down and was quiet for a while, and I suspected he was thinking about his own death. He had to have thought about it many times before, hurling himself forward at great speed into the deck of an American aircraft carrier. What would it be like at that very moment when he passed from this world to the next?

He looked up at me again. "It must have been a difficult decision for you."

I looked back at him quizzically.

"Deciding to become the Kamikaze Geisha..."

I hesitated, not sure how open I should be with him, and then I began to talk, telling him about the twisting road I had taken to becoming the Kamikaze Geisha. There seemed no reason now to hold back. He would soon be gone. I began with the night of my debut, and I told him how I met the Minister of Public Enlightenment and how the Minister then decided I would become the Maiden Maiko. I was so young and innocent and naive, and I was told it was for "the good of the nation" and I didn't really think I had a choice, and so the decision was made for me. I really hadn't made any decision at all. That's what I told him. Now I know this was not the complete truth. I didn't tell him about the Lieutenant, about how I had fallen madly in love and given myself to him, and how that had affected my thinking about the Minister's proposal. I didn't tell him about that. However open I might wish to be,

I could not go that far. But the essentials of my telling were truthful— I was young and innocent and naive, and I was indeed convinced it was for the "good of the nation." He said it must have been very challenging, taking on this new role, and I told him he had no idea how difficult it had been. The government and the press— even the Chinese— they had all built me up into something I wasn't. The Chinese had even claimed I was worshipped as a god in Japan. Could he believe that? I was merely a simple girl from the backward fishing village of Kujirahe whose real name was Panko. Panko. And to then have to perform ceremonies at Yasukuni and other shrines throughout the nation, standing before the gods and the souls of our departed heroes. He couldn't imagine how inadequate I had felt. So many times I had even considered taking my own life. And then one day the Madame had called me in and told me the Imperial Navy wished to recruit me for a new special attack force being formed in Kyushu. And the very next day after that Rear-Admiral Nishida had come and thanked me for my "service to the nation," and once more the decision had been made for me. That's what I told him. That's how it had all happened. That's how I had become the Kamikaze Geisha.

"It has indeed been a difficult path you've taken," he said.

"Yes..."

"And now you will give your life to the nation, just as we will."

I realized suddenly that he didn't know I was only there for publicity purposes, that I would not be sent aloft with him and the others. All of the press, of course, had talked about my volunteering to "serve with the boys," and I had been training just like "one of the boys," and there was no reason for him to think anything other than I would be sacrificing my life "with the boys." I didn't know what to say.

It didn't seem right to tell him I would not be sacrificing myself when all the rest of them would be giving up their lives. But I knew he did have some feelings for me— even if he did have a sweetheart back home— and I thought how sad it must make him to think of me departing this world, and so I decided to tell him about my unique circumstances. I was ashamed to say it, I said, but I would not be flying with him and the others to attack the enemy ships. I was only there in a publicity role. As I had hoped, this did indeed seem to make him quite happy.

"It's so good to learn that," he said, smiling. "I couldn't really believe they would send up a girl like you, but..."

"Yes, I know..."

He was silent for a long moment, looking down again, and then he said, "It was a difficult decision for each of us, for each of the boys here."

I nodded gravely, and he was silent again for a long while, and then he began to talk about how that decision had been made by himself and Muto and Saito. Muto was a very patriotic sort, he said, a judo champion at university and a practitioner of other martial arts. He hadn't been drafted. He had enlisted, and when the opportunity to fly with the Special Attack Force had presented itself, he had been quick to step forward. It couldn't have been an easy decision, but for him it might have been a logical decision. The nation was under attack. Almost all of our resources were gone. If we couldn't somehow stop the Americans now, they would soon be on our doorsteps, slaughtering innocent civilians and raping our women. Sinking their aircraft carriers with suicidal attacks might be the only chance we had left. Naito said he'd talked with Muto about it on a couple of occasions. Every man who joined the armed forces in defense of his country, Muto had said, must assume his life would be sacrificed.

Those who served in the Special Attack Force should be seen no differently than those who served in any other capacity. As for himself, Naito said, he had been drafted, and then one day he and other university draftees had been gathered in a room and told about the dire situation of the war and the mission of the Special Attack Force, and asked if they would volunteer. He liked to think he had made a conscious decision, but he couldn't say that with absolute certainty. He was fatalistic, he said. Each of us would one day die. We were all terminal. Japan was going to lose this war. His death would not make a difference in the outcome. But this was his fate, and rather than try to run from it, he had decided to embrace it. By embracing it, he would give his life meaning. As for Saito, Naito said, he was afraid the poor boy had been pressured into agreeing to volunteer. There were a number of boys like that, he said, boys who had been too afraid to stand up and say they wouldn't go. It was a high price to pay for lacking the mettle to speak up. He hoped Saito's praying would give him solace of some sort. There was only one more thing, Naito said, he wanted to do before going on his own mission. His sweetheart was coming the following week. Her name was Chiyo. She was coming all the way from Fukuoka, their hometown, to spend one night with him as "man and wife." It would be very special, he said, just to spend the one night together. It wouldn't be the same if they spent two nights together, or three— or maybe even a lifetime.

I told him I could understand what he meant, and then I thought of my own Lieutenant, and tears came to my eyes.

40

It was only after I'd been at Kikuna for a month that we actually started doing any training related to flying. I suppose Commander Kimura felt we had strengthened ourselves sufficiently both physically and spiritually by this time to tackle the challenges of flight. Or maybe we were simply running out of time. To paraphrase Koyo, war waits for no one. In any event we started our flight training, but as noted earlier, there wasn't much actual "flight" to the flight training. In fact, for our section there was none. Instead, we trained in the cockpit of an old shot-up plane that was never again going to go anywhere.

All of the sections were ranked weekly by the Commander from one to 50. We finished a surprising 35th the first week. I say surprising because all the other sections were surprised that a team with a geisha in it would finish anywhere higher than 50th— but of course most of them were not aware of the singular history of the House of Sugutatsu. If the truth be told, I think it is fair to say that I was, in fact, the most skilled of the four members of the Fuji Team. I would go so far as to say my hand-eye coordination is better than most, and I do have a mind that can move quickly and decisively when necessary. These are the essential skills of the pilot. Naito and Muto also did fairly well. Although Naito's hand-eye skills were not good, he did have a decisive mind, and he also had the determination to improve at anything he did. Day to day, we could see him get better. In fact, over time, I think he even got better than Muto, who started out not doing too badly but never really improved much. You might expect that Muto would have been better, seeing that he was a muscular and manly type who fit the image of a fighter pilot, but with his beefy hands he seemed to have considerable trouble maneuvering around the control panel. It might have been, too, that he just didn't have the same quickness of mind. As for Saito, he was the one, actually, who kept the overall score of our section down. The problem with Saito was that he couldn't follow directions. He might get through two or three tasks, but then he would forget what came next and he would go into a panic, flipping one wrong switch after another. I had thought he would be calm and collected, given all the meditation he did, but he was just the opposite. Predicting the behavior of people is never easy.

Early in February, Captain Mushitani came to Kikuna with several members of the press to interview me. Messrs. Wada, Tada, and Yada were again among the journalists who came. Commander Kimura was not happy about the visit, as you might imagine, but there was nothing he could do about it. Rear-Admiral Nishida and other more senior officers felt more needed to be made of the Kamikaze Geisha. There had been the initial splash of press coverage at the time of my induction, and then almost nothing since. More publicity was needed to help with the recruiting efforts.

"That's perfect," the Captain said when he learned the nickname of the section to which I had been assigned was the "Fuji Team."

"Perfect?"

"Yes, we'll have to interview them as well."

The Commander was furious when he got the request from the Captain, but again there was nothing he could do about it. The three boys looked bewildered when the

Commander ordered them to meet the press.

"Are we worthy of such publicity?" Naito asked.

"Yes, why us?" Muto added.

But, again, there was nothing they could do about it.

The journalists interviewed each of us individually early in the morning, and then they followed us about the rest of the day as we did our training. When it came to our flight training, Commander Kimura did his best to make all of us, including Saito, look capable in front of the gentlemen of the press. It would do no good, he knew, to possibly have his pilots written up as incompetents.

"That Muto is a fascinating character," Mr. Yada said to me at the end of the day. "And those other two as well. I've got plenty of material."

We were later sent copies of the articles that Mr. Yada and the other gentlemen had written. Much as with myself, there were many small kernels of truth that had been transformed into overblown myths by the time our esteemed writers were done. As an undergraduate, Naito had done all of the calculations and drawn up the final blueprints for two factory buildings and a bridge. Saito was a Buddhist acolyte who had done the pilgrim's walk around the island of Shikoku four times— once in each of the four seasons, barefoot each time. Muto was a martial arts expert who held advanced certification not only in judo but kendo, calligraphy, and the tea ceremony as well. I felt badly about the whole thing, but there was nothing I could do about it.

"More idiocy," the Commander said when he saw the articles.

All I could do was agree with him.

41

On the morning of March 10th, we awoke to radio reports of a large air raid on Tokyo by American bombers. The damage sounded substantial, but it was only when I received a letter from Hoshi some three weeks later that the tragedy of this event truly struck home.

Dear Suzu,

I'm not sure how to go about writing this letter. I've given it a lot of thought, and I've come to the conclusion that there is no good way. When one must pass on news such as I must in this letter, there simply is no good way.

Many innocent souls perished in the air raid of March 9th, as I am certain you have heard by now. Among them, I must most unfortunately report, were many members of our house, including Koyo and Mangetsu. The Madame was also seriously injured, but is now in the hospital recovering. The entire Asakusa area was destroyed by the fire of the bombing attack. Nothing remains of the House of Sugutatsu. I myself would have likely also been killed or injured, but I was away that night, visiting the doctor in another part of the city. The gods sometimes move in strange ways. Takako was also not in Asakusa the night of the bombing.

She had earlier evacuated to Gunma, and is living there with relatives.

I went to see the Madame the other day in the hospital. She still cannot remember much about that night. She says she recalls the sirens and leaving the house with several of our sisters, but then she was separated and she remembers little after that. Many of our sisters' bodies were found near the Azuma Bridge along with hundreds of others. They were trying to escape to the water of the river. The Madame says she knows it will be very difficult for you, especially since you are alone and so far away, but she says you must bear up and do what you must to keep on going.

I wish I could be with you now, Suzu, so that we could hold hands and share our tears, but of course that is not possible. One day, though, we will be together again. I'm certain of it, and you must believe it too. Please write me if you can.

Affectionately yours, Hoshi

I was devastated. Koyo and Mangetsu and several of our other sisters killed in the Tokyo air raid? It just didn't seem real. I had waited with trepidation for the bad news that I knew might come from the front— news of the death of Tomo or the Colonel— but I had given no thought whatsoever to the possibility that members of our house would die in the air raids. Even after I learned of the catastrophic raid of March 9th, I had assumed they were all right. Like Takako, it was probable they had evacuated to the countryside, I thought. And even if they hadn't evacuated, I was certain they had survived. We were all of the House of Sugutatsu, after all. We were special. Where others hesitated, we charged forward. Where others failed, we succeeded. Where others died, we lived. But they hadn't lived. They had died. I couldn't understand why they had still been in Asakusa. Why hadn't they evacuated? The raids had started months before, and it was known that conditions would only get worse. The Madame had many influential connections. Surely she could have found a safe place outside of the city. And then I wondered if it had been the Ministry that had kept them in Tokyo. Had they maybe even publicized the fact that the women of Sugutatsu had not left the capital, that they had not run before the enemy? Had they maybe even played up some sort of angle that they had stayed behind in solidarity with their geisha sister, the Kamikaze Geisha, who had gone to Kyushu to give her life for the nation?

I wouldn't have put it past them.

As I read Hoshi's words, bitter tears welled up in my eyes and streamed down my cheeks, dropping on to the letter and smudging the black ink of the finely written characters. All seemed bleak and hopeless. Several of my sisters were dead, the Madame badly injured, Asakusa burned to the ground—and now I would be sending my comrades off to fly their planes into ships. The Madame had said I must bear up and carry on, but I didn't see how I could.

And then, only two days later, I did indeed learn of the Colonel's death. As I had already largely resigned myself to his passing, the article in the newspaper seemed to only confirm what I already knew. It seems he had met his demise some ten days earlier during the battle for Mandalay. The headline read:

"Viper of Burma" Perishes in Heroic Banzai Charge

At the end, his unit surrounded, the Colonel had apparently personally led his troops forward, a pistol in one hand, a sword in the other. There were no survivors. Accompanying the main article was a short obituary in which I discovered that: 1) he had been born in 1899 (making him 46 years old); 2) he had graduated from the Imperial Army Academy in 1921; 3) he had served with distinction in Taiwan, Korea, and China before his final assignments in Malaya and Burma; 4) he was married (wife: Kumi) and had three children, a boy and two girls. I had known all along that he must have a wife and children, but he had never mentioned them, and it hadn't been my place to bring it up. It was an odd thing, but now that I knew the wife's name and how many children he had had, the Colonel seemed much more real to me.

And as I thought about the Colonel I also of course thought about the Lieutenant. Many years before I had already decided he was dead, but what if he had still been alive? Had he been with the Colonel in this final charge? There had been no survivors, according to the article. But might he have by then been assigned to another unit? Or might he have been in the hospital, previously wounded or laid low by a tropical disease? He was dead— I had already decided that. But somewhere in the back of my mind, I maintained the notion— however weak that notion may have been— that he had survived.

That he was alive.

42

The very next day after I learned of the Colonel's death, the Americans invaded Okinawa. The date was April 1, 1945. Within the Special Attack Force the invasion had been anticipated, and there were extensive plans ready to implement. Now, finally, our time had come to take our places on stage and perform.

At the end of that week, the Commander gathered together all of the men and briefed us on our unit's first attack, which was scheduled for the next day. Ten of our sections, forty planes, would be flying with other units from Kikuna and other nearby air bases. The Commander called out the names of the ten sections. All of them had poetic names— such as the "White Chrysanthemum Team" or the "Mt. Takakuma Team" or the "Yae Cherry Blossom Team." The Fuji Team was not among the names called out. I thought maybe the Commander had followed the rankings in choosing whom would fly— those with the highest rankings having the honor of going first— but this was not the case. Many from the top of the rankings went, but so did many from the bottom. The team just above us, number 34, as well as the team just below us, number 36, were among those chosen.

"I wonder when our number will be up," Naito said.

Muto shook his head. "I suppose only the Commander knows."

"I suppose so."

The next morning we all gathered at the airfield to see our chosen comrades off on their mission. A Shinto priest said prayers, and the young men drank cups of *sake*, and then they boarded their planes and roared down the runway and up into the blue sky. It was a moving sight indeed as they circled the airfield once and then headed south.

"Do you know any of the men who flew today?" Naito asked the rest of us.

Muto rubbed the back of his head. "There was one fellow I got to know a bit. He was from a place near my hometown."

"Did you say anything to him before he left?"

"No, nothing..."

"I guess there's not much to say, is there?"

"No..."

"No, I guess not..."

I looked over at Saito and there were tears in his eyes, and I thought that was a good thing. It didn't seem possible that forty young men could fly off like that and none of them come back.

But none of them did.

Missions weren't flown everyday. There were only so many planes and men, and I suppose it didn't make much sense to use them all up in the first few days of the campaign. So missions only went out every five or six days or so, but when they did go a large force of planes would be sent all at once. The idea was to overwhelm the enemy with numbers in a concentrated area. All we needed was one direct hit.

You can do the math. If we sent forty planes per mission, it would only take five missions before all our planes were gone. As it was, there were seven missions in total. With the first mission having taken forty planes, there were 160 planes left, with the six remaining missions using an average of 26.6 planes. Seven missions being sent at a rate of one every five or six days meant that our campaign would last about forty days. And that's what it was— we started on April 7th and ended on May 16th. All of the planes were gone then.

All except for the four planes designated for the Fuji Team.

Not long after the last of the other planes was gone, I was called in to see Commander Kimura in his office.

"We're holding your team in reserve," the Commander said, "orders from the top."

"Orders from the top, sir?"

"Yes, from the very top."

He stood up and started pacing about the room, just as he had the first time I'd reported to his office.

"This 'Kamikaze Geisha' business— it looks like the 'Fuji boys' have been roped into it now too."

I lowered my head. "I'm sorry, sir."

The Commander looked away and lit up a cigarette. "It's not your fault."

It was the first sympathetic thing he had ever said to me.

"It's a package deal now— you and the 'Fuji boys.'"

"I'm sorry, sir," I said again.

"I still think the whole thing is ridiculous."

"Yes, sir."

"Absolutely ridiculous."

"Yes, sir."

The Commander went to the window and looked out, slowly inhaling his cigarette and then blowing out a large puff of smoke.

"It's very quiet around here now, isn't it?"

"Yes, sir, it is."

"All those boys... and now they're all gone..."

"Yes, sir."

The Commander stood there for a while longer, blowing

out several more puffs of smoke, and then he walked back to his desk and sat down. Like the Colonel, I knew he probably had a wife and several children. I wondered where they were living then. We had never talked about it, of course.

"So, your team will be held in reserve."

"Yes, sir."

"Headquarters must have some sort of a special mission in mind."

"Yes, sir."

The Commander leaned back in his seat, and looked up at the ceiling, and blew out a very large puff of smoke.

"Good lord, a special mission…"

43

The Colonel had been right— once the Americans controlled the islands closer to Japan, they went about trying to sink us to the bottom of the ocean. Tokyo had only been the beginning. After that there were reports of other cities all across the country being bombed week after week— from Sendai up north to Kumamoto in Kyushu, with a long list of cities in between— Yokohama and Nagoya and Osaka and Nara and Matsuyama, and countless others. One night the city of Kagoshima, across the bay, was bombed. We watched the B-29s fly over, and then minutes later we heard the explosions, and then we saw the fires start and soon there seemed to be fire everywhere on the horizon. There was nothing we could do about it. There was nothing anyone could do about it. The Americans controlled the seas, and all of our planes were gone. I wondered if the four hidden in our hangar were the only planes left in the entire country.

In the meantime, we continued our training day after day, week after week— waiting to be told more about our "special mission." One day the Commander finally took us up in the air. We had begun to think it would never happen.

"We'll go up one at a time," the Commander said.

He took Muto up first. We watched as the plane ran smoothly down the runway and then up into the air, the Commander at the controls. The plane banked and circled back around, and then as it was coming back over the runway again there was a sudden dip and then a sudden climb and then a sudden dip again.

"Muto must have taken over the controls," Naito said.

Saito put his hands together and started praying.

On the second time around the runway, the plane came in and landed, and then it taxied back up to the other end and ran down the runway one more time, and climbed unsteadily up into the air.

"Muto's trying a takeoff," Naito said.

Saito continued to pray. I wondered if that was why he had so much trouble with directions. Maybe he was praying instead of listening to the directions, or maybe he was praying while trying to operate the controls.

"Naito, you're next," Muto said breathlessly, running back to us after landing.

"What was it like?"

"Exciting, once I started to get the hang of it."

Saito went back to his prayers.

Naito's time in the air was pretty much like Muto's— certainly nothing exceptional but at least he got up and down without an accident. Then it was Saito's turn. The Commander followed the same pattern, handling the control's himself on the initial takeoff and then handing them off to Saito as they came back around the runway, but soon after the plane went into a steep climb and then a severe nosedive, coming within a few meters of actually hitting the ground. We could see that the Commander was handling the controls the rest of the way back around on into the landing.

"That boy almost killed me," the Commander said to me once I was airborne with him.

It was wonderful to be back up in the air again— brought back memories of the first time I had flown, from Taiyuan to Wuhan back in '40.

"Why, you're a natural," the Commander said after I'd been at the controls for a few minutes.

I gave the Commander one of my coquettish smiles. I hadn't had the opportunity to do so since the dinner with the boys at Yoshiko's, and it felt very good.

"Let's take her for a little run."

"A run, sir? "

"Yes, let's head out over the coast."

"Are you sure, sir?"

"Yes, let's take her for a little run."

We quickly found the coast, and from there the Commander had me point the plane north until we came abreast of Mt. Takakuma. Then I headed her a bit more northeast and we approached Mt. Sakurajima, its volcanic cone rising majestically, before I banked her steeply as we circled around and came back down the west coast of the bay. It was a beautiful day, the sun high in the sky, a few wispy clouds floating about. The war was far, far away.

"Thank you," the Commander said as I brought the plane back down on the runway. "I think we both needed that."

44

One day towards the end of July the four of us were sitting around a table in the mess hall having our dinner. It was a large mess hall, and it always felt very strange for just the four of us to have our meals there, but of course by then we were the only ones left and there was nothing we could do about it.

"Isn't it odd," Naito said, "that Nagasaki hasn't been bombed yet?"

"It is, isn't it?" Muto agreed.

"Fukuoka, Kumamoto, Miyazaki, Sasebo, Oita, Saga, Kagoshima— they've bombed every city in Kyushu except Nagasaki."

"There's a rumor they're saving it to try out a new kind of bomb."

"I wonder what that could be."

A week later we heard the news about Hiroshima over the radio. My first thoughts, perhaps oddly, were about the two old drunk men we'd met at the restaurant. I wondered where they'd been when the bomb hit. Then three days after that came word of the attack on Nagasaki.

"They say a single bomb wiped out the entire city," Naito said.

"It doesn't seem possible, does it?"

"No, it doesn't, does it?"

"A few more of those and there will be no more Japan."

"All gone…"

There was a long silence as we looked around the table at each other, and then we all hung our heads.

Five days after the destruction of Nagasaki, the Commander called all of us into his office.

"Tomorrow's the day," the Commander said, lighting up his ever present cigarette.

"The special mission?" Naito asked.

"Yes, the special mission. With these new bombs the Americans have, it seems headquarters feels we have no choice but to employ our own weapon of last resort."

Muto straightened his shoulders further. "And what would that weapon be, sir?"

The Commander stood up then, as was his habit, and started pacing back and forth. There was a nervousness about the pacing that I hadn't seen before.

"We've been ordered to send the Kamikaze Geisha into battle. Our leaders at the top, the very top, feel this is our only hope."

I was stunned. It had always been in the back of my mind that this might be their eventual intention, but I hadn't thought they would actually go through with it. Was the man serious? He had said a number of times that he thought the whole idea of the Kamikaze Geisha was "ridiculous." Now did he really intend to send me up?

"Through this sacrificial act of the pure and perfect Kamikaze Geisha, the gods will see to the salvation of our nation."

Naito looked over at me, his face pale.

"The Fuji boys will go as the escort."

The fate of the nation now rested on me, little Panko from Kujirahe? There was the matter of my life, but what about the fate of the nation? What if I sacrificed myself and the nation was still lost because the gods knew I wasn't a maiden?

Naito stepped forward and bowed stiffly. "Is it really necessary to send the Kamikaze Geisha, sir? Couldn't we act on her behalf?"

The Commander ignored Naito, walking over to the window and looking out, seemingly far into the distance.

"I myself will fly with the Kamikaze Geisha," he said softly.

It was clear the Commander had by then reached his own point of madness. He was serious. He would take the Kamikaze Geisha up, and we would find an enemy aircraft carrier, and we would crash our plane into it, and the nation would be saved. He was certain of it.

"Saito!" the Commander bellowed, turning around.

"Yes, sir!" Saito shouted back, stepping forward.

"You will stay behind to pray for us."

"But sir..."

"If no one prays for us, our souls won't reach the next world. You have the most important assignment. I expect you to carry it out properly!"

Saito nodded silently. But we all knew the real reason he was being asked to stay behind was because it was highly unlikely he would have been able to get off the runway in one piece.

It would have been suicidal.

I didn't sleep at all that night. There was no way out. Either fly and die, or confess and be executed for treason. If only I'd confessed early on, when the Madame had first brought up the Minister's proposal, or later, right after I'd been returned by my kidnappers— even then, there would have been a way out. But now... And then, like so many others in this tragic war, I too reached my own point of madness, and resigned myself to my death. Memories of all sorts came floating back to me, memories from Kujirahe and Asakusa and Beijing and

Wuhan and so many other places.

I remembered the last time I saw my father, tears streaming down his face.

And I remembered riding the train to Nikko with the Madame and the Master and all the other girls of the house, eating tangerines and sipping tea.

And I remembered going with Hoshi to see Tomo perform with Enoken.

And I remembered hiding under the boat with Sumio.

And I remembered the night Mangetsu and Koyo and Hoshi and I talked about love and the different kinds of men.

And I remembered my last night at Sugutatsu, Taibo hoisting me over his head as the other girls laughed and applauded.

And I remembered the night with the Colonel in Taiyuan, our hands entwined.

And I remembered the poignant final moments of Consort Yu, the king's sword poised at her throat, his name on her lips.

And I remembered my own Lieutenant and our own brief time together, and I thought— hadn't that been meaning enough?

45

The next morning, August 15th, we were up at 03:30 hours. We had a simple breakfast of rice, seaweed, and broiled fish. In the middle of each bowl of rice was a red pickled plum, symbolic of the rising sun of our flag. When we were done eating, the Commander gathered us around and laid out a map. There was an enemy flotilla believed to be just off of Amami Island in the northern Okinawa chain. We were to proceed there and target an aircraft carrier, the USS Chelsea Creek. The Commander would fly at the head of our formation, with Naito and Muto to follow. If we were met by enemy fighters, Naito and Muto were to make every effort to distract them so as to allow the Kamikaze Geisha to reach the target.

"Is everything clear?" the Commander asked.

"Very clear, sir," Muto replied crisply.

After the briefing we went out to the airfield, and the Commander lined us up and poured out some *sake* and we toasted each other.

"Pardon us for going on ahead before you," Naito said stoically to Saito, and then Muto and I both said likewise to our already grieving comrade.

Saito bowed deeply in response, saying, "Let us meet again in the next world."

Then the Commander had me step forward, and he read a scroll:

> *In recognition of your pure and unsullied state, your unstinting efforts to save the nation, and ultimately, your willingness to make the ultimate sacrifice, you are hereby posthumously awarded the Order of the Sacred Wind, First Class, and granted the posthumous name of "Muko."*
>
> *Rear-Admiral Nishida Hajime*
> *Imperial Navy*

Muko— *"child of nothingness."* I thought I might call the Commander's attention to the fact that I was still of this world and not yet of the next, but it seemed pointless to do so. I was handed the scroll, and then the Commander wrapped a bandanna with the streaming rays of the rising sun around my head. I saluted and stepped back into line, and the others saluted as well, and we were ready for departure.

Then, just as the sun rose above the horizon, we climbed up into our cockpits and revved up the engines and taxied to the end of the runway.

"Are you ready, Kamikaze Geisha?" the Commander shouted out to me over the roar of the engine.

"Ready, sir."

"Here we go."

And with that we hurtled down the runway and up into the air. Naito and Muto followed, completing their takeoffs more smoothly than could have been expected. We circled the field once, tipping our wings towards Tokyo, and then we headed south down the bay and out over Cape Sata into the open Pacific. It was a beautiful day, not unlike the day I had first flown with the Commander, with the sun rising steadily on our port side as we passed the island of Tanegashima and quickly approached Yakushima.

It was just about then, as we were over Yakushima, that we flew into a large bank of cumulus clouds and lost Naito and Muto. I thought the Commander might veer to the left or the right, but he flew directly into the clouds, and when we came out on the other side, Naito and Muto were no longer with us.

"We'll have to go on alone," the Commander shouted. "No time to search for them."

Where would the "Fuji boys" go without the Commander? I prayed fervently that fate would be kind to them.

We flew on for another forty minutes or so, and then the Commander lowered our altitude to where we were just skimming over the water. It wouldn't be long now, I knew. My heart was racing and I couldn't catch my breath. I really was going to die. It really was going to happen. We continued on that way for what seemed an eternity. Several times I thought we would hit the water as a swell rose up to meet us, but each time the Commander skillfully pulled up, avoiding disaster.

Then we started climbing again, climbing and climbing, and then suddenly there she was, the object of our mission—the USS Chelsea Creek.

"It's a miracle," the Commander shouted. "She's by herself."

And indeed she was. Where were the other ships that were supposed to be with her?

The Commander immediately took us back down to our lower altitude, skimming over the water again.

"It's a sign from the gods— by herself and her stern's to the sun."

I instantly grasped what the Commander meant. We would approach with the sun at our back, making it difficult for the gunners to see us. Coming at the carrier's stern, as opposed to coming across her beam, would also give her fewer guns to aim at us.

"Kamikaze Geisha, prepare to attack!"

"Yes, sir!"

"Let us meet again in the next world!"

"Yes, sir!"

We sped on over the water, and now as we got closer, the carrier opened on us with her guns. Shells were exploding all about. The Commander took evasive action, moving to the left and then the right, then up and then down. I didn't know if my heart would hold up until we reached the target. It seemed it was about to burst. It really was going to happen. I really was going to die. Then one of the shells hit us— in the forward cockpit.

"I'm hit!" the Commander cried out. "Take over!"

Those were his last words. The plane lurched to the left and I grabbed the controls. I could see the carrier's deck in front of me. I aimed for the center, making adjustments as best I could as the deck pitched back and forth. If only I could bring her up just a little bit more, and then a bit more to the right, and—

46

The war was over.

That's what the Americans told me later that day. It seems I had actually landed my plane right on the carrier and then skidded off the deck. The Americans had fished me out. The Commander was dead. I never knew whether he was already dead when we landed on the carrier or if he died when we went in the water.

"The Emperor made a radio broadcast. The war's over."

That's what the interpreter said to me. He was a Japanese-American. He looked Japanese and he spoke Japanese, but he was an American.

The Americans were curious, of course, about why a girl would be flying an airplane. I must have still been in shock. I told them I was the Kamikaze Geisha and that I had flown my plane into their ship in order to save the Japanese nation. The interpreter then found the insignia on my jumpsuit that said "kamikaze geisha" and pointed it out to his colleagues. They seemed to find this amusing. They all laughed.

"Why are they laughing at me?" I asked.

"They think you're crazy," the interpreter replied.

Only two weeks later I was back in Tokyo. The carrier sailed into Yokosuka as part of the fleet to receive our nation's surrender, and I was let free. I took the train up to the city, and then headed for Asakusa, catching a ride on the back of a horse-drawn cart from a boy of maybe fifteen or sixteen whom, I must admit, I had shamelessly charmed. Sometimes it is of particular advantage to have in hand the social skills common to all but the most inexpert of geisha. The scene was shocking indeed as we plodded along kilometer after kilometer from the station to my intended destination. As I had heard, but still found difficult to fathom, the entire downtown core of the city had been devastated. All that still stood was the occasional concrete building or stone warehouse. Some people had taken to putting up crude shacks and others were living in the bombed-out wrecks of buses or trucks or cars. Winter would soon be approaching, and those who had nowhere to go would have to survive in whatever shelter they could find.

As Hoshi had written in her letter, Sugutatsu had been burned to the ground, but I was able to find in the old neighborhood one lady who used to own a vegetable shop. Where her shop had once stood, she now ran a small stand. She told me she went over to Ueno early every morning and bought produce from farmers who came in by train from the countryside and sold their goods in the black market there. Very fortunately for me, she knew where the Madame and Hoshi were. It seems they were staying with some friends in Dozaka, not far from where I lived with my relatives when I first came to Tokyo. I bought some vegetables from the kind lady with dollars the Americans had given me, and then I started for Dozaka, once again riding in the back of the horse-drawn cart.

"You're sure?" I asked the boy when he offered to give me

the second ride. But of course I knew he was sure even before I asked him— he was in love.

As we crossed Ueno and started down Shinobazu Avenue, we found many more buildings standing. It seemed the fires from the March 9th bombings had stopped here, and the odd shop or home damaged the rest of the way was due to a bomb or two gone astray outside of the main target area. Such appeared to be the case right at the Dozaka intersection, where there was a large crater in the road.

"Thank you so much," I said to the boy, hopping off the cart.

"Will you need another ride?" he asked expectantly.

I told him no, and gave him another coquettish smile and a small wave of the hand, and then headed up the hill from the intersection. He'd been a very nice boy indeed, and although I felt somewhat guilty about having taken him out of his way, I knew I had also given him a sweet memory he would have for life.

Reaching the house where the Madame and Hoshi were staying, I slid open the door and called out a greeting. Soon an older woman appeared. When she learned who I was, she became very excited and shouted out to the Madame, who was upstairs.

"It's Suzu!"

"Oh, my, Suzu," I heard the familiar voice of the Madame ring out.

And then I dashed up the stairs and into the room at the end of the hallway, and there was the Madame. It had been just about eight months since I had seen her, and it seemed the pain of all that had happened during that time was etched into her face, now much thinner, the wrinkles about her eyes much more pronounced. But the smile was the same, and the eyes were bright, and the voice was steady, if not quite as strong as in the past. I sat down on the tatami next to her and grasped her two hands in mine, very similar to the pose we had taken my last night in Tokyo before leaving for Kyushu, and tears filled the eyes of both of us.

"Oh, Suzu, you're alive... you're alive..."

I asked where Hoshi was, and the Madame explained that she had gone to the black market in Ueno and would be back later in the day. And then I asked if she'd heard anything about Taibo or Ummu Sensei. She said they had both survived the war. The Sensei had evacuated to his mountain in Nikko, while Taibo was living in Chiba with some other former sumo wrestlers. Hoshi had seen him recently, she said. I asked her if there was any significance to that. She said she wasn't sure, but suspected there was still some affection alive in both their hearts.

And then when our emotions had calmed down a bit and the timing seemed appropriate, I asked the Madame about her injuries. It was obviously difficult for her, but she knew it was important for me, and she proceeded to recount the events of that evening, finally breaking down when she got to the point where she was separated from Koyo and Mangetsu.

"The fates were very unfair to them," she said, sobbing.

She herself was recovering well, she said, although the doctors had told her it would be several more months before she got sufficient strength back in her legs to walk.

"Oh, we've all gone through so much," she said, grabbing one of my hands again.

"Yes, yes, we have..."

And then she asked me about my own experiences with the Special Attack Force. How had I managed to survive? And I spoke about my time in Kyushu— about the "Fuji boys," and the horrible days sending young men off who would never come back, and the final, climactic mission with the Commander, and my time with the Americans.

And then, without warning, I was overcome with the guilt of the secret I had carried these so many years, and I blurted out to the Madame, "I am not a maiden!"

The Madame hesitated, unsure how to respond to this outburst. "You're not a maiden? How could... What do you mean?"

"I am not a maiden," I said again, this time more quietly.

"The Americans got you?"

"No, no..."

"The Chinese? The Chinese did get you after all?"

"No," I said more emphatically, "no... I was never... never a maiden."

"Never a maiden?" the Madame said, furrowing her brow. "When did this happen?"

"Right... after my debut..."

"And who was... this man?"

"A young lieutenant in the army... I met him the night of my debut."

The Madame paused for a long moment. "It was your 'brother,' wasn't it?"

"You knew?"

"I didn't know, but it all makes sense now..." She paused again, painfully shifting her injured legs.

"Mangetsu warned me..."

"Warned you?"

"She warned me not to fall in love... especially not with a soldier..."

The Madame smiled slightly. "Yes, it's..."

"But the very first night..."

"It's so easy to warn someone, isn't it? But a woman's heart..."

"The very first night... He was so... I..."

"Yes, I know..." She let out a sigh. "In matters of the heart.. we don't always make the right decisions, do we?"

I felt certain she was talking about herself and the Master.

"Yes, in matters of the heart...," she said again.

There was a long silence, and I thought back to that night so many years before when I'd met the Lieutenant in Jinbocho and we'd gone to the *yakitori* shop and had a few drinks and he'd taken me to that boarding house and... It all seemed like a dream now. Had it all really happened?

And then, overcome with guilt once more, I said, "I should have told you. If only I'd told you, then maybe the gods wouldn't have punished us so!"

The Madame peered deeply into my eyes, and then she started laughing. "Oh, Suzu, our tragedy had nothing to do with your maidenhood. It had everything to do with the fools who were in charge of the country— everything to do with those cowardly fools!"

She was right, of course, and in my heart I knew it as well as she did.

"The Maiden Maiko and the House of Sugutatsu and the Kamikaze Geisha— how ludicrous, all of it!"

There was nothing for me to say.

"And I...," she went on hesitantly, "I didn't... I didn't protect you as I should have."

I tried to reassure her as best I could. What more could she have done? There was nothing more she could have done. I reached across and once more grasped her two hands in mine and we shed more tears, and I told her again there was nothing more she could have done.

Later I asked about the Minister and Captain Mushitani. Did she know what had become of them? She said she didn't. The following week we found out. It was in the newspapers— they'd both killed themselves before they could be arrested by the Americans as "suspected war criminals."

47

By the next spring I still hadn't heard from Tomo. I had even heard from the Fuji boys by then, but I still hadn't heard from Tomo. It seems that after we lost Naito and Muto in the clouds, they had crash landed on an island. I didn't ask them about the thinking that went into their decision. Had they tried to find the original target and failed? Or had they simply decided it made more sense to live in this world for a while longer? The questions didn't seem relevant. Naito said he intended to finish his degree in civil engineering and then help rebuild the houses and factories and bridges and railways and roads of Japan. Muto said he intended to become a businessman and help rebuild the commerce of the country. Saito said he intended to become a Buddhist priest. I wished all of them good luck in their endeavors.

Then one day early that next summer Tomo came home. We went and had a bowl of noodles at the old Tour Eiffel. They had had to adapt to the realities of the post-war world, just like all the rest of us, and they were now a ramen shop. Someone must have saved the "Tour Eiffel" signboard when the fires came, and it had been carefully placed at the entrance of the little lean-to shack that housed them.

"It's a beginning," Tomo said.

"Yes, a beginning."

He told me his unit had been in fierce fighting around Manila before retreating into the mountains. Later they had been forced to surrender.

"Are you going back into comedy?" I asked him.

"That's my intent," he said. "I think the country could use a few laughs."

I had to agree he was probably right about that.

"What about you?" he asked.

"The Madame is talking about getting her house started up again and..."

"Is that so?"

"And she's asked if Hoshi and I..."

"You've got to figure the Americans will like geisha."

"I'm not so sure... Geisha may be too 'feudal.' I'm told they don't like 'feudal.'"

"They like women in exotic costumes. I think it will work out."

"We'll see..."

Later we took a walk out across the Azuma Bridge, and as we did so I said a prayer for Mangetsu and Koyo and the Master.

"Did you ever hear from that lieutenant again?" Tomo asked abruptly.

"Lieutenant?"

"You know, the one who..."

I paused for a long moment. "No, no, I..."

"I wonder if he's alive."

I turned away and bit my lip.

48

But I never did see my Lieutenant again. No, I never did. It's all so long ago now, those war years. Seventy— I just turned seventy last week. Who would have thought the Kamikaze Geisha would ever reach the ripe old age of seventy? It's been two years since I came back here to Kujirahe. I wanted to be with family again, and Jinbei and his wife were so kind to take me in. They gave me my own room in the back of the house with its own little garden, and this is where I've been writing, a few pages each day. I could have stayed in Tokyo, but with business bad after the bubble burst, and Tomo gone and no children of my own, there was really nothing to keep me there. Seventy— a significant milestone. They organized a party for me down at the local sushi shop. Jinbei had caught a mid-sized skipjack tuna the day before, and the chef went to the trouble of slicing it up into a spectacular sashimi presentation, the head still attached. Wonderfully fresh fish— the one clear advantage of living in a fishing village. It wasn't a large gathering, just Jinbei and his wife and a few of their friends and some of the ladies I've gotten to know here in town. Certainly not like the old days, when there would have been crowds following me, and the press recording every detail of such an event.

So much has changed. The Americans came after the war, and they've never really left. We were suffering from militarism, they said, and would need an infusion of democracy— a rather large infusion, as we were afflicted with a serious case. My past history as the Maiden Maiko and the Kamikaze Geisha did not fit well with the new norms. There was some trouble for me for a while. I won't go into the detail— maybe someday if I get around to writing another volume— but in the end it all worked out. The Madame started her house back up, and Hoshi and I took on larger roles in rebuilding the business with her. Various men came and went, some more important than others, but I never did get married. No, I never did.

All of history is a myth, the Colonel said, a fable, simply the telling of a tale. What about this tale— what would he have thought of it? Would he have agreed with what I've written here? Or would he have questioned my portrayal of him and the others? Would he have said this or that didn't happen? Would he have said I left out something? Would he have— might I dare ask— questioned my motives? I don't know. I just don't know. Sometimes as I walk down by the harbor, or up in the nearby hills, these are the questions that run through my mind.

And sometimes, too, I think about you, my reader. Who are you, and what will you think of this tale? What will you believe and what will you discard?

The Kamikaze Geisha— oh, you so want me to be real, don't you?

Acknowledgements

At the University of Massachusetts in Amherst, Professor Richard Minear first taught me the importance of understanding the background and biases of the author when reading any history. Ciaran Murray and Ko Shioya, both of Tokyo, have read my attempts at fiction and drama over the course of many years and always provided unstinting encouragement. John Sugimoto (Loveland, CO) and Ron Henkoff (Westport, CT) reviewed earlier drafts of this book and gave me a number of very valuable suggestions. Rafael Andres has created an eye-catching cover for the book; Mapping Specialists have designed maps that will be highly useful to the reader in navigating the plot. My sons, Owen and Ken, and my daughter, Eileen, have given me their support in so many ways. And what would I do without my wife, Setsuko? She is always there for me with insightful feedback (never varnished), special nuggets of information about her home country, and an evening meal (if I'm behaving); it means everything.

To all of those listed above, I give my heartfelt thanks.

About the Author

Born in Boston, Massachusetts, Michael Cooney grew up in Tokyo and later lived there off and on for many more years. Over the course of his career, he has worked as a translator, editor, and businessman, all the while continuing to write his own fiction and drama. A tennis enthusiast, he is a past member of the board of the Tokyo Lawn Tennis Club. He and his wife, Setsuko, currently live in Westport, Connecticut.